HER
FINAL
BREATH

BOOKS BY CAROLYN ARNOLD

Just Cause

Deadly Impulse

In the Line of Duty

Power Struggle

Shades of Justice

What We Bury

Girl on the Run

Her Dark Grave

Life Sentence

SARA AND SEAN COZY MYSTERY SERIES

Bowled Over Americano

Wedding Bells Brew Murder

MATTHEW CONNOR ADVENTURE SERIES

City of Gold

The Secret of the Lost Pharaoh

The Legend of Gasparilla and His Treasure

STANDALONE

Assassination of a Dignitary

Pearls of Deception

Midlife Psychic

HER FINAL BREATH

CAROLYN ARNOLD

bookouture

Published by Bookouture in 2023

An imprint of Storyfire Ltd.
Carmelite House
50 Victoria Embankment
London EC4Y 0DZ

www.bookouture.com

ISBN: 978-1-80314-786-4
eBook ISBN: 978-1-80314-785-7

Dedicated to Emily Gowers

PROLOGUE

Leanne's eyelids are so heavy, but there's a voice inside telling her to open them and move. She spreads her fingers at her sides. They touch a soft surface. She extends her arms and find they move freely. No restraints.

Still, tremors of fear slice through her. Something is wrong.

Her head is spinning.

Where am I?

Images flash through her mind. A man, a dog, ice cream... *Gracie!*

She jolts to a seated position, opening her eyes and recoiling at the sudden burst of light. But she fights against it, squinting as she scans her surroundings.

She's on a single-sized bed in a room decorated for a young girl, though it feels like a huge space. The bedding is a bright pink, and the walls are papered in a pale-pink nondescript pattern, with a border at the level of a chair rail.

To her left is a large window with metal bars.

The blood in her veins becomes ice.

Across the room are two doorways. She sees a vanity and a toilet through one—a bathroom. The other is shut. There is a third door on the right side of the room that is also closed. One of these is likely a closet and the other a way out.

But first, where is my Gracie?

The question ricochets in her head as a sob, as she now trails her gaze along the right wall. There's another bed with a small form beneath the comforter and a little pudgy hand poking out over the fabric.

"Gracie." A plea, a cry, not much above a whisper.

She shuffles to the edge of her mattress, throws her legs over the edge and stands. Pain flares in her ankle, blinding her vision, and she crumples to the floor. She crawls to the other bed, tugging herself up by clawing at the comforter. It comes toward her in massive waves of fabric. Suddenly it's like she's drowning, trying to keep her head above water.

She swims free, and her daughter is facing her. Lying on her side, her eyes pinched tight.

Gracie!

She stares at her motionless daughter. If she's breathing, it's so shallow Leanne can't see her chest rise and fall.

Oh my God! Please no!

She shakes her daughter's arm. No response.

She tries again. This time, near violently. The girl groans.

Leanne scoops her daughter into her arms and squeezes with what strength she can muster, tears falling. "Baby, baby, it's Mommy."

Gracie turns her head and looks in her eyes—the bluest blue peering into hers and the missing pockets of time return. She trusted that man, allowing herself to be blinded by his charms. But he'd been so kind to them. Her daughter had loved petting and playing with his black Lab.

Meanwhile, he was working his agenda.

Leanne wants to tell Gracie everything will be okay, but she's feeling hopeless and responsible. This is all her fault.

She needs to get them out of here. If only she can figure how to do that. "Just stay right here, okay, sweetie?"

Gracie nods.

Leanne leaves her daughter's side, hobbling. She discovers the closed door across the room is secured shut with screws.

She heads to the other closed door, grabs the handle, and it twists easily.

She will get them out of here!

She pulls on the door, but it doesn't budge. She pushes. No give.

It must be locked on the outside.

She bangs her palms against the door. Angry, frustrated. Tears burn in her eyes, but she has to be strong for her daughter. She begs a higher power this isn't the end for her. For Gracie.

ONE

TRIANGLE, VIRGINIA

The day was off to an early and interesting start. The dead body wasn't unusual, but the circumstances were.

Detective Amanda Steele drove her Honda Civic into the lot for Prince Park, joining a Kia sedan, a fire engine, the fire marshal's SUV, and an ambulance. Three young men were being tended to by two paramedics.

Busy place for six in the morning. Any other day, she'd be in bed at this time. In some ways, she wouldn't mind being there now. Even the October sun was slow to surrender to a new day. Though its rays cut through the light cloud cover and penetrated the spaces between the tree branches, they did little to cut out the damp chill of fall that permeated to the bone.

She pulled her car into a spot near the Kia and got out.

"Amanda!" Spencer Blair hustled toward her, and it had her stomach sinking. Their paths had crossed on a case a year ago, but since then she'd found out Spencer was the product of an affair her father had twenty-six years ago. Her father had come out with this last year, and Amanda hadn't spoken to Spencer since.

He slowed to a stop once he reached her, not winded from

his jaunt. But Spencer was fit and lean—something that served him well as a firefighter for the Dumfries-Triangle Volunteer Fire Department.

"You found the body?" A toss-away question. After all, he'd been the one to call her here—the unusual part.

"Not exactly. A little background first?"

She gestured for him to go ahead, wondering how he got caught up in all this. Spencer had shared little when he'd called her, just that there was a dead body buried in the woods.

"Some teens thought starting a fire in the woods was a smart idea. We got called out."

She nudged her head toward the men with the paramedics. "Them?"

Spencer nodded. "Yep, those buttheads. They got started around three AM. The fire was called in around five. We arrived shortly after and got it under control. Thankfully, the flames never got to any trees."

"Three is a little early for a party and a fire. And it's a Tuesday. Don't they have school?"

"You'll need to bring that up with them."

"And the body...?"

"Quite sure it's a woman. In a shallow grave." His eyes glazed over, as if his imagination was venturing down a gruesome path.

Her thoughts immediately took her there with the delivery of his words *shallow grave*. It could be the work of a serial killer, but her mind was getting ahead of things. The killer likely had little time to dig a deeper hole, or may have wanted the victim to be discovered sooner. If the latter, why? Just one of the many questions that were sure to come. "What do you mean, you *think* it's a woman?"

"You'll understand once you see for yourself, but not much of the body is exposed. And we weren't poking around. Leave that to the right people."

It was possible the entire body wasn't there. She could have been hacked into pieces and certain parts buried. *Push that one from my mind...* The nasty creeped in when a person had seen enough of it. "Good call. But speaking of the right people, where is everyone? The medical examiner, Crime Scene?"

"I figured you'd call them. I called you, thinking you might want to have a look first. Don't let that fact go to your head or read more into it."

"Uh-huh." She was curious, though. Had he called her to get close to her, establish some sort of bond? She rubbed her forehead, not eager to traipse down that path just yet.

"I mean it. After all, dead bodies are your wheelhouse."

"Can't argue there." But technically, her shift started at eight thirty. It was her strong drive—obsession—for justice that had won out over her personal desire for a few more hours' sleep. She just hated that the hour had caused inconvenience to her seven-year-old daughter, Zoe, who Amanda had to drag from bed and cart to her aunt Libby's. "Who found her?"

"That one there." Spencer indicated the young man who was wearing a yellow-and-red plaid shirt. He was tall and gangly, like he hadn't grown into his arms and legs yet. "Name's Nolan Copeland. It was his idea to drink and start a fire."

Nolan was sitting at the back of the ambulance. His friends were loud, while he was quiet. Amanda would talk to the group, but later. She preferred to be armed with seeing the site and gleaming more information before doing so. It would also be best if she waited for her partner, Trent Stenson, to arrive. What tells she might miss, he could pick up. "We need them to stick around. Will you see to that while I call everyone?"

Spencer nodded and went to the young men. She watched the interaction as she called her partner.

"Amanda?" Trent answered on the second ring, but his voice was groggy, like she'd woken him up.

"Rise and shine. There's a situation." She told him about the discovery at the park.

"I'll meet you at the station? We'll head over together..."

They worked out of Central, one of three stations belonging to the Prince William County Police Department. It was in Woodbridge, about ten minutes from Triangle, where she was now. "A bit of a story there, but I'm already on scene."

"Really? Why are you at work already? You know what? I'll be there as soon as I can."

She rushed out a quick "goodbye" and hung up, not wanting to face an awkward "see you later." Blame that on a kiss that shouldn't have happened. Four months ago. Two kisses, truth be told. He kissed her, backed off. Then she went in for seconds. Now she just wished to forget all of it. She had started seeing Logan Hunter again, and it was going on four months. Things were good between them. But still... the kisses in her kitchen with Trent clung to her, haunting her like a persistent migraine she couldn't shake. She would, though. Eventually. Hopefully.

Amanda made the other necessary calls to get a medical examiner and crime scene investigators en route. Her sergeant, Katherine Graves, was last on her list. She was prickly to deal with most of the time, and her voice set Amanda on edge. At least she was just a stopgap until Scott Malone returned to work. Malone was more than her sergeant; he was a family friend. Recovering from surgery to remove a malignant brain tumor had him benched for seven months already. Amanda was counting down the days until he returned. She didn't want to consider he might decide on early retirement.

Graves sounded more flummoxed than Trent had been. "At Prince Park? And it's just after six AM. What are you doing there, Steele? I didn't think your shift started until eight thirty."

Amanda bit her bottom lip, counted to three in her head. It had become a ritual so Amanda wouldn't risk saying something she couldn't take back. "My..." She stopped talking. It was probably best to leave out that her half-brother called her there. The sergeant was sensitive to any perceived personal connections when it came to her detectives and their investigations. "One of the firemen had my number." Since Amanda had already laid out what little she knew, her statement would make sense to Graves. "I, ah, worked with him on a past case." It was the truth, also a worthy addition to support why a fireman might have called her directly instead of PD.

There was a rash of silence. Amanda let it grow despite wanting to get on with her day. But any rush to speak might come across as her craving approval, or desiring control of the situation. Neither would gain her Graves's favor.

"Very well. I'll be there soon." With that foreboding promise, the sergeant hung up.

Spencer was looking at her, along with the fire marshal. Craig Sullivan was a pleasant man she'd met on the same case as she had Spencer. She bridged the distance.

"Detective Steele. We meet again. Would be nice if it didn't always involve a dead body." His words seemed an attempt at humor, but they came out flat and heavy.

"Wouldn't it? Spencer said you responded to a call and wound up with a surprise."

"You heard right. At the very least, the young man is facing a fine. Fires are not allowed in the park."

Amanda suspected a monetary fine might be the least of Nolan's worries. Specifically if he was why the woman was in the ground. The "discovery" might be nothing more than an elaborate attempt to cover up his crime.

TWO

Trent was still shaking cobwebs from his mind when he arrived at Prince Park. He'd been in the middle of a dream when Amanda's call came through, rousing him to the cruel reality of the waking world—one in which dead bodies beckoned and demanded his attention.

But at seven in the morning? That's what the clock on the dash read when he cut the engine.

He spotted Amanda speaking with the fire marshal—Craig Sullivan, Trent recalled—and Spencer Blair. Trent headed over. The sound of tires crunching on the gravel slowed his steps, and he looked over a shoulder. The sergeant's SUV.

She was just what he needed before coffee—a superior on a power trip.

"Detective." Amanda waved an arm to flag his attention, as if she didn't see he was already walking toward her.

He lifted a hand, a meager, awkward attempt at acknowledging her. Things between them were tense and uncomfortable at times. It was hard to know what to say, what to do, just in case the other was offended. He never should have given in and kissed her. He'd been an idiot to think he could and then completely forget. And it wasn't like a romantic relationship between them was possible as long as they were partners.

"Hey." Trent greeted the group as he stopped next to Amanda.

She stepped to the side, placing just a few more inches between them, as if he'd gotten too close.

"Any developments since we spoke?" he asked, clutching at the hope there would be, but the question also served as an icebreaker. Hopefully, it masked his relative unease.

Amanda shook her head. "Haven't even seen the body yet. I was waiting for you and everyone else to arrive first."

"It was one of them who found the body?" Trent nudged his head toward a group of three young men near an ambulance. They were standing in a circle, two of them kicking at stones with the toes of their shoes.

"Nolan Copeland. He's the one in the plaid shirt, dark hair."

Based on first impressions, Trent would say Nolan was the leader of the group. His friends were looking at him, while Nolan had his eyes on Trent.

A van from Crime Scene pulled in and began parking, along with the ME's vehicle. Both were stationed out of Manassas, about thirty minutes from here. But it was rare that they showed up at the same time.

It was turning into one big party, and he hadn't even had a sip of coffee.

Graves was the first to join them, travel mug in hand. Trent imagined it was full of coffee. Steam curled from the hole in the lid. What he'd give for one hit. He inhaled deeply and was rewarded with the robust aroma of roasted coffee beans. It would have to carry him until he could get his own.

"Detectives, we're all up a little early today. Let's make it count." Her brow wrinkled as she lifted her cup to her lips.

He was all onboard with her pep talk—if four words constituted that.

Graves took a swig, lowered her cup. "The body?" She pursed her lips and looked at Amanda.

Amanda gestured toward Spencer.

"I'll take you now. Unless you'd prefer that someone else take care of that?" Spencer glanced at the marshal for permission.

"You go ahead," Sullivan said. "I'm going to send the guys back to the station. You and I can go back together in a bit."

"You got it."

The marshal walked off to give the news to the other firemen. Coming toward them was Crime Scene Investigator Emma Blair—Spencer's mother—and CSI Isabelle Donnelly.

"Spencer?" Blair hustled to her son, leaving her counterpart to catch up.

"I'm fine." Spencer barely opened his mouth to speak, the words slipping through clenched teeth. "The body's this way." Spencer led the way into the woods.

Hans Rideout, the medical examiner, and his assistant, Liam Baker, had tagged on to the group too, and they all followed Spencer.

Trent had been to Prince Park many times. There were play areas for children and walking trails. Visitors could hike or take to the water for fishing, pedal boating, and canoeing. There was a mini-golf course, a driving range, batting cages, volleyball, and tennis courts. Some activities were seasonal, but the fact remained it was a popular destination for adults, teens, and children. It would be high traffic, making it a risky place to dispose of a body—let alone a place to execute a murder.

No one said a word until Spencer stopped and pointed about six feet in front of him to a small knoll. "She's right there. You'll see the tip of a shoe once you get closer."

Trent moved in, watching where he placed each footstep to

avoid contaminating the scene. Just as Spencer had said: the toe of a woman's running shoe, bedazzled with rhinestones, stuck out from the dirt. He also noticed a slash of blue going up from the ankle. He crouched down, angling his head. Blue jeans, presumably covering her leg.

"When Nolan tripped over her, it pulled more of the remains out," Spencer said.

CSIs Blair and Donnelly set down their collection kits. Blair took out a camera and snapped shots while everyone stayed back. She and her colleague continued scouring the immediate area around the grave.

Rideout and his assistant stood sentinel. They'd wait for the investigators to process the scene before moving in. Once they finished, Rideout and Liam would exhume the woman.

Trent stepped up next to Amanda. Her arms were crossed, and her face was shadowed. "Who buries a woman in the woods?"

She leveled a serious gaze at him. "Don't say a serial killer."

He held up his hands. "I never did. Besides, it's far too soon to leap there." He smiled at her, an expression she returned, even if both were dampened by the circumstances. They were standing on the edge of someone's grave. Speaking of... "It looks like she may have been put here recently. The soil appears loose, not packed down."

"I noticed that too." Amanda wasn't looking at him now, but chewing her bottom lip, her eyes on the grave.

The sergeant nudged over, her elbow grazing Trent's. "We need to figure out who she is and how she wound up here."

Silence passed, and Graves passed a look at each of them like she expected them to have those answers already.

"We got here at the same time as you," Trent said. He didn't look at the sergeant when he spoke, figuring it was best not to make eye contact and really provoke the bear.

"Well, we need to find out as soon as possible. I don't want this hitting the press without having answers."

Trent resisted pointing out the lack of answers was standard this early in an investigation.

"We'll do what we can, Sarge," Amanda said in a measured tone.

Impressive. Redheads got a bad rep for being temperamental, and while Amanda could be fiery, she somehow stuffed it down for the sergeant. His partner would likely vent to him later.

"Where were the teens having the fire?" Amanda slowly pivoted toward Spencer.

"I'll show you." He stepped off with Amanda.

A feel for the entire scene would be helpful, but Trent's heart was with the woman in the grave. Who was she? Were her loved ones looking for her? Worse yet, had a loved one put her in the ground?

"Trent, are you coming?"

He looked up to find Amanda bugging her eyes and tilting her head. "Ah, yeah." He wasn't sure if she'd called his name before, but given her body language, he would guess she had. He half jogged to catch up, and thankfully didn't see Graves on his heels. She was staying at the burial site. *One small mercy.*

Spencer took Trent and Amanda to a clearing away from the body. He didn't need to point out the firepit. Stones circled black and charred pieces of wood.

If it wasn't for the fire, how long would that woman have stayed buried?

"What are you thinking?" Amanda asked. Her and Spencer were looking at him.

"Is smoke coming from my ears?" The half-siblings didn't appear amused. "Just happy that kid tripped over the body—not that there was one. You know what I mean. At least we can find some closure for her loved ones."

Amanda met his gaze. Her eyes lit, and a few seconds later, she nodded.

She'd told him before she admired his optimism, but what she didn't realize was he clung to it like a buoy. To roll over in defeating thoughts wasn't how he was wired. Nothing got accomplished that way. "We should talk to the kid who found her and his friends." As the word *kid* left his lips, he felt ancient. He was only thirty-five, barely old enough to be any of their dads.

"We'll get there. But I'd like to get more information from the ME and the investigators first." Amanda turned her gaze to Spencer. "And we need to take your statement."

"I told you all I know."

"Okay, but for the record this time."

Trent pulled his notepad and pen and readied to write. Amanda covered the who, where, when, what, and why of the discovery. In summary, Nolan could be the innocent victim of the wrong place, wrong time, or a killer with solid acting ability. "Did he seem to be playing a part? Like he was pretending to be shocked?"

"From his screams, I don't think so. His reaction seemed genuine to me."

"Were you the first to come across Nolan?" Amanda asked.

"Yep." Spencer bobbed his head as if his verbal response wasn't enough.

"What was his state of mind?" Trent tapped the point of his pen to the page, the ink leaving a blot of blue.

"Distressed, freaking out. He was on the ground a few feet away, his knees tucked into his chest. Oh, and he was rocking back and forth."

Amanda bobbed her head.

"If that's everything, I should check in with the marshal." Spencer jacked a thumb over his shoulder. "It's probably about time I left."

"That's fine. We know where to find you if we have more questions," Amanda told him. "Thanks."

"Ah, sure. For what exactly?"

"Reaching out."

The half-siblings held eye contact for several seconds before Spencer left, and Trent wished he were somewhere else, affording them space.

Amanda didn't seem fazed, though, and turned to Trent. "Early thoughts?"

"Someone needs to be missing her. At least I hope so."

"Do you think we're looking at a disposal site or a murder scene?"

"Given she was buried in a more secluded part of the park, it could be either. We'll need more to go on. Her cause of death, et cetera. The grave is so shallow, if there had been heavy rain, she'd have been exposed. So was the depth because the killer ran out of time, or did they want her found quickly?"

"I was thinking the same."

"Good to be on the same page." He closed his notepad and tucked it away.

"That has never been a problem for us." She walked on ahead of him in the grave's direction.

He was left with the company of his thoughts, which were chewing apart her words. But it was best he not read too much into them—they were a double-edged sword.

THREE

As Amanda and Trent returned to the crime scene, to her it all felt somewhat reminiscent of a case they had last fall. The one with the college student. She hadn't been buried, but left naked and on display in a wooded park next to the Potomac River.

The CSIs were snapping photographs and setting out yellow markers. Rideout and his assistant, Liam, were carefully brushing dirt away from the woman. Graves was lurking, hanging over them like a vulture seeking a meal.

"Do you think she's all there... the complete body?" The question ripped from her throat and was accompanied by a wave of nausea that had her entire body feeling ill, not just her gut. They had exposed two feet so far, but ugly surprises could still lurk beneath the soil.

Rideout rested his hands on his thighs and looked at her. "An educated guess? Yes. But we'll need to wait to know for sure."

The macabre image of the body missing its head flashed in Amanda's mind. She shook the thought away.

"We'll get there, Detective. Just give us some time. We do

this right, and we might even unearth evidence to track her killer."

He was right, of course. They had to handle this methodically and with a gentle touch. The smallest of trace evidence could be what nailed the son of a bitch. "I understand."

"Why did you ask that, Steele? Whether there is an entire body?" Graves cradled her mug in one hand, her arm tucked close to her torso, as if waiting for story time.

Amanda wasn't pulling from a grisly case in her past though. Her motive for asking about the remains came down to one sad truth. "Anything is possible at this point."

"Huh. Okay. Well, as I said before, we first concern ourselves with finding her identity and cause of death."

"I realize that, but those answers can't be pulled from thin air." Amanda's respect for Graves had been tested four months ago when the sergeant was ready to close a case prematurely to look good to the chief. Amanda drew herself taller, prepared to stand her ground. Even shoulders squared, chest out, her five-foot-nine frame felt small next to Graves's nearly six-foot height.

"And I realize that," Graves hissed in return.

Amanda would move on. Otherwise, she'd likely be pointing out how rhetorical statements didn't get the investigation anywhere. "CSI Blair," Amanda called out, and the investigator slowly lowered her camera.

"Yes...?" The subtle hint of a smile. Their relationship had changed since they had met for coffee and cleared the air in the spring. Before that, Blair had harbored animosity toward Amanda's father, which she took out on Amanda.

"Any signs that the murder happened here?" Amanda asked.

"No blood or biological trace. We have shoe prints, though." Blair pointed toward a few markers. "Just partials, two different designs on the sole and two different sizes. Both suggest men's footwear."

"One likely belongs to Nolan Copeland, the young man who tripped over the vic's leg," Amanda said, stepping toward the closest flagged print to her. It was set in the soft earth and clearly visible. Circles of varying sizes, transected by a slash the shape of a lightning bolt.

"I'd say the ones that look like that." Blair gestured to the marker next to Amanda's foot.

The skin crinkled around Trent's eyes. "What makes you so sure of that?"

"There are quite a few that look like that, and given the direction they lead, but..." Blair indicated a marker next to a partial which, by the look of it, was the heel portion of the sole. It had deep grooves with a thin swipe arched toward the inseam. Blair added, "There's only one that looks like this."

"What are you saying exactly?" Graves spoke up.

"The killer may have taken his time to cover his shoe prints."

"Or they wore away over time," Graves said. "Still, if this partial ties back to the killer, lucky for us, he missed one."

Some luck. They'd still need to find Cinderella.

Blair went on. "Databases may tell us the make and style of shoe, but I'd say this lone partial belongs to a man's work boot or hiking boot. The other pattern is likely a running shoe."

"Estimation on foot sizes?" Trent asked, his notepad and pen in hand again.

"Eleven for the boot, size ten for the shoe."

Amanda nodded, appreciating Blair's confidence in her assessments. "Thanks."

"Don't mention it. Oh, there's one other thing. Over here..." Blair pointed out a section of ground where the grass laid flat. "Not certain what to make of it yet, but we flagged it."

The overall size would be right for a person's ass. "Ah, well, the person who tripped over the woman was found sitting on the ground rocking back and forth."

"That could explain it." Blair returned to work.

While they had spoken with Blair, the ME and his assistant had cleared up the woman's right leg to her knee. At the current rate of progress, it might be awhile yet before they had her fully exposed. Amanda faced Trent and nudged her head down the trail in the direction of the parking lot. "Let's go talk with Nolan Copeland."

"And check out his shoes." Trent closed his notepad and stuck it and his pen into the back pocket of his pants.

"I'm going to make sure PIO is briefed on the situation," Graves said.

The Public Information Office was the point of contact for the media and represented the PWCPD.

Graves shook her head and turned her chin downward, her gaze on the body. "A woman buried in the woods... I doubt it will take long before the media vultures arrive."

Amanda smiled, feeling a teeny tug of a connection to the interim sergeant. It might have been the first since her arrival in the spring. Amanda didn't much care for journalists and reporters either. They had a knack for crossing lines and smearing the PWCPD whenever they got the chance. It was easy to judge the actions of others when not in their shoes.

Graves left the site ahead of Amanda and Trent, but they followed close behind.

Amanda wished they were armed with more before speaking with Nolan, but that was how murder investigations worked. They unraveled in stages and often much slower than desired.

Dumfries-Triangle Volunteer Fire Department had cleared out, but there were PWCPD cruisers accompanied by four officers.

Graves got into her SUV, and shortly later, it was kicking

exhaust out of the tailpipe. Probably to give the sergeant a little warmth while she made her phone calls. Amanda watched for a moment, then turned her attention to the group of friends.

Nolan Copeland was sitting on the hood of the Kia sedan, his two buddies standing near him. They were a good-looking bunch and appeared harmless, but appearances were often deceiving.

Officer Wyatt was with the young men and dipped his head in greeting. He had his notepad out and would have been taking preliminary statements. Amanda and Trent would pose questions of their own, some of which might be repetitive. But if they uncovered the smallest of discrepancies, it might prove integral to solving the case.

"We can take it from here, Officer," she told Wyatt.

"As you wish." Wyatt closed his notebook and walked toward a cruiser.

"Nolan Copeland?" Amanda directed toward the young man in the plaid shirt. She had her badge held up, as did Trent.

"I am, but we just answered a bunch of questions. Can't we go now?"

Noland struck her as a guy's guy, life of the party, the goof. "We're detectives Steele and Stenson. And you two are?" She leveled her gaze at Nolan's friends. They'd need to give their version of events too.

"Chet Farley." He repositioned his black-frame glasses on his nose and wouldn't hold eye contact. He ended up tucking his hands into his jeans pockets. Possibly shy, but more likely he was uncomfortable, as his bright-yellow knitted sweater spoke more to a vibrant personality.

"And you?" Trent prompted the third friend.

"Jared." Spat out as if it was of little consequence.

His harder edge spoke to a person who thought it was him against the rest of the world. His black hair was cropped very short, and his face was unshaven. He wore a black hoodie and stood with his shoulders rounded forward.

"Your last name, Jared?" Amanda asked pointedly.

"Hart." It came out like a hiss.

"Well, Jared Hart, why don't you tell us what happened here?" She didn't care for people with chips on their shoulders, no matter their age.

"Nolan just told you. We told that cop." Jared flailed a hand toward Wyatt, who was now sitting in his cruiser.

"And now, you're going to tell us." Amanda met his gaze, held it. She'd stare the defiant kid down until his legs buckled. She hadn't lost a stare-down contest once.

"Fine," he huffed. "We wanted to have a little fun, let off some steam."

"On a Tuesday morning. Strange day of the week, isn't it?" The timing had bothered her from the start. Surely these kids would have school today. They couldn't be any older than twenty.

"No."

"You don't have anywhere to be today? School perhaps?"

Jared kicked some stones.

"We're taking an in-between year." This from Chet, the timid one—at least around her and Trent.

She wasn't about to lecture them on how their time could be better spent than drinking and having illegal fires in public parks. "I get that. You're still deciding on the direction of your lives." She put it out there non-judgmentally, appreciating that Chet had spoken up. She also wanted to relate so they would be more open to talking.

"Yep," Chet said.

"Not that it's any of your business." Jared's mouth set in a scowl.

"It *is* our business, actually." Amanda pointed her finger between herself and Trent. "In case you haven't figured it out yet, we're with Homicide." She paused there, letting that sink into their skulls. They likely deduced that already, but she felt it necessary to stress their purpose at the park and the importance of the situation. "Your friend found a dead woman buried in the woods."

"You make it sound like I did it. I didn't!" Nolan protested.

"Never said that."

Nolan licked his lips and glanced away.

"But you never saw her before?"

"What?" Nolan spat. "No way." His hands were trembling, and he set them on the edge of the hood.

"What time did you arrive at the park?" Trent asked.

"Three AM, thereabouts," Nolan mumbled.

"Before that?" Amanda wanted a picture of their night.

"We were just hanging out playing video games at Jared's." Chet jacked a thumb toward his friend.

Trent glanced at Amanda briefly and picked up the questioning from the timeline of the friends' arrival at the park. "After you got here... then what?"

"We started a fire, had some beers." Nolan rubbed his arms. "That's it."

"Then what?"

"We heard the sirens and ran into the woods," Chet said.

"In different directions," Nolan amended. "That's when I, ah, found that woman." His face paled, and he put a hand over his stomach. "I was using the flashlight on my phone but got turned around."

Amanda imagined it was possible to become disoriented, especially buzzed and in the dark. "We need to see the bottom of your shoes. All of you."

Each of them lifted their feet for her and Trent to look at the soles. They were all wearing running shoes, and Nolan's were a visual match to the many prints near the grave, just as they had suspected.

"Okay, thank you," Amanda told them.

"Who is she... the dead woman?" Chet asked and met Amanda's gaze.

"We don't know yet."

"Was she, ah, *was she*—" Nolan covered his mouth, swallowed roughly, his Adam's apple bulging. "Was she being buried while we were—" Nolan rushed to a thicket of bushes next to the lot and emptied his stomach.

That was a good question. The victim hadn't been buried for long, but they didn't know how long she'd been dead. Just more blanks that needed filling in. "Did you see anyone else in the park?"

Chet and Jared met each other's gazes and shook their heads.

"No," Nolan said between bouts of retching.

She highly doubted these young men were responsible for the woman's fate. Nolan, specifically, didn't have the stomach for murder. Rather these boys were just victims of circumstance.

With them in the clear, though, it raised another point. Who had called about the fire? Had it been the killer? If so, why risk drawing attention to himself? So many questions...

"Detective?" Chet prompted, bringing her back to the question that Nolan had raised.

"When was she buried? At this point, we don't know." She could have tagged on *much* but that had her feeling so powerless. She pulled out her business cards and handed one to each of them. "Call me if you think of anything that might help the investigation."

"Does this mean we can go?" Nolan pried himself from the bushes, his cheeks now flushed.

"Yes, but stay in the county. I assume you all live in Prince William County?" Wyatt would have taken all their information, but she asked anyhow.

The trio nodded.

"Did you all come in this car?" She pointed to the Kia.

"Uh-huh. It's mine," Nolan said.

"Before you leave, I want you to check in with Officer Wyatt." She waved him over.

Nolan's eyes enlarged. "What? Why?"

"This is messed up, man," Jared griped. "He didn't do anything." His volume tailed off as Amanda spoke to Wyatt.

"The boys are good to leave, but please run a Breathalyzer test on Nolan Copeland to ensure he's in a good state to drive." He wasn't showing signs of intoxication, but the discovery of a dead body would sober a person's mind quick. It didn't mean the consumed alcohol had left his bloodstream. And she'd had an up-close snapshot of what happened when a drunk got behind the wheel. She squeezed out thoughts of her husband, Kevin, and six-year-old daughter, Lindsey, who had died over seven years ago because of a drunk driver.

"Will do. Come with me." Wyatt and the boys headed toward his cruiser, just as Liam was jogging toward her and Trent.

"You've got to come quick... back to the burial site." Liam was winded, like he'd run the whole way.

"What is it?"

"The woman isn't alone. There's a young girl with her."

FOUR

Amanda's heart was pounding as she tramped down the path to the graves. *A young girl...* Liam's words kept repeating in her head.

She stopped short at the feet of the woman. She was dressed in a turtleneck long-sleeved shirt and jeans. Any exposed skin was a pale gray—her hands, neck, face. Her fingers appeared intact, and presumably her prints were as well. Whoever had placed her here wasn't overly worried about her being identified. Her face appeared early thirties. She had shoulder-length blond hair, a thin nose that ran slightly crooked, and a subtle chin dimple. Her eyes faced the sky and were milky.

A young girl of maybe six was on her side, her right arm draped over the woman's stomach. Her facial features had her looking like a miniature version of the woman, and her eyes were open too. She was clothed in jean overalls and a sweater.

There was a stuffed elephant, about six inches long, in the pit with them.

Amanda's lungs froze on an exhale. Zoe had a stuffed dog, Lucky, she had carted everywhere until her seventh birthday two months ago when she'd proclaimed herself as too big for it now. Lucky had been resigned to pride of place on the book-shelf in her bedroom. Amanda shook her personal thoughts aside, focusing again on the sight before her.

Mother and daughter could have just laid down for a nap amid the rustling leaves and birdsong.

Assuming for now they are mother and daughter...

Amanda considered herself hardened by the many things she'd seen in her career but seeing that little girl in a shallow grave, curled against the woman's side... It brought out the mother in her, a protective need to defend and protect. But those actions would all come too late. She'd be hugging Zoe extra tight tonight. "Any identification?"

"Not yet." Rideout brushed more dirt off the victims.

No purse or phone were immediately visible.

"Do you know when or how they died?" Trent asked.

Rideout shook his head. "It's early yet, but preliminarily I'd say they died within the last few days. Rigor has certainly come and gone. I'll conduct more tests back at the morgue to narrow that down some."

"So we are talking less than a week?" Amanda was desperate for some sort of timeline.

"I feel comfortable saying that, yes. Before concluding cause of death, I'll need to take a closer look. *Manner* of death, I think we all know..."

Amanda nodded. "Murder. The dead don't bury themselves."

"Precisimo." A fictional word, a desperate stab at levity, but it fell flat.

Amanda looked at her watch. 8:05 *AM*. It felt like it should be much later than that. "A few days." She mulled that over and said, "Are there any signs animals got to either of them?" The grave was only about ten inches deep—no wonder the tips of the shoes poked from the ground.

"Not from what I'm seeing." Rideout set down the brush that he'd been using to sweep aside dirt.

CSI Blair stepped in and snapped a myriad of photographs of the victims in situ and shortly later declared herself finished.

Rideout fished in the front pockets of the woman's jeans and came out empty-handed. Next, he delicately removed the girl's arm from the woman. The action had Amanda wanting to turn away, but her gaze was hooked on the nightmare in front of her.

Had the mother witnessed her daughter's murder before her own?

Rideout checked the girl's front pockets too and produced nothing for his trouble. Next, Liam helped him slowly turn the woman to her side on a tarp that had been placed next to the grave. Nothing was beneath her but more dirt.

Rideout checked the woman's back pockets and shook his head.

He checked the last two pockets—the ones in the back of the girl's overalls. He sat back on his heels, looking over the makeshift grave. "Nothing in their clothing."

A ball knotted in Amanda's gut. She may have been wrong about the killer wanting them discovered sooner than later. He certainly didn't want them identified easily and their families afforded closure. Though that thought chilled her. What if it was a loved one or family member who had killed them? Were their deaths intentional or was the burial to cover an accident?

"Hopefully Missing Persons will give us something." Desperation gripped Amanda's chest because the database would only help if they'd been reported.

"Do you think it's mother and daughter or...?" Trent stopped there.

"They look alike," Rideout responded.

"I agree," Liam chimed in. "It's in the shape of the nose and chin. Of course, DNA testing will tell us for sure."

Which takes time... This case was just starting, and it was already frustrating. "Surely, someone knows they're missing." Amanda would cling to that life raft even as it rolled over swells in the middle of the Atlantic. "They both appear to be well-nourished. Their clothing isn't designer, but it's in good shape..."

"The paint on the woman's fingernails is intact," Rideout said.

"Any signs of a struggle?" Epithelium under fingernails could lead them to the killer—if she'd fought back.

"Not that I'm immediately seeing. Obviously, I'll scrape under the nails." Rideout pushed up the woman's sleeves. "Oooh. I might have spoken too soon."

"What is it?" Amanda stepped closer. The woman's wrists were marred by bruising.

"Not defensive necessarily, but it would seem someone gripped her hard."

"Someone? Not the killer?"

"Sure, if he was around her a while. But see the contusions are a rainbow of hues?"

"Right. So they were inflicted at different times?"

"Yes. I'd say these bruises would indicate up to two weeks of abuse. After that contusions are no longer visible."

Trent's jaw was tight, his expression shadowed. His mind was likely going where Amanda's had briefly leaped—domestic violence—but it was unfounded at this point.

"Let's not jump to any conclusions," she said. "We don't know when they went missing or how long they might have been with their killer. We need to keep our minds open. We'll find their identities and go from there."

Trent was staring intently at the ground, at the bodies, as if he were avoiding making eye contact with her.

"Can you tell approximately when the most recent bruising on her wrists occurred?" she asked Rideout.

"The most recent appears to be days old."

"So whoever inflicted those specific bruises is potentially the one who put her in the ground," Trent reasoned.

"More than likely. Now I noticed something just now when I moved their bodies." Rideout placed his hands on the girl's face and gently rolled her head. "As suspected."

"Hans." Amanda pulled out the medical examiner's first name, not able to stand the suspense. It was like she was walking a high wire and leaning precariously to one side, about to topple to the ground without a safety net to catch her.

"By the way I can manipulate her head, her spinal cord has been severed, likely due to a broken neck."

Amanda laid a hand over her stomach. She thought she'd seen the worst the world offered when she'd uncovered a sex-trafficking ring. But breaking a little girl's neck also required a next-level monster.

Rideout added, "Again, I'll know more back at the morgue. I'll X-ray her entire body."

"And when do you think you'll get to their autopsies?" One horrible realization led to another. This little girl's next stop was being dissected and pulled apart.

Rideout looked at Liam who kept the medical examiner's schedule.

"Dr. Rideout can perform these this afternoon," Liam said and pulled out a tablet, pecked on the screen. "Specifically, he'll start at one."

"There you go." Rideout gestured toward his assistant and nodded, firming up what he had said.

"Okay, we'll check in with you then or shortly afterward to see what you've gathered." Amanda straightened up.

"Can you tell if the woman's neck is broken too?" Trent asked.

"It is. I noticed how it moved when I rolled her onto the tarp."

Silence followed Rideout's words, like a natural marker for the conclusion of a conversation. It was time to move, but Amanda's feet were weighed to the ground. "We find out who they are, and we're more than halfway there."

"Let's go check Missing Persons." Trent started toward the parking lot, and Amanda kept stride with him.

Graves was coming at them. Trent bypassed her straight to the department car he'd brought to the scene.

Traitor...

The sergeant looked like she had a lot to offload. She was holding her cell phone cupped in both hands and flipping it back and forth from one palm to the other. Her shoulders were squared, and her face shadowed.

"Yes?" Amanda said.

"You're leaving already?"

"Getting ready to. Why?"

"Bring me up to speed."

"You heard about the girl... Yes?"

"The girl?" Graves's brow furrowed in confusion. "No."

"There were two in that grave. The woman you know about. She looks to be in her early thirties. There was a girl of about five or six with her. Presumably they are mother and daughter, though we can't be sure without ID."

Graves's posture faltered, her normal self-assurance melting away like hot wax and shrinking her height. Slumped shoulders, head dipped forward and down. "So no phone or purse?" Her voice was rough, gravelly. Amanda didn't think Graves was a mother herself, but that mattered little. Cases with children were tough on everyone involved. But this one was also allowing Amanda a glimpse of Graves's humanity.

"No."

"Were they sexually assaulted?"

"We'll need to wait on autopsies to know for sure. But there are signs of physical abuse. The woman has multiple bruises, with some dating back weeks."

"Rideout make any comment on what he believes may be cause of death?"

"Preliminarily, their spinal cords were severed by their necks being broken."

"Dear God." Graves stared into the woods; her eyes glazed over. The reverie lasted mere seconds before the sergeant's face turned to stone. "We need answers yesterday. When is Rideout doing the autopsies?"

"This afternoon, one o'clock."

Graves nodded, her eyes back to carrying that faraway haunted look. It could just be that Amanda was seeing herself reflected in them. Cases like this were tough, but also motivating.

"Trent's searching Missing Persons right now," Amanda eventually said, filling the silence. She glanced at Trent, who was in the driver's seat of a department car. He'd be using the onboard computer to conduct the search. "We'll see what comes of that. We'll also be speaking with the person who called in the fire. What had them out here at five in the morning, that type of thing."

"I assume you've cleared the teens?"

Amanda nodded. "There's nothing to suggest any of them were involved—beyond one of them stumbling over the body. We have their information, though, if we have follow-up questions."

"What are your initial thoughts?"

"It's early. Victims of domestic violence? Abducted and with their killer for two weeks?"

"Could be a blend of both."

"It's impossible to say until we know who they are, when they died, and their last movements."

Graves licked her lips, then pursed them, nudged out her

chin. "Well, it looks like you have your work cut out for you. Keep me posted at every step along the way. I might see you at the autopsies." The sergeant returned to her SUV and drove off.

The quick exit surprised Amanda, as she'd expected Graves would want to see the child and the grave again. And Graves had never graced the morgue for any previous investigations. Was it the little girl and/or something that smacked personal for the sergeant?

Trent was jogging toward her. "I think I got a hit."

"You...?" She snapped her mouth shut, speechless. She'd been prepared for the regular answer—nada. Low expectations, little disappointment. "Who? When were they reported missing?"

"The report was filed this past Friday by one Roy Archer for his wife and daughter, Jill and Charlotte. Wife is thirty-four, daughter is five."

"You're sure it's them?"

"Look at their pictures for yourself."

She did just that. "Oh, yeah, it's them all right. Let's go talk to Roy."

He didn't respond but stood there, his jaw clenched.

"You heard me? It's time to move."

"Reported *last* week," Trent hissed. "Bruising going back *weeks*." His left hand formed a fist.

She didn't like that he seemed to be internalizing and making this about his aunt, who had an abusive partner. "Let's see what he has to say before we jump to any conclusions."

Trent shook his head angrily. "I *am* looking at the evidence."

She brushed her fingers over his fist. He drew back like a torch had burned him. "Are you? This isn't about your aunt." It came out all wrong.

His eyes flicked to hers. "You can't argue with the bruising."

"Well... Maybe Jill took her daughter and left Roy weeks

ago. She'd been in communication, then more recently fell out of reach. That's when Roy reported them missing."

"You want me to believe a killer abducted them and held them for weeks during which time he inflicted the bruising?"

"It is entirely possible." Silence stretched between them, which she broke. "As we've said many times, we need to keep an open mind until all the evidence is in."

"Fine. But I have a sinking feeling..."

"And that's okay. Your instincts are there for a reason. It's just our responsibility to know when to listen and act on them."

"You know what makes this even worse? That is, if the husband was abusive and killed his family."

"What?"

"Roy Archer is an officer with the Dumfries PD. He must have joined after I'd left. Tell you what, I'll meet you at Central, and we'll take one car." He didn't wait for confirmation but got into the department vehicle and shut the driver's door behind him.

She didn't stop him. It was a solid course of action. And maybe the separation would give him a chance to cool off. Trent didn't let his temper show often, but it was beneath a thin veil when it came to violence toward women and children. Something she admired, but with this case, depending how it played out, it could be her partner's undoing.

FIVE

Trent might have been pushing the gas harder than normal, but he was pissed. His mind kept kicking out the same scenario, regardless of Amanda's repeated caution to keep an open mind. If he heard that admonition one more time, he might snap. As it was, he still quaked from her touch—and not in a good way. She'd tried to calm him down, but he was entitled to feel how he felt. *Damn it.*

There were the bruises, the prolonged infliction of the injuries; it had to be cumulative domestic abuse. Jill and Charlotte were reported missing last week, so presumably they hadn't been gone for weeks—the age of some of the bruising. And how many more scars were hidden beneath the woman's clothing? As a husband and father, positions that garnered trust, that man should have provided comfort, solace, and protection for his family. Instead, they were now dead.

He called his aunt's number as he drove. The call was answered, but there was silence.

Trent jumped in. "Aunt Gert—"

An automated voice struck his ears. "You have reached a number that has been disconnected."

He came close to throwing his phone through the windshield. The bastard had truly gone above with this—having his aunt sever the line that allowed her family to reach out to her. Things had gone from bad to worse. She used to be the life of the party but had retreated into a wallflower. The vibrant colors she used to wear became tans and shades of gray, black, and white. Then one day she stopped cheerleading family reunions and turned into the person who made shallow excuses to avoid them.

He pulled into the lot for Central and parked, coming to such an aggressive stop the nose of the car dipped down, then shot up.

Amanda parked in the spot next to him. He didn't want to talk about his aunt and hoped she'd leave the topic alone.

She loaded into the passenger seat and tossed out an awkward smile. "Someone has a lead foot."

"Looks to me like you kept up all right."

"Got me there."

He waited for her door to shut before he reversed out of the spot.

"We need to talk."

"Not more about keeping an open mind. Please."

"I was going say we need to discuss more of what we saw on scene." Her voice was harsh, a touch raw.

He gestured for her to proceed.

"The way they were buried together, in the manner they were, suggests they were posed. The fact he included the child's stuffed toy and had the girl hugging her mother tells me there might be some remorse."

"The killer may have experienced regret, but that's of little consequence. Jill and Charlotte Archer are dead." Saying their names, he realized he may have been too emotionally vested. He softened his voice and volunteered, "I can do this, Amanda... Stay objective."

"I know you can."

Something about her confidence and the way she was watching him, had his tough front disintegrating further. He had proven himself to her before when a case touched close to home, and she'd believed in him then before she even had a reason to. A part of him would love to open up about his aunt and how he felt a responsibility toward her. It wasn't his fault she'd married Don, but his job was to protect and serve the community. He'd failed his own flesh and blood. What did that say about him?

But it wasn't like he hadn't tried to reach his aunt, to help her see. How often, though, can a person be shut out before they raise their hands and walk away? And maybe that's what he should do—once and for all. Regardless, for now that was his only choice. This investigation deserved his full attention.

Trent led the way into the station for the Dumfries PD. He found Officer Ben Fuller at the front desk. A few years ago, it would have been Trent seated there.

"Trent Stenson? Long time no see. Guess you're too big for us now." Ben had started a few months before Trent transferred to the PWCPD. He was the oldest in his class at the academy, going through the training in his late twenties, but he spoke like he was fifty-something.

"Hey, Ben. Is Officer Archer in?" Trent cut to the point.

"Think you just caught him. Want me to get him for you?"

"Please. Tell him it's Detective Stenson and Detective Steele." Trent's insides were quaking with rage, just thinking Roy might have killed his family, but he wanted to prove Amanda had every reason to put faith in him. He'd pull himself back from the ledge and stop projecting his personal life onto the case. This wasn't about his aunt.

"Detective Steele. Nice to meet ya." Ben shook Amanda's hand.

"Ben?" Trent prompted, remembering the man was chatty.

"Ah, yeah, sure. Roy. Say, this have anything to do with his wife and daughter? Awful tragic they went missing."

"It's best we speak with him."

Ben got up from his post and headed down a hall, calling out, "Roy."

"What is it? I'm just about to head out." Gruff.

"I know, but you've got visitors."

There was a distinct mumble and groan. "Who?"

"Detectives Stenson and Steele. I think it's about your wife and daughter." The latter part was spoken lowly.

Silence was the immediate response followed by, "Send 'em back."

Ben called out for Trent, and he and Amanda followed his voice to a doorway. Ben gestured inside and left for the front.

This room housed a few computer stations for officers to key their reports at the end of their shift. Roy Archer was leaned back in a desk chair, hands clasped across his lap, and lightly swiveling. His presence at this time of day would be because he hadn't finished up before heading home last night. Not impressive cop work.

"You find Jill and Charlotte?"

"Let's take this to the conference room." Trent led the way, familiar with the blueprint of the building from his years of working there.

Once inside, he rolled out a chair for Roy and said, "Sit."

Roy looked at him with dead eyes, as if no soul existed behind them.

Amanda closed the door and sat next to Roy, leaving Trent to pick a spot farther away. A blessing. He didn't think he'd handle being close to the man; there was just something about him. First, Trent's suspicions, but also the rudeness he had demonstrated toward Ben.

"So you found them?"

Trent's eyes landed on the man's knuckles. Scraped and scuffed.

"Hello?" Roy waved a hand in front of Trent's face.

Now if Trent were closer, he'd twist his wrist. Instead, he took a calming breath.

"Where are they?" Roy raised his brows, impatient.

"They're both dead." Sadness welled up for Jill and Charlotte, but he was without empathy for Roy. He had that same overbearing energy as the man his aunt had married.

"We're sorry for your loss," Amanda interjected.

"Oh." Roy rubbed his face. "Ah, where did you find them?"

"Most people also want to know *how*," Trent said drily.

Amanda shot him a side-glance and answered Roy's question. "In Prince Park. They were buried together in a shallow grave."

Roy's mouth fell open.

Trent resisted the urge to ask what part of Amanda's statement came as a surprise, in the vein of objectivity.

"Are you familiar with the park, Mr. Archer?" Amanda asked.

"I'd actually prefer you both call me *Officer* Archer."

"Sure..."

"Prince Park is where Jill often took Charlotte."

"When was the last time you saw them?" Trent would try to keep his mind open. Everything within him screamed Roy was a piece of shit, but mother and daughter could have been abducted by a killer.

"I filed a missing person report on Friday."

"Yes, and that's what led us here," Trent volleyed back. "Not an answer to my question, though."

"It wasn't ID?" Still detouring.

"Your wife and daughter weren't found with any," Amanda said. "No phone or purse either."

"Huh."

"Did she have a cell phone? A purse?" Amanda asked.

"Yep. Any sign of her car?"

Amanda glanced at Trent, back to Roy. "What vehicle did she have?"

"A white Chevy Malibu. I have an APB issued for it."

An all-points bulletin.

"And I haven't been able to get through on her phone since last Tuesday."

"Last time you saw them?" Trent asked.

"Same. Last Tuesday." Roy sat back in his chair, his elbows resting on the armrests like he was having a casual conversation. "I came home from work, and they were both gone. No note or anything. I figured maybe she'd left me."

"But you filed the report on Friday," Trent said.

"Uh-huh, but you should know twenty-four to forty-eight hours must pass, unless there's unmistakable proof of foul play."

Trent would just keep his mouth shut. But Rideout figured they died days ago. What was to say Roy didn't kill them, then report them missing? His claim that he hadn't seen them since Tuesday could be a lie.

"Why did you assume she'd left if there was no note? Were there problems in the marriage?" Amanda put it all so calmly, not a feat Trent could have pulled off.

"Ah, just like any other married couple, we had disagreements. Sure."

"That all? Disagreements? Is that why there are bruises on her body telling us she was beaten for weeks?" Trent was impressed he remained in his chair and hadn't yet throttled Roy.

Roy stared into Trent's eyes, challenging him. "What are you saying, Detective?"

He hadn't denied the allegation; he'd deflected. Again. "I'm quite sure you know." Trent pointed to the man's abraded knuckles. "What happened there?"

"I got into a scuffle with someone."

Trent clenched his jaw. Roy phrased it as if he had been in a fight with another man.

"Why are you looking at me like that?"

With utter disgust? Somehow Trent managed to keep that thought internal.

"But I know the spouse is always the prime suspect. Is that it?"

"Please, Officer Archer," Amanda said, stepping in as a mediator, "we're just trying to figure out what happened."

"How the hell should I know?"

"Right. You returned home, saw they were gone. Then what?" Amanda asked, losing patience.

"I tried calling her, but it went straight to voicemail. It has in the times I've tried since Tuesday too."

"Was it common for your wife to turn her phone off?" Amanda asked.

"I usually got through."

If Roy was telling the truth that left the potential for an unknown third party to intercept. "You mentioned problems in your marriage..." Trent coughed to clear his throat. "Did you suspect she was having an affair?"

"Guess it's possible. She was a pretty woman."

Trent didn't imagine Roy would tolerate a cheating wife. "We'll need to know all your movements from last Tuesday until now."

"I'm a fellow officer of the law."

"Even if it's to rule you out. But as you said, the spouse, partner, significant other is always the first suspect," Amanda served, using his earlier words against him.

Roy threw his hands up and shook his head. "While you're riding me, their killer is out there."

Trent wasn't ready to let go of a neat and tidy close to this case that would see Roy Archer behind bars. After all, the timing of their disappearance and the bruising heavily implied Roy beat his wife. But what if that was his greatest sin? What if there was far more to this investigation than first met the eye?

SIX

Amanda didn't care for Roy Archer. The second she'd laid eyes on him, she'd had the sense he was a predator—controlling, abusive, and chauvinistic. He hadn't defended himself when Trent brought up the bruising on his wife's body or clearly explain the reason for his scuffed knuckles. But she'd leave that line of inquiry for now. "We will need Jill's number and the name of the service provider to review her communications. Was she on your plan?"

"Yep. And that's fine. Whatever it takes."

For someone who had just lost his wife and daughter, he was rather blasé. It might be an emotional defense mechanism playing a cruel trick on him, blinding him to acceptance. But Amanda had been in his place, losing her family in one swoop, and it had her reeling from the moment she found out. Roy seemed to take the news of his family's deaths in stride. Was it simply shock? He'd admitted to problems existing in the marriage. Had he been the one stepping out on his wife? "Were you seeing anyone else, Officer Archer?" she asked Roy.

"Absolutely not. Jill was enough work." He puffed his cheeks and blew out a breath.

A vibration under her feet picked up more speed. It was caused by Trent bouncing his leg on the floor, from the other side of the table.

"What do you mean she was *work*?" she rushed out before her partner said something he might live to regret. He was a ticking time bomb around this man.

"Please, Detective. Girls, women, you can be high-maintenance. Not that I didn't love my wife and daughter. I did. I do."

Even with the declaration, Amanda was seeing little to support the claim. "There was a stuffed elephant in the grave with them. Was that your daughter's?"

Roy's brow pinched. "I don't think she had one of those. Unless Jill bought it without my knowledge."

Amanda bristled again. It would seem Roy kept his wife on a short leash. He probably watched her every move—or at least most—which meant he'd be familiar with the toys she bought the girl. But if the elephant hadn't been Charlotte's, who did it belong to? And what might that mean for the case? "We'll get a picture to you for verification."

"I'm telling you. She didn't have a stuffed elephant."

"There's no need to become defensive, *Officer*," Trent chimed in. "Unless you—"

Roy flailed an arm toward Trent. "Really? Well, newsflash. I. Didn't. Kill. Them. That means you'll have to pick your ass up and do some work."

Shadows passed across Trent's face, his cheeks flushed, and his lips curled into a scowl.

"Detective Stenson," Amanda punched out quick. "Could we talk in the hall for a minute?"

Trent slowly pried his eyes from Roy, met Amanda's gaze and got up.

She closed the door behind them.

He rushed out, "Don't even think about telling me to back off. He—"

She held up her hand. "Not going to. Just thought you needed a break from the guy."

"You got me there." He shot daggers at the door.

She moved down the hall and continued speaking. "He's got no emotion about them being dead. Not one tear or clear sign of remorse." Those words tripped her up; the way their bodies were posed suggested just that. "He's quick to point elsewhere, defensive, vague, dismissive. You notice any of that?"

"Not lost on me."

"But he knows nothing about the elephant."

Trent smirked. "Means nothing. Jill bought it without him finding out. So what? The guy's a wonderful actor and knows how to cover his tracks. He's used to hiding the fact he's been abusing his wife—something he hasn't denied. He tosses in the elephant to throw off the investigation, ditches the wife's car somewhere..."

She eventually nodded, feeling the need to concede to the possibility Roy had killed his family. "Here's how we're going to proceed. We request Jill's phone records, see if there's anything in her communications that's helpful."

"Which ideally will reveal her last steps," Trent inserted.

"Yes. We'll also speak with her friends and parents, see what they might have to say about her and her marriage."

"Still following."

"If Roy Archer did this to his family, we'll get him, but we need to build a case against him. We can't just go accusing another officer of the law of murder."

"Not that he deserves the badge if he's abusive."

If only that was grounds for dismissal... "Won't argue that, but we need to back off on the allegations. You with me?"

He scanned her eyes, the energy coming from him hesitant. "Yeah."

"All right. Let's do this."

"Oh, one more thing. We might want to find out where

the Archer family lived before Dumfries. He wasn't here when I was, and I'm thinking he transferred from another department. The people there might have things to tell us about Roy."

"Yep, good idea. We still need to speak to the person who reported the fire, even if for due diligence." Amanda glanced down the hall, toward the closed door, back at Trent. "You ready to go back in?"

He took a deep breath, shook his arms, and stretched his neck side to side. "Yep, let's do this."

Amanda and Trent rejoined Roy, who they found staring into space. His eyes were glazed over. Still no fallen tears for his lost family.

"Sorry to keep you waiting," Amanda offered. "Since there were no IDs with their bodies, you'll need to make the formal identification. As you know, this is just procedure. Hans Rideout is assigned to their autopsies." She figured he'd know the name.

"How did they die?"

It took Roy long enough to ask. "Rideout hasn't yet concluded, but he suspects their necks were broken."

Roy sniffled, showing his first sign of emotion.

"You brought up the fact there were some problems in your marriage. Had there always been?" Amanda wanted to get a better feel for the relationship.

"We can both be strong-willed and don't always agree."

Not exactly an answer to Amanda's question, but it passed close to one. "Things any better or worse, recently?"

"I dunno. I know the move was rough on her."

"Where did you transfer from?" Amanda asked.

"The Anne Arundel County Police Department in Edge-water, Maryland. It's less than an hour and a half from here."

Trent leaned forward. "When did you move?"

"About nine months ago."

"What made you think she wasn't happy with the move?" Amanda asked.

"Didn't really need to *think it*. She told me more than once."

"She missed family and friends... coworkers?" Amanda was grasping, as she didn't know where Jill's family lived, and really a ninety-minute drive wasn't far for visits. "She have a job there she loved?"

"Being a wife and mother kept her too busy for that."

It was the way he'd said it, as if he'd made that decision on his wife's behalf. "Those jobs are most certainly full time." Amanda tacked on a smile hoping to dampen the judgment rising within her toward Roy. "And her friends, family... are they back in Edgewater?"

"Yep. Well, her parents. Jill didn't have any siblings. She never had a relationship with her cousins, aunts, or uncles. No idea where they live."

"And names of her friends?" Amanda asked.

"Don't know of any."

Tingles spread down Amanda's arms. Had Roy controlled Jill to the point she wasn't allowed to have friends outside the home?

"No friends?" This from Trent, bordering on a snarl.

"Nope."

"Well, we'll need a number for her parents," Amanda interjected.

"Ah, yeah." Roy pulled out a cell phone and prattled off a number. Trent scribbled in his notepad.

"Before we leave, we'll also need Jill's cell number and the name of your service provider."

"Sure. If you think it will help." Roy informed him of those things, and Trent recorded them on paper.

"Okay, well, you hang tight." Amanda paused at hearing her own words. *Hang tight?* As if there hadn't been a tragedy. She tried to redeem herself. "Detective Stenson and I will do all we can to find out what happened to your family. Once we know more, we'll get back to you."

"All right." He watched her, scanning her eyes, as if trying to pry her mind.

"We're sorry for your loss and appreciate this must come as quite a shock." Amanda extended Roy the courtesy, but seeing the man so unmoved was difficult to reconcile. Then again, people wore their grief differently, and shock enforced dark blinders.

"Thank you."

Amanda and Trent left and ran into Becky Tulson in the station's parking lot. Becky was an officer with Dumfries PD, but also Amanda's best friend since kindergarten.

"Hey, what are you guys doing here? Thought you'd pay me a visit?" Becky grinned, but it faded fast upon seeing Amanda's and Trent's serious expressions. "Uh-oh, what is it?"

Amanda put up a hand, wanting to quash any worries that might have crept up for her friend. "We were here to speak with Roy Archer."

"Oh. About his wife and daughter?"

Amanda nodded.

"Not good news if you're here."

"I'm afraid not. They were murdered and discovered in a shallow grave out in Prince Park." It didn't matter how many times Amanda imparted this news, the intensity was almost crippling.

"Oh. That's... Well, there are hardly words."

"What do you know about Roy?" Trent cut in, possibly without the emotional capacity to wallow in the tragedy of what happened, more focused on getting whoever did it held accountable.

Becky's eyes widened. "Do you think Roy did this?" She flicked a finger toward the station.

"Yep."

Amanda shook her head at Trent and amended. "It's only one possibility. We're still investigating."

"If you ask me, I wouldn't be surprised if he killed them." Becky crossed her arms. "He's got a temper, is aggressive as hell. He merely tolerates women. But honestly, I don't know a lot about his home life, and I think anyone within the Dumfries PD would tell you the same thing. We just were aware he had a wife and daughter— Ah, her too. It's just sinking in." Becky processed for a few seconds. "How did they die?"

"It appears their necks were broken," Amanda said.

"Son of a bitch." Becky clenched her jaw and shook her head. "Whoever did this needs to be locked away."

"Understatement. We're going to do all we can to make sure that happens." A promise if Amanda could at all help it.

"Call me if you need anything."

"Thanks, Beck. Will do."

Becky left them and entered the station.

"I know we're supposed to remain objective here, but I'm having a hard time. No friends? He moves her away from her parents. Roy isolated Jill from the rest of the world. He's controlling and abusive."

"I know, Trent. I heard everything too. Let's just keep our heads about us and check off all the boxes. If he did this, I want the charges against him to stick like hot tar."

SEVEN

Amanda called Graves from the passenger seat of the department car while Trent drove. They were headed to speak with Lance Crane, who had reported the fire. A quick background showed Lance was a resident of Triangle, thirty-eight, single, with no priors. His home address put him within walking distance of Prince Park.

She filled the sergeant in on their visit to Roy Archer and their suspicions. Graves saw merit in them but stressed they were to "play nice" unless the evidence cemented his guilt. She volunteered to handle the subpoena request for Jill Archer's phone records—communications and GPS tracking—and forwarding of that on to the service provider. She'd have the file sent to Amanda and Trent when it became available.

Amanda ended the call. "Huh."

"What?"

"Graves volunteered to help. She'll get Jill's phone records for us, including GPS."

Trent turned to face her. "Really?"

"I'm about as shocked as you. But I get the feeling this case hits close for her too." She could have hit herself for adding *too*. He didn't strike her as open to discussing his aunt.

He fell silent and retreated inward.

"You know you can talk to me about your aunt. That's if you want to." *What am I doing?* She hated it when people pushed her for personal information.

He ran his hands over the steering wheel. Said nothing.

"Or if you don't want to, that's fine too obviously."

"I tried calling her this morning and found out her number isn't in service."

"Sorry to hear that, Trent. Could you drop by for a visit? Is she in the area?"

"She's in Woodbridge, from what I last knew. Suppose I could go over. I'd just need to be careful. I wouldn't want Don taking my visit out on my aunt. You know, in case he suspects I'm there to take her away from him. Who knows what runs through that man's screwed-up mind?"

"I could go with you if it would make it easier."

Trent looked over at her, and he bobbed his head lightly as if to acknowledge and thank her for offering.

Just a few seconds later, Trent pulled into the driveway of an end-unit townhouse and they got out.

They knocked on the front door three times before there was an answer.

A man wearing jogging pants and an oversized T-shirt squinted in the sunlight and danced his gaze over them. She got the impression they had woken him up.

"Who are you?"

They both held up their badges.

"Are you Lance Crane?" Trent asked.

"I am. What's this about?"

Trent gave the introductions, then said, "We'd like to ask you a few questions. If we could..." Trent gestured into the home.

"Ah, sure." Lance opened the door wider and stepped back.

The place was modest but tidy. Lance took them to a small living room with an overstuffed couch, a bulky wood coffee table, and a media unit that took up a chunk of floor space. A large flat-screen television sat on top.

Lance gestured to the couch. "Sit if you'd—" A barking dog interrupted, and Lance excused himself. "That's mine. I better get her before she ticks off the neighbors."

Amanda nodded, though prepared to bolt after him if he ran out the back door. No need, though, as Lance returned within seconds, with a panting black Lab pup. She was still growing into her paws, and her hurried pace was comical as she tried to gain purchase on the wood floor. Regardless of the slick terrain, she still successfully navigated jumping up on Amanda's legs.

"Bad, Sophie. Get down." Lance waved his canine companion away. "Sorry about that," he said to Amanda.

"It's fine." She'd be smiling if they weren't there for such a serious reason. She loved dogs, and puppies made her heart melt. This one's entrance had certainly lightened her spirit.

"You said you had questions." Lance petted the dog, who had dropped onto her rear beside him.

"Why don't we sit?" Amanda suggested as she did just that.

"Sure." Lance lowered himself onto a chair, and the dog jumped onto his lap.

"We're here because you called about the fire at Prince Park," Amanda began.

"I figured, though I'm not sure why that brings two detectives to my door."

Amanda would supply more information once she'd felt him out. "We'll get to that. But where were you when you saw the fire?" He couldn't have been in his neighborhood. There were too many obstructions in the way including woods and a highway.

"I was out walking this girl." Lance scratched the pup's head. As a reward, the pup panted harder and flashed a wide doggy smile.

"Where did you walk?" Amanda asked.

"To the park."

"Over the highway?" She was a little skeptical, though it was possible he'd crossed the two lanes.

"That's right."

"Why so early in the morning?"

"I work the evening shift. Start at three in the afternoon and get off at midnight. Then I come home, eat, unwind for a bit, go for a walk, turn in."

This seemed to confirm her first impressions that they'd roused him from sleep. "So we woke you up just now?"

Lance bobbed his head. "Yes, and no. Sophie heard the door first and started whining. I popped her out back just before I got to you guys. As you saw, she's a little exuberant with visitors."

"Doesn't exactly have the makings of a good guard dog." Trent glanced at the canine.

"Black Labs aren't known to be aggressive. Sophie would slobber any intruder to death."

His remark was harmless, but Amanda stiffened at the man's light banter about death. "We'll need to verify your work schedule with your place of employment. Is there anyone who could confirm why you were out this morning?"

"No," he dragged out. "I live alone."

"Anyone who can attest to your movements since and including last Tuesday?" She was basing the timeline on what Roy had told them.

"Basically the last week?"

"Yes."

"I was at work Tuesday and Wednesday. Also Saturday, Sunday, Monday. I had Thursday and Friday as my weekend, but I didn't go anywhere. Stuck around here, watched TV and read. Oh, I stopped for groceries on the way home Sunday night. Of course, I took Sophie out for her daily walks. Now, I've cooperated with you, but I'd like to know what's going on." Lance's voice tightened, his mouth thick with saliva. He patted the pooch on the butt to get her to move, and she hopped onto the floor, sought a knotted rope, and settled with it at Lance's feet.

"My partner and I are with Homicide. After your call, two bodies were found in the woods. Would you know anything about that?"

"Bodies? Uh, no."

"Now I'm sure you can appreciate why we're here asking questions. We need some answers." She didn't feel it was necessary, at this point, to let him know the victims were a mother and her daughter.

"Well, I have none to give you... Not concerning bodies." He choked on the word *bodies* this time, his eyes bulging. "I just called about a fire."

"All the same, we will need the name and number of your employer. Just procedure," Amanda added.

"Procedure," Lance parroted. "But, sure. I work for Living Standards and report to Chris Graham."

That company specialized in the manufacture of sinks and faucets. "Do you know a Jill and Charlotte Archer?" She wanted to gauge Lance's reaction to the names, and his face was blank. Roy hadn't made the official identification yet, but that was merely a formality. The pictures with the missing person reports were an unmistakable match.

"No. Is that who was, ah, found?"

She nodded. "You told us you take Sophie for daily walks. Do they always take you near the park like this morning?"

"Usually."

If Lance wasn't the killer, he could have seen this person

without even knowing it. "Did you run into anyone on these walks in the last week?"

"Heavens no. Not a soul around that time of day. Well, except today... whoever had that fire going."

She pulled her card and handed it to him. "If someone comes to mind after we leave, call."

"Will do."

They thanked Lance for his time and left.

She spoke once they were back in the car. "We could verify he was working, but I'm not even sure that would get us anywhere. So much of his time can't be accounted for." She clicked her seat belt into place.

"I noticed you never told him it was a mother and daughter."

"No need to go there. He showed no visual reactions to the mention of their names." Amanda's thoughts trailed off. The identification was a formality, but one immediate anomaly just may be that stuffed elephant. Was she making more out of the fact Roy wasn't familiar with the toy than it warranted? Or was its placement in the grave a message of some sort?

EIGHT

Rideout looked up at Amanda and Trent and waved a gloved hand. "I was starting to wonder if you were going to show up."

"Well, we're here now," Amanda replied.

Jill Archer's body was on display. Rideout was in the middle of conducting a preliminary autopsy on her. So much of her flesh was marred with bruises in varying shades. Amanda glanced away only to have her gaze land on a second gurney.

Little Charlotte.

The girl was covered with a sheet to her shoulders, leaving her neck and face exposed. What she wouldn't do to travel back in time and save mother and daughter. But that wasn't her job. She came after hell happened. She sorted out the mess, made sense of it, and gave closure to loved ones left behind. *Justice.*

She cleared her throat. "We have their names now. Jill Archer is the woman, and the child is her daughter, Charlotte. They are the wife and daughter of an officer with the Dumfries PD. I'll text you the husband's number so you can arrange for him to formally ID them."

"All right."

Amanda quickly took care of that, then pocketed her phone.

"Any highlights we should know about?"

"As you can see, the woman's body is a map of abuse. In addition to the contusions on her wrists as I noted at the grave, you see there are many on her legs, inner thighs, abdomen."

"All within the last two weeks," Trent seethed.

"Afraid so."

Trent shook his head, grimaced. "You should know we're looking at the husband."

"As you probably should be. Husbands, partners, first suspects and all that."

"Yes, well, we're keeping our minds open," Amanda said. "Is there evidence of sexual assault?"

"For the woman, there is evidence of forced sex, yes. And I believe it was repeated instances."

That woman would have lived in horror. "The girl? Was she... Have you gotten to her yet?"

"She was first for the external autopsy. I'll go back to her and pick up where I left off after I've looked over the woman." Rideout's voice was gravelly.

"Never easy when it's a kid." She took a bet that's what had Rideout allowing himself some separation. Otherwise, he normally stuck with one body until the autopsy was complete before moving on to the next.

"It's not, but the one silver lining is there is no sign she was abused physically or sexually. Aside from the perimortem bruising on her back, her body isn't telling that story."

"Her back?" Amanda asked.

"I'll get to that."

"Semen in the woman?" Trent asked.

Rideout shook his head.

"Wore a condom then." Trent removed his notepad from his coat pocket.

"Could be that or the last time she had sex was some time before her death."

"Have you been able to more accurately pinpoint time of death?" Amanda asked.

"Approximately four days ago."

"As you thought on scene." That would mean their deaths took place on Friday, three days after Roy told them he'd returned home to find them gone. It would be more favorable if he'd lied to protect himself. The alternative birthed the possibility of a killer taking them and holding them before eventually taking their lives.

"X-rays did show breaks in the C2 and C3 vertebra, just at the base of the skull. I can now confirm that cause of death for both was transection of the spinal cord caused by the killer twisting their necks. Definitely done at someone's hand. Likely a man's, a person of strength. He'd also possess knowledge of how to pull this off." Rideout mimed how that would work—his left hand on his right jaw, right hand on his left temple. "This would have been done from standing behind them."

A few seconds passed in silence, but the space was filled with tangible sorrow.

Rideout continued. "I scanned their entire bodies, in fact. The mother showed bones that had been broken but were in various stages of healing."

"The son of a bitch," Trent muttered and paced a few steps away, turning his back to them.

Rideout glanced at Amanda. "It's always difficult when cases involve possible domestic abuse."

"Nothing *possible* about that," Trent said.

She wasn't even going to touch his comment, not wanting a confrontation with her partner. "Anything else we should know?"

Rideout turned Jill on her side and pointed to a reddish-colored section beneath her buttocks. "Livor mortis, as you know, blood settling and pooling in the body after death, always shows in the lowest extremities. In this case, the woman was sitting for a couple hours after her heart stopped. Not lying down, as she was found in the grave. Same goes for the girl."

"Okay, well, we didn't figure they were killed in the park." The scene of the crime remained a mystery along with how their bodies were transported to the grave.

"Something else you'll no doubt find interesting is under ultraviolet light, there are faint markings on their backs to indicate they were both hugged tightly. That perimortem bruising I'd mentioned earlier."

Amanda did her best to assimilate what Rideout just told them. "He hugged them hard enough to bruise them, then broke their necks? And all this while they were sitting down? I'm not sure how this would all work."

"I'm not saying they were hugged and their necks broken while sitting. The killer could have put them in a seated position right afterward."

"You are sure? He hugged them first?" Trent asked.

"That's what the evidence is telling me."

Amanda mulled on that. If this was a matter of domestic violence being taken to the extreme, their deaths would have happened in a rage. They wouldn't have been shown affection first. Then again, anything was possible. "Do you think you'll be able to determine a handspan from the bruising on their backs?"

"The crime lab should be able to come up with an approximation. I will forward photographs to the lab for further analysis. I'm sure CSI Blair or Donnelly will be in touch. I feel comfortable in concluding it is most likely a man's hand. As I mentioned, it would take someone with a fair amount of strength to do this, especially with the woman."

Amanda nodded. Those measurements would either strengthen the case against Roy Archer or release him from suspicion. Her mind circled around to something else Rideout had said. "Let me get this right, though. So after their necks were broken they were left to sit?"

"Exactly."

"That could fit a heat-of-the-moment kill. They're dead and now he's left to figure out how to get rid of them."

"Possible."

But not definitive... And maybe the seated part meant nothing of real importance. She was still weighing her suspicions about Roy Archer though. "Is there any way you can compare older bruising and tell if they were all caused by the same hand? Finger size or handspan?"

Rideout smiled tightly. "Now you're wishing for a magical genie, Detective."

"Anything else you will be forwarding to the lab?" Amanda was greedy for answers, even though she had worked cases where they had far less at the start of an investigation.

"Some hairs and fibers."

"And under their nails?" Amanda asked.

"I scraped, of course. No epithelium."

It wasn't what Amanda wanted to hear, but it might make sense. Both had been embraced before death; they may not have felt threatened enough to fight back. Roy could have killed his family. Both mother and daughter would have trusted him enough to let him get close. Or was it someone else they knew? Then again, fear or shock could have hindered their defense. After all, one of them had to go first. Amanda worked the scenarios in her mind—child first, the mother would have gone ballistic; mother first, the child might be convinced it was an accident and welcome comforting. It was also possible they were separated at the time their necks were broken.

"Now, this is where I tell you I've given you everything I've discovered thus far. You going to stick around or...?" Rideout put his face shield in place. He was obviously getting to work regardless of their answer.

"Send us your full reports once you have them," Amanda told him, and she and Trent left the morgue. Since they were already in Manassas, she was tempted to pop over to the crime lab and see if they had any updates to share, specifically regarding the stuffed elephant. Was there anything to confirm definitively if it had been Charlotte's? If so, maybe Amanda's thoughts would calm down.

Trent unlocked the department car and got inside.

The engine was already running by the time she joined him.

"Roy Archer lied about when they went missing," Trent said. "He beat them. He killed them."

"The evidence seems rather damning, but we still don't have a solid case against him."

"I know he's a cop, that the sarge wants all the i's dotted and t's crossed before we go after him. But I say we look in the family home. We shouldn't need a warrant for that—not if Roy is innocent and interested in knowing what happened to his family."

"I'm not so sure. He already knows he's a suspect."

"The fact remains he is the *prime* suspect. If this was anyone else but someone with a badge, we'd be in the house."

Amanda couldn't argue with Trent because he was right. Politics were at play. Though she didn't know what they could find in the home to point them in the killer's direction. The location where the murders had taken place was still a mystery. With their cause of death, it wasn't like they had a bloody crime scene to find either. But knowing more about Jill and Charlotte Archer from looking at their things might move the case forward. "We'll talk with Graves, bring her up to speed on the autopsy findings, and go from there." In speaking of the sergeant, Amanda noted she hadn't been present at the morgue.

"Let's do it. Surely she has to see what I do. Roy Archer killed his family."

This new side to Trent wasn't entirely attractive. She'd dismiss it as concerns about his aunt affecting him, but that didn't make his attitude excusable. He stubbornly refused to accept there were potential holes in the evidence against Roy.

Trent looked over at Amanda. "Tell me you see it."

"I see it's possible. But some factors cast doubt on Roy being the killer. For one, the circumstances in which they were killed. There's no sense of urgency to support heat of the moment, as in cases of domestic killings. There's also the stuffed elephant and the timeline between when they went missing and were killed."

"Assuming Roy didn't lie about when he last saw them. And, Amanda, you know as well as I do just because Roy denied knowledge of the doll doesn't mean it wasn't his daughter's. And you realize if it wasn't Charlotte's then that leaves the question of where it came from." He glanced at her, and they locked eyes.

"Of that, I'm well aware."

"See? A worse thought? Was it another child's toy? A killer who has murdered before? If we dismiss Roy we're looking for a third party who abducted mother and daughter, held them for days, killed them, then buried them in the woods."

"I'm not so sure it's a better or worse thought at this point. We still have two people whose lives have been cut short. It's good we're talking this through."

"We have to, right? It's all about keeping an open mind." More sarcastic than authentic.

"It is," she shoved back. "Take us to Central. We'll have that talk with Graves in person."

Trent got them on the road while Amanda called CSI Blair. She landed in voicemail and left a message requesting a list of what was deemed evidence from the crime scene. She also specifically mentioned the elephant, the hairs and fibers, and photos of bruising that Rideout would be sending over. She kindly asked that a rush be placed on everything. Trent wasn't the only one hungry for justice.

NINE

"You've done the right thing by coming to me first." Graves was seated at her desk, frowning. "If you had just gone ahead to the man's home, we'd be having a very different conversation."

Amanda had just finished laying out everything in the case they'd gathered to date, including what Rideout had told them. She was aware Graves's most-used control tactic was holding threat of unemployment over her officers' heads. Of note was the fact Graves had referred to Archer as a man, not an officer. That felt significant somehow. "We appreciate the delicate nature of the situation and that it needs to be handled the right way. Armed with warrants, likely preferred."

"Glad to hear you say that, but I don't see a warrant happening just yet. But if Roy Archer has nothing to hide, he shouldn't have a problem letting you inside."

"We'd want to see in his vehicle too," Trent interjected. "Jill and Charlotte Archer weren't killed at Prince Park so they had to have been transported there somehow."

Amanda nodded to support what Trent had said, though technically they just knew they weren't killed near the burial site.

"If he's innocent, he shouldn't care what you look at," Graves said. "But before we go there, why don't you feel out Jill's parents about their daughter's marriage? Don't raise accusations against Roy. Notify them of their daughter's and granddaughter's deaths, and see what they say in response."

"We can do that." Roy would expect they'd talk to them, as he'd provided them with the parents' number. It would be a safe and neutral path. "They live in Edgewater, Maryland. Not far. We could go there today."

"Do it. If this guy killed his family, he doesn't deserve the badge and needs to be pulled off the street immediately."

Amanda was surprised at Graves's judgment but also felt a new level of respect for the sergeant. Graves had given the impression in the past that she was more interested in pats on the back than much else. But it would seem she also had strong convictions about getting justice. "We'll head out right now."

"Keep me posted. You both have my cell phone. If I'm not here when you've finished, call me. Oh, and I already forwarded a signed subpoena to the service provider for Jill Archer's phone records and GPS history."

"Great. Thank you," Amanda told her.

"Doing what I can to help."

Amanda slowly rose from her chair, keeping her gaze on Graves until she reached the door. She wasn't sure what to make of Graves's new cooperative spirit.

In the hall, she turned to Trent. "I just need to make a quick phone call, and I'm good to go."

"Zoe?"

"Yeah. But it's the job, right? There are no set hours. It's also the first twenty-four in this case, and I want answers as much as you do. Go ahead and get the car warmed up, and I'll be out in a minute."

Trent nodded and headed for the parking lot, while Amanda took out her cell phone.

She didn't relish the thought of disappointing Zoe. Today was Pizza Tuesday, something they'd dubbed the day in place of conforming to Taco Tuesday. Tonight Logan was going to join them, and even he had been looking forward to making a home-made pie. Normally when an investigation took her into over-time, she would call Libby Dewinter, Zoe's adopted aunt, and let her know. As it was, Libby brought Zoe home from school and stayed with her until Amanda got off work. But maybe tonight Logan would be interested in assuming the extended shift.

She landed in his voicemail, as expected. He worked in construction and wasn't always available to take a phone call. She left a message for him to call her back and then called Libby and filled her in. "Sorry I can't be more definitive right now. I'll let you know when Logan can get there."

"You know me. I always go with the flow."

"I do." Amanda respected that and admired the quality, wishing to be more like that herself. But she preferred plans over spontaneity, even if the latter could present some fun adventures. "Can I talk to Zoe for a minute?"

Libby's answer was to call out Zoe's name. "She's running for the phone."

Amanda smiled, loving the relationship she had with the girl. It was crazy to think that she just came into her life a year ago, on the tail end of a tragedy. Zoe had witnessed her parents' murders, and it had been Amanda and Trent who were tasked with the investigation. Amanda had fallen hard for Zoe, and Zoe had taken an instant shine to Amanda.

"Mandy!" It was what Zoe always called her. Not Mom, and Amanda was completely fine with that. Whatever was comfortable for Zoe. But just hearing the girl's voice lifted Amanda's heart. She asked Zoe about her day and was regaled with a colorful story about a rabbit on the school grounds.

"It ran under a portable." Zoe's giggles traveled the line. "I'm going to catch him tomorrow."

"Maybe it's better that you leave him be."

"No. I want to catch him."

"Be careful. He could bite you."

Silence.

"Nah, he wouldn't do that."

Amanda smiled, admiring Zoe's courage. "All right, I need to get back to work, but be good for Aunt Libby."

"Duh, always."

Duh... A new word to recently enter Zoe's vocabulary, and they'd had the discussion several times that Amanda didn't care for it. "You mean *always*?"

"Yes, sorry."

"Okay. Well, Logan might still be over for pizza tonight, but I will be late."

"Frick."

It would seem they'd have to have another conversation. *Later.* "Okay, I love you. Bye."

"Bye."

Zoe was growing up far too fast, the little girl disappearing before her eyes. All too soon she would be replaced by a teenager. But at least she was getting older. Charlotte Archer wouldn't have that chance.

Amanda took the lead up the Meyers' front porch at about five o'clock that evening. According to their records, Darla and Irvin were both fifty-five and self-employed. The sedan in the driveway gave Amanda further hope someone would be home. Not that she looked forward to delivering notification, but best they hear it from her and Trent than from the news.

Amanda rang the doorbell, and before it finished its diddly a fit and attractive woman answered the door. Her hair was a blend of blond and gray, a transition before surrendering to all gray, no doubt.

"Darla Meyers?" Amanda asked.

"That's me. And who are you?"

Amanda and Trent held up their badges.

"Detectives with the Prince William County Police Department," Amanda told her. "Would your husband Irvin be home?"

"He is. Can I ask what this is regarding?" The woman's eyes landed on Amanda's badge clipped to the waistband of her pants.

"It would be best if we spoke with you and your husband together. Is there somewhere we can sit for this conversation?"

Darla's posture slumped. "Ah, sure, follow me. Irvin!" Darla yelled for her husband to join them once they were inside.

Amanda and Trent were seen to a modest living room with outdated furniture. Framed portraits on the wall captured snapshots of the Meyers, Jill, and Charlotte. One showed Jill and Charlotte on a beach building a sandcastle. Mother and daughter were sun-kissed and smiling.

"That is from last summer." Darla touched the frame of another picture. It was of a young girl, her mouth wide open with a finger pointing to where her front tooth had been. The outfit the child was wearing dated back a couple decades. "This one always makes me laugh." She chuckled now as if adhering to a self-mandated order.

"Is that Jill?" Amanda asked.

Darla stepped away and hugged herself. "It is. How do you know Jill?"

"We'll talk in a few moments, Mrs. Meyers." Amanda could have hit herself for the slip. Of course, Darla would be on edge, and if she was aware of her daughter's home situation, her mind may naturally go to her and her granddaughter's welfare. Amanda took in more photographs, and could feel the loving relationship between the Meyers, their daughter, and grand-daughter coming off the glossy prints.

Amanda and Trent had just sat down when a man graced the doorway. He looked from them to his wife and cocked his head.

"Who are these people, Darla?"

"We're detectives with the Prince William County PD." Amanda rushed out the answer to save Darla the need to do so.

"Well, I'm not sure what you'd want with us." There was a slight tremble in his lower lip that belied his words. He had some suspicion.

"If you would please sit, Mr. Meyers," Trent interjected. "We'll explain everything."

He sat on the couch next to his wife. Each reached for the other's hand.

"We're sorry to inform you that your daughter, Jill, and granddaughter, Charlotte, were found dead this morning." Anyone would say that Amanda's delivery had been profes-sional and detached, but she was just an expert at hiding her feelings. She'd been in their position—finding out family was dead—and from that moment everything changes. No matter the sympathies people offer, it doesn't bring them back.

"They were..." Darla's face fractured, and tears fell.

Irvin shimmied down the couch and put an arm around his wife. "What happened to them?" His voice was gruff, riddled with emotion, and his body tensed.

"He did it!" Darla spat, her cheeks flaming a bright red, as tears continued to fall without shame.

"Who, Mrs. Meyers?" Amanda asked.

"That no-good husband of hers."

"May I ask why you think Roy had something to do with their deaths?"

Darla opened her mouth, but no words came out. Irvin took over.

"We aren't blind. We know he controls her every move, and we were quite sure he physically abused her."

"Why didn't you do anything?" This from Trent, and Amanda shot him a look to keep quiet.

"We tried." Irvin's face pinched in pain. "But no matter what we tried, she was blind to him. She had a slew of excuses. He had a bad day at work, he was tired... The list goes on."

"We should have done more." Darla's voice was tiny.

"Sometimes everything is still not enough," Trent offered, calming from his immediate reaction, relating to the situation.

Irvin sighed deeply, licked his lips, stared in the distance. The pain emanating from him was tangible. "We begged her to leave him. We made it clear to Jill that she and Charlotte were welcome here whenever she was ready to leave Roy."

"He only moved to Dumfries to put distance between us," Darla began. "At least he didn't take them hours away. But in some ways, it didn't matter. He did whatever was within his power to keep us from her and our granddaughter even when they lived in town."

Amanda flicked a finger toward the wall of memories. "You found times to spend together anyway, from the look of it."

"Yes. Thank heavens for that much. But she'd never talk about her marriage. When we brought up Roy, she either defended him or shut the conversation down quick," Irvin said.

Everything they were saying added more to the physical evidence: Roy had abused his wife. But they were also seeing another side to Jill. She made time to see her parents even when Roy seemed to forbid it. Had Roy found out and moved his family for that reason—an act of control and isolation? And what else might Jill have been hiding? A secret life? "Do you know why Roy transferred to Dumfries?"

"To get Jill and Charlotte away from us," Darla punched out.

"Have you seen them since they moved?" Trent asked.

Both Meyers shook their heads in unison.

"We didn't even have the girls for Christmas last year. And that was just before their move." One lone tear streamed down Irvin's left cheek, and he pawed it away.

"Sorry to hear that." Amanda let a few seconds pass before she continued. "When did Jill and Roy meet?"

"Seven years ago?" Irvin looked at his wife for confirmation, and she nodded.

Darla took over speaking. "Jill was coming off a bad relationship. Some sloth of a man. She should have taken time for herself—to be single—but it always felt like she needed to be paired up to feel whole."

Amanda could understand Jill searching for what her parents seemed to have. "Did Jill have many friends here in Edgewater?"

Darla shook her head.

Irvin spoke. "She used to, but over the years they pulled away from her."

"They must have seen what was happening with her. Like she was stuck on a downward spiral," Darla added. "'Course that wasn't helped by the fact the men she chose were possessive. Roy was the worst of 'em all. He wanted every minute of her life to be devoted to him."

"But she found ways to spend some time with you." Amanda nudged her head toward the photographs again.

"She'd sneak off, or add an hour or two to her errands. She'd tell Roy things just took a little longer."

Amanda wondered if Jill might have done the same the day she went missing. Assuming for the moment that Roy was innocent of his family's murders, had Jill taken Charlotte and ventured somewhere that had gotten them into trouble? "You said you haven't seen them since the move, but did you speak with your daughter?"

"No." Irvin pulled his arm back from his wife but held her hand on her lap.

"Were you aware that Roy reported Jill and Charlotte missing last week?" The answer could be assumed, but Darla's clenched jaw and scowl spoke before her words.

"No. Last week? That bastard didn't even bother to call to tell us they were missing. He's covering for himself. Has to be." Tears brimmed in her eyes. "Whenever he was here in the past, he'd sit in the corner of the room drinking beer all night, hardly saying a word, but he'd watch her in such a way, it would just send shivers through me." Darla rubbed her arms as if she was getting a chill recalling.

"How did he watch her?" Amanda asked.

"He was so smug and full of hate. He'd say, 'Oh I love her,' then wrap his arm around her and pull her close to him. But she'd wince like he was hurting her, holding on too tight. It was like he was flaunting his control over her in our face."

"He must have gotten quite the kick out of taking our girl away." Irvin retracted his hand from his wife's and balled both his hands into fists.

"Sorry you had to go through that," Trent offered softly.

Neither Meyer verbally responded, but they met Trent's gaze, and it felt like an unspoken bond had been established.

"So did he do this to them? Do you know?" Darla searched Amanda's eyes for an answer.

She wished she had one. "It's an open investigation."

"You said they were found," Irvin began. "Where, and how?" His Adam's apple bulged with a rough swallow.

"They were discovered in a shallow grave in Prince Park. Their necks had been broken."

"Irv!" Darla cried out and threw her arms around her husband.

Amanda gave the couple a few beats to ride out this crest of grief. "Do you know if Charlotte had a small stuffed elephant?"

It was possible they had bought it for their granddaughter. If so that might be why Roy had no knowledge of it.

The Meyers looked at each other. Darla responded.

"Not that we know of, but we weren't around much. Especially since their move."

"We are very sorry for your loss." Amanda was the first to extend sympathies and stand. They offered to call friends or family to come be with them, but the Meyers said they'd be fine. So, she and Trent headed back to Woodbridge.

Amanda looked over at Trent while he drove. "I'd like to know where that elephant came from."

"And I think you're making too much out of it. We have enough to justify a look at the Archer home. The Meyers just told us about the abuse in Jill's marriage. He reported them missing to cover himself. I'm with Darla Meyers. He killed them."

"You sound quite confident."

"I don't think I've made how I feel about this guy a secret."

"Nope, you haven't. Well, I'll run this by Graves and see what she says." The weight of Trent's judgment settled on Amanda, and the argument against Roy was certainly strong. But she simply couldn't shake her nagging doubts. Justice for Jill and Charlotte was what mattered, and convicting the wrong man wouldn't give them that.

TEN

Amanda's call to Graves had met with success. She was going to get search warrants rolling for the Archer residence and Roy's vehicle, while Amanda and Trent made their way back to Central. After ending the call with Graves, Amanda's phone rang with a call from Logan. He confirmed he'd cover pizza night with Zoe. "No problem at all," he'd added.

She and Trent stopped for a bite to eat, which would allow more time for the warrants to come through. It was creeping up on seven thirty by the time Trent parked in the lot at Central, and they headed to Graves's office.

"Nothing yet," Graves told them the second they graced her doorway.

"Why is this taking so long?" Trent fired back, his frustration obvious.

"This needs to be done right," Graves said firmly. "You could go over there and ask permission, but if Roy turns you down, you'll be right back here anyway."

"I'm willing to take the chance."

Graves shook her head. "Roy Archer is currently a Dumfries police officer."

"So what? Does that give him the right to abuse his wife, possibly kill her and their daughter?" Trent spat.

"Absolutely not. But it's the *possibly* bit that is the sticky point. We don't have solid backing to our suspicions yet."

"There's no question he beat on his wife." Trent huffed and flailed his arms. "Her body is a testament to that. All the bruising and broken bones."

"I hear what you're saying, Detective, and trust me when I say I'm on your side. There is a leap from abuse to murder, though I'm not sure it's a big one."

Amanda would disagree, but Graves's statement felt personal. Or maybe she was far off the mark for thinking that. But regardless, the niggling settled in her gut with how Graves discussed the case. The more the investigation pointed toward domestic violence, Graves had a different aura about her—determined, harsh, and laser-focused.

"I've spoken with Chief Buchanan, and he's calling the judge to get this moving. I expect it won't be long before we're hearing from them."

"Giving Roy a chance to hide evidence," Trent countered.

"Jill and Charlotte Archer have been dead for approximately four days," Amanda started. "Any evidence could already be gone."

Graves gestured toward Amanda with a flat palm as if to say *Bingo*. Her desk phone rang, and she answered. "Sergeant Graves... Yes... Uh-huh. All right. Thank you, Chief." She replaced her receiver, and the line rang again.

Judging from this side of the conversation, the calls had to do with the warrants. Not good news based on the growing grimace on Graves's face. She ended the call with, "I understand." Which usually meant the opposite...

"First call was the chief, second was Judge Anderson. The warrants are being held up because formal identification hasn't been made yet."

"You've got to be kidding me," Trent lamented. "It's just a formality, Sarge. The victims are unquestionably Jill and Charlotte Archer."

"We do this by the book," Graves said coolly.

"Roy should have gone over this afternoon." Trent's voice was almost shrill.

"But he didn't," Graves pushed out. "Apparently he's having a rough time."

"Sure. The man probably has a shitload of regrets." Trent rolled his eyes and shook his head. "This is unbelievable."

"Detective," Amanda said. One word, but it contained a warning. If he didn't get his emotions under control, they would get him benched from the case. She held brief eye contact with Trent, then turned to Graves. "When will Roy Archer be identifying the bodies?"

"An appointment has been set for nine tomorrow morning."

Amanda purposefully didn't look at Trent; she didn't have to. His seething was felt from across the room.

"The second he has confirmed the victims are Jill and Charlotte Archer, the warrants are as good as signed."

"He gets another night free." Trent was speaking softly, not due to acceptance. Rather, Amanda sensed his temper brooding just beneath the surface.

"Nine AM, he makes the identification, we move ahead. If he did this, we'll get him." Graves made piercing eye contact with Trent, and after a few seconds, they both nodded. A silent communication passed between the two. Graves added, "You're both dismissed. Get your rest. You're going to need it."

Amanda was the first into the hallway.

Trent joined her and said, "I won't sleep tonight."

"Try, okay? She's right. We've got a lot on our plate tomorrow."

"I realize that."

"Are you going to be all right?" The question was out, and she regretted it instantly. His eyes narrowed slightly, and he got this wall around him that told her he wasn't her problem to worry about.

"I'll be fine. See you tomorrow. Eight thirty."

"Yep." She believed that technically he would be *fine*, but that didn't rule out his living in mental torment.

Amanda arrived home to find Logan and Zoe on the couch, some mindless sitcom on the television. Zoe was lying with her head against his arm, fast asleep.

It pleased her the two of them hit it off. Not everyone had a knack with kids, but Logan was good with her. Not bad for a one-night stand—going back almost two years now. It was hard to believe it was that long ago. Time went too fast. And, wow, had a lot changed in her life since.

She smiled at Logan but brushed some of Zoe's blond hair back with a hand. "Zoe," she whispered. No response. She repeated herself, a little louder this time.

Zoe's eyes sprung open, and she sat up. "Mandy. You're home." She got off the couch and wrapped both arms around Amanda's neck. Amanda hugged the girl back, but kept her hold loose, as thoughts of the case soiled the moment.

Jill and Charlotte's killer had hugged them tightly just before breaking their necks.

Amanda pinched out the ugly and guided Zoe's head to the alcove of her shoulder, running her hands over her hair. Then pulled back. "So I'd like to know something... How was the pizza?"

Zoe's eyes widened almost comically; her facial mannerisms had always been expressive. Much like Amanda's mother—not that there was a blood tie between her and Zoe. "It was delicious. But look." Zoe opened her mouth wide and pushed the tip of her tongue through a gap on top. "It fell out during dinner."

"Oh?" Amanda stood, glanced at Logan.

"She handled it like a champ," he said, as if reading her mind.

"Of course I did. I'm not a baby."

"As that proves." Amanda pointed at Zoe's mouth and smiled.

"That's right." Zoe bunched up her face and stuck her tongue out at Logan.

"Now, now." Amanda put her hand on Zoe's shoulder.

"I'm just kidding around. Can't he take a joke?" She pushed her tongue out again.

Logan laughed. "You better be careful."

"Or what? What's ya gonna do?"

Amanda was giggling now. The two had a sibling type of relationship—and she should know. She had four herself, one of them an older brother. As much as they teased and chided each other, they were great friends. Though their relationship was challenged over the last number of years, things between them were getting better again. "Let's get you to bed."

"It's not even eight o'clock," she whined.

"You fell asleep on the couch." Amanda wouldn't mind some alone time with Logan.

"I always do." Zoe looked at Logan to support her claim.

He bobbed his head. "It is true. She does."

"That's right." Zoe nudged out her chin and crossed her arms. "I'm a big girl now."

"I see. Well, *big girl*, you have one more hour. Tops. You have school tomorrow."

"What?"

"You heard me."

"Fine," Zoe pushed out, her lips turning into a scowl.

Logan touched Amanda's hand. "There are leftovers in the fridge if you haven't eaten."

"Nah, I'm fine. Picked up something earlier." She took the spot on the couch vacated by Zoe and sat next to Logan. "Hey."

"Hey."

They pecked a kiss to each other's lips.

"Yuck." A large groan of protest from Zoe only had Amanda and Logan laughing.

For the next hour, the three of them watched TV. Amanda didn't glean much from the programs as her mind was on the case. So much had happened since Spencer had called her to Prince Park that morning.

The moment the clock flipped to nine, Amanda roused Zoe, who had once again fallen asleep—her head on Amanda's lap, her feet on Logan's. "Time for bed. School tomorrow."

There was a grumble, barely a protest on the scale of Zoe's capabilities. "Okay."

She sauntered down the hall, the scuffle of her socked feet on the wood floor disclosing her progress. Then the bathroom door shut.

Lucky wasn't the only thing to go when Zoe had turned seven in August. She was no longer interested in playing dress up or watching *Frozen* for the millionth and one time—and she didn't need Amanda to read to her before bed. She did continue to kiss Zoe on the forehead once she'd slipped under the covers, but that ritual was probably nearing an end too.

Once Amanda heard Zoe flush the toilet, she got up and told Logan she'd be right back.

"Not going anywhere." He smiled at her, and she felt warmth rush through her.

"Good." She found Zoe already under the covers, but Amanda adjusted the lay of the comforter and flicked on a light that projected stars onto the ceiling.

"No."

"What?"

"I don't need that anymore. Turn it off."

"You don't enjoy looking at stars?"

"I'm a big girl, and I don't need a nightlight." Zoe pushed out her bottom lip, meeting Amanda's gaze with stark seriousness.

"Okay. Big girl, it is." Amanda turned the light off but left the unit on the nightstand, not buying Zoe was finished with the apparatus for good. She tapped a kiss on Zoe's forehead and got up. She stopped in the doorway and turned to check on her. In the faint light seeping in from the hallway, Zoe already had her eyes shut.

They grow up too quickly... As the thought passed through, an ache formed in her chest. Her daughter, Lindsey, never had the chance to become a *big girl*. She'd stopped aging at six-and-a-half years old. Amanda was already going places with Zoe she hadn't with her own flesh and blood.

She walked back toward the living room but stood at the end of the hallway. "Wine?" she asked Logan.

He looked over a shoulder at her from the couch. "Sure."

She grabbed a bottle of red, popped the cork, and poured some into a couple of glasses. She returned with them to the living room and handed him one. She didn't click her glass to his, no need for a toast tonight. And she wasn't drinking to celebrate. Her heart felt broken. Not just for the fact Zoe was growing up too fast, but that another little girl wouldn't get that chance.

ELEVEN

Trent told Amanda "good night," but he wasn't in a hurry to leave the station. He hated letting things sit overnight, but he had no choice when it came to going to the Archer residence. There was something else he could do though. He called Anne Arundel County Police, Roy's old department, hoping to get some information.

Trent identified himself to the officer on desk duty, a woman named Alison.

"You said you're with what PD?"

"Prince William County."

"How can I help you, Detective?"

"I'm calling about a Roy Archer. He used to be an officer with you there."

"Uh-huh, I know the name." There was an obvious change in her tone—from light to heavy and loaded.

"Can I ask why he left the department?"

"I'm sorry, but I'm not at liberty to disclose that information."

"But I'm sensing you knew him well. Is that right?"

"Yeah."

He had a hunch but wasn't sure how to broach it over the phone. It would have been difficult in person, but Trent suspected that Alison and Roy were acquainted biblically. "You were friends? Go through the academy together?"

"What's this about?"

Trent should have thought ahead. Under pressure to come up with something his mind went blank. Any cover stories he came up with were riddled with holes. Until he landed on one. "I heard rumor he's going to be my new partner. And if you could keep my call off the record, I'd appreciate it. I'm just trying to find out what kind of guy I'm going to be entrusting my life to." He hadn't said which unit he was in, but he had given Alison his name, rank, and PD. If she tried to verify his story, and this made its way to Graves, he could land in a heap of trouble. Calling might have been a bad idea.

"He's... How do you say, snaky? Guess just like that. Wouldn't trust him past seeing him, if you catch my drift."

The hunch felt confirmed: Alison and Roy had an affair. "He is married from what I've heard," Trent tossed out.

"He is, but I'm not sure it means anything to him."

"Why? He sleeps around, or doesn't treat his wife right?"

"He has a wife and daughter, and he has a temper." Alison stopped there, but Trent sensed she had more to say on the subject.

"Do you think he ever used his temper on them?" Trent appreciated the need to tiptoe, but he also wanted to build such a strong case against Roy Archer, he'd never squirm free.

Silence.

"Did he beat them?" Trent asked after a few seconds. "To me that's just not okay."

"I shouldn't be talking about him. Anything else, Detective?"

"No, that's it. Thanks." Trent hung up armed with more proof that Roy was a no-good sack of shit. But did that mean he was a murderer? Had he, like some psychopath, hugged his wife and daughter and then broken their necks?

He got up from his desk and headed to his Jeep. Graves was walking out behind him.

"You still here?" she said to him.

"Yeah, just..." He let it dangle. He didn't have an excuse at the ready.

"I know this situation is rough."

He scanned her eyes, had the feeling she wanted to insert another word besides *rough*. "It is. But we'll get him. That's what you said."

"That we will." Graves resumed walking toward her vehicle. "Night."

"Night." Trent got into his Wrangler and watched her leave the lot. He should go straight home but a voice in his head wouldn't leave him alone about his aunt and her disconnected phone number. He should check on her. It would require a detour, but it might allow him to sleep better.

He put his vehicle into gear and headed for the last place his aunt had lived. With every mile he got closer, the gnawing grew in his gut. What if he showed up to find new people had moved in? Honestly, nothing would surprise him at this point. That bastard wanted so much to isolate his aunt, rip her away, it was surprising her phone hadn't been disconnected years ago.

Or make that one year *ago...*

That was the last time he'd tried calling.

Lights were on inside the house when he pulled in front. The SUV in the driveway had plates registered to Don, which Trent knew from looking them up in the past. It would seem he was living here.

Trent's impulse was to bang on the front door and demand to see his aunt.

But where would that lead? And would it cause her harm?

Trent gripped the steering wheel, grinding his palms against it. He needed to listen to his intuition that was telling him to leave because nothing good would come from knocking.

He just put his vehicle into drive when a woman crossed in front of the window. He kept his foot on the brake.

The silhouette was the right size and shape to belong to his aunt. An overwhelming urge to rip her from the place was almost impossible to ignore.

"She needs to want help," he mumbled under his breath, repeating a mantra he'd said many times before about this situation. It was what allowed him to sleep at night.

Don stepped into view, and Trent slipped the gear back into park.

He prepared himself to act. Just one aggressive move toward his aunt, Trent would get out of his Jeep and pound the living daylights out of the guy.

His aunt and Don interacted, speaking, arms gesturing in a conversational manner. Nothing that spoke to anger. Shortly later, his aunt walked away and disappeared from sight.

He wanted to go after her, but his mantra was back. Instead of a soothing sentiment, a haunting reality. His aunt had made it clear the last time she'd spoken with Trent's mom, her sister, that she was happy with Don and he took care of her. But for how long? Would there ever come a day when the abuse was taken too far? When there would be no chance of saving her?

TWELVE

Leanne was on a bed with Gracie, squeezing her daughter tight. Hours had passed without a grand epiphany of how to save them.

"Mommy, you're hurting me."

She released her hold some and ran a hand over Gracie's hair. "Sorry, sweetie." If she had a mere penny for every time she'd apologized since they'd been trapped here, she'd be a rich woman. But it was really the if onlys that were devouring her alive. If only she hadn't kept Gracie home from school the other day. If only she hadn't agreed to join him for ice cream. If only she hadn't left her cell phone behind in the trunk of her car—an idea she thought smart at the time. But if she'd brought it along, it didn't mean he'd find it and discard it with certainty. She might have been able to hide it from him and lead the police right to his door.

But, no, like a moth, she flew too close to the flame. She'd seen flickers of hope and adventure that came from spending time with a relative stranger. It had been served up like a temptation, luring her from her oppressive life. It had been titillating for a few moments.

But look where that got her—and worse, Gracie. All because Leanne had dared to pull strength from within and turn her back on her husband. He'd been telling the truth those times he told her she was nothing without him. The proof was there: she'd failed to keep her daughter safe. It was one job she'd been given, a blessing and responsibility, and she'd screwed it up.

She was stupid, just like Billy had told her. He was right about everything he'd said about her. Even as a spark inside screamed he spoke lies, the truth was clear. She was to blame for this. And because of her selfishness and stupidity they very well might die.

If the man was going to let them go, he would have by now. But he hadn't yet killed them either. Suppose there was some hope in that.

If only she knew what he wanted from them. He'd visited twice. Both times were brief, and he had dropped off bottles of water. Never spoke a single word. Leanne had tried to get him to talk, asking him what he wanted. He'd just stare blankly at her.

That only scared her more, making escape that much more imperative. But she could feel herself getting sucked into a pit of hopelessness.

They might as well be in a prison. The door was secured with three deadbolts. When he came to visit, each clunk was like a hit to the heart. They were on the second floor of a house. There was just the one window, lined with bars, and an attached bathroom.

She might be able to work the bars out of the old wood frame if she had a tool to use. But if she got the bars out, then what? How would they reach the ground and where would they go from there?

There weren't any other houses within sight, just a run-down barn and miles of fields and trees. The area wasn't one she recognized, but the house had to be set next to a road. They could head for there and flag down help...

She sighed. Escaping felt on par with spotting a live unicorn.

But maybe, just maybe, the fact she'd left her phone behind would lead police to them. Or was that giving them too much credit? After all, the phone wasn't with her. But, surely, it would speak of foul play.

Any whispers of hope were blown aside by a storm of overwhelming chastisement. She was a horrible mother, who didn't deserve Gracie. If she'd been a good mom, she would have seen the man for who he was in time to avoid this outcome. But it had been too late when she'd caught the darkness in his eyes. He had seen things, *done* things.

Chills flushed through her at the memory and had her trembling.

What do you want from us? she screamed in her head.

Their only possibility of being saved was the police. Surely, they would be looking for them.

"When can we go home?" Her daughter's blue eyes were pooled with tears, her voice tiny, as she pulled back and looked at her mother.

"Soon, baby." She had to remain strong for Gracie, even for herself. What she wouldn't tell Gracie until later is they were never going home. She never wanted to see Billy again.

Her daughter's breathing deepened as she dozed off, leaving Leanne with one thought of gratitude. Thank God the man hadn't touched Gracie.

But Leanne couldn't just sit here and wait to find out their fate. She had to take some control. If it was the last thing she did, she'd get Gracie to freedom. Somehow. Someway.

She moved Gracie off her, being careful not to disturb her sleep, and walked to the window. If only their surroundings had changed. But the view offered nothing new. In fact, there was less to see. It was night, and a blanket of stars glimmered over-head. She sought out the brightest one and made a wish, tears squeezing from her eyes as she did.

The clunk of a deadbolt.

Leanne stiffened and turned.

Another one.

She hurried toward the bed.

Gracie had bolted awake, as if harassed by a nightmare, and cried out for her.

The third lock clicked, and the door opened.

"Let us go. Please," Leanne belted out, petitioning for their release yet again.

He didn't even look at her but kept walking toward them, his head slightly cocked, his expression eerily soft. He held a stuffed toy elephant toward Gracie. Her daughter was worming into the corner behind her, trying to make herself small.

"She wants nothing from you," Leanne spat, her heart pounding so hard she feared it jumping from her chest. "Just let us go."

"I thought you'd like it." The man leaned across the bed and wriggled the doll in front of Gracie. "You always loved elephants."

"No." Gracie tucked her legs into herself, burrowing her head against her knees.

"Please, leave my daughter alone."

The man's gaze snapped to meet Leanne's. And it was there again. The darkness. Rolling in as fog overtaking a field in early evening, suppressing it in an eerie calm.

Leanne's next breath froze. She was afraid to inhale, to make any movement. It was then she spotted a silver chain around his neck just as it dipped beneath the collar of his T-shirt. The necklace held a pendant—possibly more than one.

If she showed interest in the adornment, culled out its meaning to him, that might lead to conversation. In turn, that might establish a bond and give him a change of heart. She'd witnessed this tactic play out often enough on crime dramas she'd watched over the years.

"Nice necklace." She pointed toward the chain. "I have a locket on mine." She pinched the small gold heart between her fingers. It had been a gift from her mother years ago, before she'd passed, before Billy. "See? It opens." Leanne pried at the clasp and revealed a tiny photograph of herself holding Gracie when she was a baby. Showing something so personal and intimate to this man had goosebumps crawling over her skin, raising the hairs on her arms and back of her neck.

The man snarled and mumbled incoherently as he headed toward the door. She was quite sure she made out two names: Cheryl and Holly. Whoever the hell they were. Then a theory hit.

Shit, he... he... She'd seen it before on one of those crime shows. The episodes where the killer thought his victims were someone else.

"We're Leanne and Gracie," she screamed.

Each deadbolt thunked shut, sealing off their freedom, likely their fate.

Leanne dropped onto the bed, sitting on the stuffed toy. She hurled it across the room, and it thumped against the wall.

"I'm scared, Mommy."

"Me too, baby. Me too." She hugged her little girl, trying to conjure a single pleasant thought that put them somewhere far away from here.

THIRTEEN

Logan was gone before the sun rose. He'd slipped out quietly, but Amanda had gotten herself a kiss before he left. She also found a thank-you note on her kitchen counter—not for their sleepover. He was thanking her for not canceling pizza night.

It gave me and Zoe a chance to hang out together. My God, she's a smart kid.

Amanda was smiling at the memory of the note as she pulled into the lot for Hannah's Diner. "*Too* smart," she muttered to the interior of her Honda Civic.

She parked and noticed Sergeant Graves standing next to her Mercedes at the edge of the lot. No coffee in hand, and she was staring at the diner while fiddling with her purse strap. Amanda started on her way over, just as Graves got into her car and drove off.

How strange...

The chime rang overhead as Amanda entered. May Byrd, the owner of the establishment, flashed a large grin.

"Miss Amanda. An extra-large?"

"Isn't that the only size you offer?" Amanda volleyed back lightheartedly, but May's coffee was the best of anywhere. "Actually, make it two, to go." She'd bring one in for Trent.

"Sure thing." May got to work.

May was in her sixties, and her daughter, Hannah, who the diner had been named after, was a defense attorney at a fancy DC firm.

"Here ya go." May set two coffees on the counter, and Amanda handed over the money.

"Keep the change."

"Thank you, sweetie."

Amanda turned to leave but spun back around to May. The older woman kept her finger on the pulse of the community. What didn't reach her ears through the diner got there from the ladies in her book club. She might be able to explain Graves's odd behavior.

"Something else?"

"This will strike you as random, but was Sergeant Graves just in here?" She could have put her coffee in the car before Amanda arrived, but it was still odd she'd then be standing outside staring at the building.

"Haven't met her yet. Only heard of her."

"Okay," Amanda dragged out, more confused.

May squinted and angled her head. "Why are you asking?"

"It's, ah... never mind." Amanda offered a small smile and hightailed it from the diner before May coaxed it out of her.

As Amanda drove to Central, she tried to make sense of what she had seen. It was as if Graves were afraid to go in the diner. But why? Nothing about it was intimidating. Even though May heard everyone's business, people loved her. Her tongue wagged but never spread hurtful gossip, simply truths. If there was unsavory news, May sugarcoated so as not to injure any party.

If she didn't have a busy day ahead of her, Amanda might

go slightly mad trying to unravel the puzzle. Hannah's Diner was the best place to get coffee in Prince William County, and Graves drank coffee. She'd been in the area for about seven months and never went inside?

But solving that mystery would have to wait. Amanda had much more important things to focus on today, starting with getting justice for Jill and Charlotte Archer.

The clock on the dash read seven fifty when she parked in the lot at Central. It would be over an hour before Roy Archer would see the victims to formally identify them as his wife and daughter. But she and Trent would keep busy until the search warrants came through. She had thought of at least one step they could take but wanted to run it past Graves first.

Amanda passed Natalie Ryan, another detective in Homicide, and continued to her cubicle. Trent wasn't in his, but she might as well put the coffee she'd bought him on his desk.

She plucked a cup out of the tray and ran right into him at the entrance to her cubicle. The lid popped off, and hot coffee sloshed onto her hand. "Ouch." She pushed it toward him. "Take it."

Trent took the coffee, a question knotted in the arch of his brow, and bent to pick up the lid.

She licked her fingers that were dripping with coffee and rushed back into her cubicle for a tissue. "Jeez. You could have said something to let me know you were there." Her flesh had recovered from the heat, but her heart was pounding from the shock. Her mind and gaze must have been elsewhere; she hadn't seen him or heard him. "That's for you, by the way." Amanda flailed a hand toward the cup in his hand. "What's left of it, anyway."

"Thanks."

"You're welcome." She dropped into her chair and took a savoring sip of her coffee. *Trent, a stealth ninja...*

Trent had gone into his cubicle and she looked at him over

the partition—saw the top of his nose, eyes, forehead, hair. Based on the slightly bloodshot eyes and some untamed blond strands of hair, she'd guess it had been a rough night. "You ready for today?"

"Damn right I am. More than ready."

"Good. Me too." She took another drink of her coffee and nearly upset it when her phone rang. She needed to get a grip on her nerves this morning. She answered to CSI Blair.

"Returning your call."

Amanda signaled for Trent to come over. "Just going to put you on speaker. Trent's joining."

"Sure."

She noted how much her relationship had changed with Emma Blair since they talked and cleared the air. Amanda wished she'd initiated the conversation right after finding out about her father's affair with the investigator.

Amanda set her phone on speaker, informed Trent that it was CSI Blair on the line. "All right, Trent and I are both here."

"I wish I had more for you..."

Those seven words were the last thing she wanted to hear.

Blair proceeded. "I received the items you noted in your message—the hair and fibers that Rideout pulled from the bodies. CSI Donnelly and I also pulled some from the stuffed elephant. I assure you that all of this will be given priority."

"Thanks," Amanda said. "Did you get the photographs of the bruising from Rideout?"

"Yes. I'll be taking a closer look today and, with any luck, getting you some measurements for the handspan and finger size. Then it's on you to get a suspect."

"We have one of those," Trent interjected.

A brief silence on Blair's end, followed by, "That was fast."

"It's a work in progress," Amanda corrected, doing her best to remain objective. "And the man's shoe size from the scene... you're still sticking to size eleven?"

"I am. Now, I can tell you this. Rideout pulled a strand of carpet fiber from the child—the pile of which is normally found in vehicles."

They'd already surmised that the killer had to transport the bodies somehow. "Can you narrow it down to a vehicle make and model?"

"We're not that good, I'm afraid. Not yet anyhow. I will look more closely at it. For now, I can tell you it's dark gray."

"Thanks." Amanda bit back her disappointment.

"Don't mention it. I'll keep you posted on more as I go along."

"Oh, before you go, when should I see the evidence list?"

"Hopefully later today."

"Thanks." With that, Amanda ended the call and turned to Trent.

"When we get the go-ahead, we'll need to check the color of the carpet in Archer's car," he said. "Bet it will match."

Separation from the case overnight had apparently done little for moving his suspicions away from Roy. "I guess we'll find out. Come on, I want to speak with Graves." She got up from her chair and led the way to the sergeant's office, figuring she'd fill in Trent and Graves at the same time with her idea.

Graves was at her desk, and her door was wide open. When she saw Amanda and Trent, she waved them in. Amanda let Trent enter first, and she shut the door behind them.

"Has something changed since we spoke last night?" Graves seemed slightly irritated, and her gaze dipped to the coffee cups in their hands. If she'd spotted Amanda at Hannah's Diner, the sergeant wasn't giving that away.

"Not exactly, but I have an idea to build our case while we wait on the formal identity and warrants," Amanda said, drawing Trent's attention now.

"Go ahead."

"We know the missing person report for Jill and Charlotte

Archer was filed Friday last week. Roy said he last saw them on the Tuesday. Rideout put time of death as four days ago."

Graves angled her head. "I'm not sure where you're going with this."

"I'd like to go to Charlotte's school and speak with her teacher. We could confirm when she last saw the girl."

"See if there is a discrepancy?"

Amanda nodded. "Just building a case."

"Not a bad idea. You might just cement what Roy told us, but it could help establish a timeline regardless of his guilt. Yeah. Do it." Graves swept a hand toward the door.

Trent headed out, but Amanda hesitated. "By the way, I saw you this morning at Hannah's Diner." She lifted her cup to point out the logo, more to add a conversational tone to her words. "They have the best coffee, don't they?"

Graves didn't look at Amanda when she replied, "The best."

Huh... May would have remembered Graves if she had gone in there. So why lie about it?

Trent popped his head into the doorway. "You coming or...?"

"Yep"—she brushed past him—"and I'm driving."

"You're what? I always drive."

"Not this time." She needed a distraction from the case and the lie Sergeant Graves had just told her.

FOURTEEN

Amanda had barely brought the department car to a standstill in the parking lot of Dumfries Elementary when Trent was climbing out.

"I know why I drive most of the time."

"Hey."

"No *hey* about it. You have a lead foot. You do know the posted speed limit, and that you were well above it?"

"Arrest me." She smiled, but it faded at the sight of the school's sign. Zoe went here, and it finally hit that she might have known Charlotte Archer.

Amanda and Trent entered the administrative offices and were greeted by the main receptionist. Flora, a robust woman in her mid-forties, was seated at her desk, back ramrod straight, shoulders pulled back, breasts front and center.

"Flora, this is my partner, Detective Trent Stenson." Amanda didn't need to give her name, as the woman was well aware who she was given they had prior dealings.

Flora's gaze trailed over to Trent, and she nodded in greeting.

"We need to speak with Charlotte Archer's teacher for a few moments. Guessing that's Kim Brewer." She'd been Zoe's teacher last year.

Class had just started, and a brief grimace crossed the woman's face. "Can I say what this is regarding?"

"Charlotte Archer." Amanda thought she'd said as much already, but she pressed on a kind smile. It was one the woman didn't return.

"One minute." She picked up the phone, and a few moments later was hanging up. "Ms. Brewer will be with you shortly. You can wait over there." She indicated a line of five chairs along a wall and had the receiver pressed to her ear again. From the sound of it, she was making a request for someone to watch over Brewer's class for a bit.

"This brings back a lot of memories." Trent dropped into a chair.

"You spend time here?" Amanda hooked an eyebrow, knowing most of the students who graced these seats were facing some sort of discipline.

"You could say so."

"Surprising. You seem the type to adhere to the book." Though that was based on her initial impression at the onset of their partnership when Trent had been quiet and eager to please.

"Do you know me at all?"

She straightened her posture and said, "Name one reason you were dragged to the principal's office."

"I..." He closed his mouth.

"Can't think of one?" she challenged.

He snapped his fingers and pointed at her. "I was caught making out in the hall with a girl."

Of all the things to say, why this story? Heat flooded her cheeks. "I see."

"Yep."

"Ms. Steele?" Kim Brewer was in her late twenties and a thin woman, almost frail in appearance. She was wearing a skirt that billowed around her legs as she walked. It was her regular look she paired with either a semi-casual short-sleeved shirt or sweater. "Everything all right with Charlotte Archer?"

"Is there someplace we could talk that's more private?" Students were in and out of this spot.

"Sure." Kim took them to a teacher's break room, which was empty.

The three of them sat down, and Kim gave Trent a shy, subtle smile.

"Oh, where are my manners? This is my partner, Detective Stenson."

The two of them nodded in greeting.

"We believe something may have happened to Charlotte Archer." There wasn't any doubt the young girl in the morgue was Charlotte, but until formal ID was out of the way, she'd present the girl's fate as an uncertainty. "When was she last in class?"

Kim worried her bottom lip. "Not this week or last, but the one before."

Chills flushed through Amanda. "And you're sure of that?"

"I am. That Friday."

Two Fridays ago... Had Roy Archer lied to them about when his family disappeared, after all? Had they really "disappeared" or had he filed the report as a ruse to protect himself? Not a new thought.

"Did you try reaching her parents to find out what was going on?" Trent asked, the hint of accusation in his voice.

"I left several messages for both her mother and father."

"And no one called you back?" The hairs were rising on Amanda's arms. Roy Archer was indisputably an ass—beating on his wife, raping her too, thinking of the evidence. Had he killed his family?

"Nope. I ended up going by the house and spoke with Roy, the girl's father."

"When was this?" Amanda asked.

"Just this past Friday after school. He told me he'd filed missing person reports and had no idea where they were. I only went over there when..."

"When?" Amanda pressed.

"I don't want to get anyone in trouble, but I spoke to the principal earlier in the week and thought he reported it to the police. But he didn't."

"Did he say why he didn't call?" Trent asked.

"He said that Charlotte's father was a police officer, and everything should be under control."

"No pun intended, but that sounds like a cop out," Trent mumbled.

Amanda let what Kim had just said sink in. The Friday she spoke to Roy was pegged as the day Jill and Charlotte had died. "When you visited, how did Mr. Archer seem to you?"

"Preoccupied, flustered."

Trent had a pulse tapping in his cheek, which Amanda recognized as his temper churning up. But the evidence was pointing back to Roy. "Any idea why he might have been that way?"

"I just assumed it was because his wife and daughter were missing. I'm guessing that you're here because something happened to them?"

"Yes, we believe so." Amanda continued to hide behind a veil of uncertainty. Fewer questions to answer that way, and it would plug the rumor mill some.

Kim's eyes pooled with tears, but none fell.

"When you last saw Charlotte, how was she?" Running

with Roy's testimony, Jill and Charlotte went missing Tuesday. That meant the girl had still missed one day of school before then, on the Monday. But why?

"Shy, but that's not new. It takes a lot to get her to interact with the other kids. It was something we were working on."

Amanda nodded, imagining if the little girl had witnessed her father abusing the mother that could be the reason. "What was your impression of the girl's home life?"

"I don't like to talk candidly about any of my students and their lives at home, but..."

"It's okay, you can talk to us," Amanda assured her.

"I know Mr. Archer is a policeman."

"Yes, with the Dumfries PD." Amanda wanted to stress that, as she sensed Kim feared some sort of brotherhood retaliation. "Go ahead. Speak freely."

Kim toyed with the frayed fabric on the arm of the couch. "I filed a report with Child Protective Services. I suspected Charlotte may have been abused at home. As a teacher, it's my duty to report such things. But then it's out of my hands. They decide how to follow up or if it's necessary."

"What made you suspect abuse?" Amanda asked. "Bruising or other injuries?"

Kim shook her head. "Nothing physical, but more in the way the girl presented herself. Quiet, as I said, but her drawings were also dark. She used very little color. And when I met her father and mother my suspicions grew stronger. Do you remember the heatwave we had this past June?"

"Oh, do I." Amanda recalled clearly because she had to replace the central air conditioning unit in her house. It was also the month she and Trent had kissed.

"Well, I had a meet and greet with parents and students who would be attending my class this fall. That's when I first met Charlotte's parents. Her mother wore a turtleneck—in that heat—and she struck me as quiet and timid. Mr. Archer did all the talking. He kept putting his arm around her, and I swear she inched away from him. It wasn't because she was warm. Something didn't feel right."

Amanda had learned early on if something felt off, it usually was. In this situation, Roy's need to touch his wife when she didn't want it was a classic sign of a controlling husband. "Was that the last time you saw Mrs. Archer?"

She shook her head. "I usually saw her when she dropped Charlotte off. So two Fridays ago."

The last day Charlotte went to class... "And was she always alone or...?"

"Usually, but that day I saw Mrs. Archer speaking with a man in the yard. I didn't recognize him. It's probably the only reason I remember. Jill had run after Charlotte that day as she'd forgotten her bag in the car. It was on her way back she stopped and talked with the man."

Amanda wasn't struck by the fact the teacher had observed all this. People in small towns were nosier than most. "You said you didn't recognize him?"

"No, but I got the impression they knew each other."

"How did the interaction appear—friendly, confrontational...?" Trent asked.

"She was laughing and smiling. Both a rare sight."

Kim not recognizing the man niggled some, but there were about five hundred students who attended the school. The man's family could have been a recent transfer, or him a mother's new romantic interest, called upon for a favor. Amanda stood and gave the teacher her card. "Thank you for your time, Kim."

Once she and Trent left the school, she turned to him. "Looks like we may have another mystery man on our hands."

"*Another?*" Trent looked over at her, squinting in the sunlight.

"At least one a case, it seems."

Trent waved a dismissive hand. "Likely means nothing this time. He could be a parent the teacher wasn't familiar with. I doubt she knows everyone."

Amanda nodded. Same as her conclusion. But what if that man was someone they needed to worry about?

FIFTEEN

Roy Archer had positively identified the woman and child in the morgue as Jill and Charlotte Archer, and the search warrants were signed and in hand. It was finally time for justice, even if getting to this point had felt like forever. Probably because Trent had no doubts about Roy's guilt. More than one person suspected physical violence in the marriage, Jill's body supported the abuse, and then there was the discrepancy between when he reported them missing and the day Charlotte was last in school. At least one day unaccounted for—the Monday.

It was about ten thirty when he and Amanda pulled into the Archer driveway behind Roy's sedan. Two cruisers parked on the road out front of the house.

Trent tried to catch a look inside Roy's vehicle on the way to the front door, but the dark tint made it impossible to spot anything meaningful. All he could make out were the vague outlines of the steering wheel, dash, and console.

Trent banged on the door, rattling the window in the screen door.

"You break it, you bought it," Amanda said to him, the light-ness to her voice an obvious attempt to alleviate the tension.

She must have sensed his dark thoughts. How he'd like nothing more than to pound on Roy Archer. Any man who hurt a woman deserved that much.

The door opened and Roy stood there, a smug expression on his face. Normal people who had just identified their dead loved ones would be showing signs of grief and sorrow. Roy was devoid of emotion and stepped back when Trent held up the paperwork.

"Read it, but we have the right to search your house and your car." It wasn't time to slap the cuffs on the man's wrists—yet—but Trent could feel Roy's arrest was imminent.

Roy passed the warrants to a man who came up behind him.

"Who are you?" Trent asked, though he had a budding suspicion.

"Willis Merritt, Mr. Archer's lawyer," the man replied.

As suspected. It hadn't taken long for Roy to lawyer up, but the guilty were always quick to line up their defense. When they finished here though, it would take more than swift words to save Roy from his fate. Trent turned and signaled for the two accompanying officers to enter the home. "I'll take your car keys, Mr. Archer." Trent held out his hand.

"Whoa, hold up there, Officers," Merritt said. "Let me read the warrants first."

"Not necessary. You can read while we search. Keys." Trent put his open palm in Roy's face.

Roy dropped a key ring into Trent's hand. He and Amanda had decided they'd let the officers search the house while he and Amanda would look at the car. Crime Scene would be arriving soon to assist with their fancy gadgets.

"Did your wife ever drive your car, Mr. Archer?" Amanda asked.

"She had her own."

"That a yes? A no?" Trent said.

"A no."

"Was she ever inside your vehicle?" Trent asked.

Merritt jumped in. "What sort of questions are these? Jill Archer was Mr. Archer's wife. It would make sense that she had been inside his vehicle. And, please, let's show some respect for your fellow officer of the law and a grieving man."

"This *fellow officer* beat his wife, raped her," Trent spat. "Did he tell you that?"

Roy stared through him, an effort to intimidate, but it would take more than that.

"You're making baseless accusations, Detective," Merritt said.

Trent moved closer to the lawyer. "Jill Archer's body told us all we need to know about your client." He dared not look at Roy now for fear he'd lose his temper.

Another vehicle pulled up to the curb, and a quick glance over a shoulder verified it was Crime Scene. *Perfect timing...*

"Now, if you'll excuse us, Mr. Merritt," Amanda said. "My colleagues and I have work to do."

Trent and Amanda went to Roy's sedan and met with CSIs Blair and Donnelly in the driveway.

"Guess if you're here, you can't be processing in the lab," Amanda said to Blair.

"Nope, but before I left, I emailed the measurements for the handspan and finger size to you."

"What more could a girl ask for?" Amanda smiled at the investigator.

"A bottle of Merlot and a hot bath?"

"Huh. Sign me up. For now, we have keys for Archer's car."

"Not exactly Christmas, but I'll take what I can." Blair smiled.

Trent unlocked the vehicle and popped the trunk. The

others joined him at the rear of the car, and the investigators snapped on gloves.

It was a cloudless day and there were lights in the trunk, but Blair still shone a flashlight inside. She ran a gloved hand over the carpet, then stood back.

"Color wise—and to the eye—I'd say this carpet is a match to the dark gray fiber found on Charlotte Archer. I'll look at it under magnification first chance once I'm back in the lab."

The hairs on Trent's arms stood. "He killed them and transported them in the trunk to the park."

"One step at a time there, cowboy." Blair smiled at him. He didn't return the expression. He was done being told how to react. "And how about instead of you two looming overhead like thunderclouds, you go inside and look around?"

"Let's," Amanda said, leading the way to the house.

He followed, but he sure hoped that Roy Archer would stay out of his face.

"You're asking for all of Mr. Archer's shoes?" Merritt was peacocking and blocking Officer Wyatt in the entrance.

"How about you tell us?" Trent stepped in. "You have the warrant in your hand."

Merritt grimaced and stepped aside. "Whatever floats your boat."

"Are all your client's shoes in this closet?" Trent pointed to one by the front door and ignored Roy, who had come up behind his lawyer.

"They are," Roy said.

Trent beat Wyatt to the bi-fold door. There were three pairs of men's shoes, including a pair of steel-toe work boots. He bent down and picked up the boots with gloved hands. The tongue on the boot stated they were size eleven—the shoe size of the partial print left at the grave site. "Cinderella's a fit," he mumbled as he flipped them to see the soles. The heel had lines and squares with deep grooves, accompanied by a thin arch swiped toward the inseam—a visual match. "Bag these," he told Wyatt. "And be extra careful with them."

"Will do." Officer Wyatt took the boots.

Trent stood. "We've got you, Roy."

"You've got nothing. I've lost everything, don't you see that?" Roy shot back.

Despite his claim he'd lost everything, he didn't give Trent the impression he was that broken up about it.

Amanda stepped in front of Trent, putting distance and a barricade between him and Roy. "Point us in the direction of the primary bedroom."

"Find it yourself," Roy mumbled.

"Have it your way." Amanda entered the home, and Trent followed.

They passed Charlotte's room, where a uniformed officer was searching, and carried on to the primary bedroom. There was a king-size bed without a headboard or footboard, the box spring and mattress on the metal frame alone. Two dressers, non-matching, and they were made of laminated chipboard. There was one nightstand with a Bible on it. Trent wagered that had been Jill's side of the bed. Maybe he was rushing to judgment against Roy, but he didn't think so. He certainly didn't see him as a spiritual man.

He opened the Bible, and inside was a printed label with *New World Church* and Jill's name printed on the line provided beneath the words *This Bible is the property of.* "Looks like Jill may have been a member of New World Church."

Amanda looked thoughtful, then said, "They're in Triangle."

He thumbed through the pages, stopping on different passages that had been highlighted in pink. Most spoke of retribution and others the promise of salvation. A few testified to God's enduring love and intention to free the blameless.

Trent wasn't too sure about any of that and set the Bible

down, as if it had sparked a fire in his palm. He wasn't a deeply religious person. He held no interest in organized religion but still considered himself spiritual.

"What is it?" Amanda must have noticed his urgency in putting the "good book" down.

"Jill highlighted different verses." He shared the gist with her, and she nodded and walked to the closet.

Trent stood at her side. The space was full of women's clothing—neatly pressed dresses on hangers. "She had the wardrobe for church," he shared his observation as his thoughts derailed down a rabbit hole. For all her faith, Jill and her daughter still ended up murdered and buried in a shallow grave. Where had God been then? Where was He or She when her husband beat her and raped her? He took a few breaths, trying to calm his anger.

They looked around the bedroom for a while longer, but there was nothing else that stood out. Next, they went into Charlotte's room.

"Find anything of interest?" Amanda asked the officer there.

"Just this." The officer lifted the comforter and pointed under the bed.

Trent and Amanda hunched down. A coloring book, crayons, and a stuffed seal. The toy was roughly the same size as the elephant in the grave, but did the similarity matter?

"This was probably where she hid when her father and mother fought," Amanda said.

"You mean when he beat the crap out of his wife," Trent spat, correcting Amanda.

Tense silence followed, and the officer left.

Trent let out a puff of air as he straightened up. "I just..." He cupped his forehead, a headache setting in.

Amanda stood next to him and put a hand on his shoulder, said nothing. It was the best thing she could have done.

"Detectives?" It was CSI Donnelly's voice calling through the home.

"Right here," Amanda said, stepping into the hall.

Isabelle Donnelly gestured for her to step back into the child's room. She spoke in a low voice. "Emma and I just found rather solid proof that Charlotte Archer was in the trunk of Roy Archer's sedan."

"The carpet was a definite match to the fiber?" Amanda asked.

"Don't know that yet, but we found a piece of fabric that fits the pattern and material of the sweater the girl was buried in."

"It was torn?" Amanda pushed back.

"Yes, but the girl was in overalls, and her shirt was tucked in. That's why it wasn't noticeable at the scene. Rideout might not have thought to mention it to you. But I assure you there was a chunk missing, and we're quite positive it's a match for what was in the trunk."

Trent's entire body was pulsating with rage. Roy Archer didn't deserve one more breath as a free man. "That's it, Amanda. We have more than enough to bring him in." Surely, she had to see that Roy was guilty as hell.

"Thanks for the update," Amanda told Donnelly in a calm manner. To Trent, she added, "I'll make a quick call to Graves," and pulled out her phone.

Trent took off down the hall.

"Trent," she called out.

He kept moving.

Amanda's steps followed as she spoke to Graves. "Yes, Sarge, we are going to bring in Roy Archer..." Amanda ran through the highlight reel of the finds since they'd arrived.

Trent picked up his speed and found Roy Archer on the back stoop, the lawyer nowhere to be seen.

He slid the patio door open. "Roy Archer, you're coming with us."

The man turned slowly, his reptilian eyes scanning Trent's face.

Trent smirked. "It's your choice. Cooperate or go in cuffs."

"I heard you, Detective." The man was so calm, it sent shivers racing down Trent's spine.

Then Roy's arm lifted. A police-issued Glock was in his hand.

"Stop!" He lunged for Roy and knocked him to the ground. The weapon flew and landed on the grass. Beneath him, Roy squirmed, trying to get free. An unmitigated rage fired through Trent.

How dare this coward hold a gun on me!

Trent punched Roy in the nose. Bone and cartilage shifted, and Roy screamed out.

"What the hell is going on?" Merritt burst into the back-yard, and Trent rolled off Roy.

"Your client is"—Trent heaved for solid breath—"under arrest for threatening the life of an officer and for the murders of Jill and Charlotte Archer."

SIXTEEN

What the hell just happened? It was the question that kept replaying in Amanda's mind. She hadn't witnessed everything, arriving just a few seconds behind Trent. But she saw Trent land a punch. "You could have broken the man's nose."

"The least of what he deserves," Trent spat.

They were on the way to Central. Roy Archer was loaded in a police cruiser and his lawyer was following.

She wasn't sure how hard she wanted to press things. Hadn't she thought of inflicting hurt on Roy Archer? She would think anyone with a reasonable conscience would. He'd exploited his family as an outlet for his frustrations and rage. He was to provide a haven for them, but instead of making the home a refuge, he'd made it hell. But a firm line needed to exist between thought and deed, and as cops they had to rise above impulse. "We can't just lose our temper and—"

"Judge? Execute? I know. And I didn't. He held a gun on me."

From what she'd seen the gun had been on the lawn, out of reach. "I never saw that."

"So what are you saying? I'm lying? I crossed a line?"

"Hell yeah, that's exactly what I'm saying," she punched out as he pulled into the parking lot. "Not the lying part," she added.

"Still. Are you going to turn me in?" Trent peered in her eyes, a daring look in his own.

His question gave her pause. This was Trent. Her defense could be that she'd hadn't been the one face to face with an armed man. What was hard to ignore was the situation had been neutralized before Trent punched Roy.

"Never mind." Trent parked and got out of the vehicle.

Amanda had upheld her duty to the badge when it meant turning in her own mother to face murder charges and yet she considered stepping into a gray area to protect Trent? "I've got you," she whispered to the empty car, then got out herself.

The cruiser with Roy Archer entered the lot, Willis Merritt's Audi close behind.

Amanda had already told Officer Wyatt, who was responsible for the transport, to take Roy to interview room one before they left the Archer house. She entered the station and headed straight for her desk. Trent was nowhere in sight.

It would take several minutes for Roy Archer to get situated, so she'd do something useful in that time. She opened her email and clicked on a message from Emma Blair. It was the one with the measurements for the handspan and fingers. Amanda printed it and then went to the secure server to download the evidence list. She printed this and was reading it when Trent came up behind her.

"What do you have?" He flicked a finger to the pages she held.

"The evidence processed at the grave site. We've also got the size of the handspan and fingers." She handed him that sheet and returned to the list. Nothing they didn't already know about. She noted the partial boot print on the list and looked for a corresponding picture. She returned to the files on the server and found the image, printed it, and gave it to Trent. "Look familiar?" She hadn't seen the bottom of Roy's work boots, but Trent had seemed excited about them.

"Yep."

"Okay, I think we've let enough time pass." She shuffled the papers, snatching the ones back from Trent and putting them into a folder. "Let's go question this guy."

They headed down the hall and found Graves outside the interview room. "You two come with me." She motioned for them to follow her next door to the observation room.

Once inside, Graves leveled a finger at Trent. "He's going to sit this one out."

"What? No way. I—"

"You punched the guy. I've already had his lawyer in my office telling me of his intention to sue the PWCPD."

Trent puffed out his chest. "That's ludicrous, Sarge."

"Ludicrous or not, *Detective*, it's where we find ourselves. What exactly happened?" Graves crossed her arms tightly across her chest.

Amanda was careful about not making eye contact with either of them, afraid that both were volatile and susceptible to provocation.

"The suspect was armed," Trent began. "He was going to shoot me."

"And you know this for a fact?" Graves pursed her lips. "That he planned to shoot you?"

"You wish I'd given him that chance?"

Graves shook her head, exasperated. "Do you really need me to answer that?" Turning to Amanda, she raised her brows. "What did you see?"

"I was in the house at that time." Amanda's chest felt heavy, just whitewashing the scenario.

"Then you saw the gun in the suspect's hand, felt fearful?"

"By the time I got there, Trent had the situation under control."

"So you never saw that Roy Archer was armed?"

"I didn't." Amanda shied away from Trent's piercing gaze. "But there was a gun present in the vicinity, and I believe Trent feared for his safety and was justified in his actions." She felt her cheeks heat at the embellishment.

Graves never said a word for several seconds, passing her gaze back and forth between Amanda and Trent. "Okay, well, if it happened as you say, there should be nothing to worry about."

Amanda let out a breath she hadn't realized she'd been holding and nodded. She was relieved that Graves hadn't pressed further and ironed out the order of events. Technically, Roy was already disarmed when Trent had punched him. She'd advise Trent not to press charges at the risk of this backfiring on him. His defense—that Roy could have gone for the gun again— was weak and unsubstantiated.

"Thanks, Sarge," Trent said.

"Oh, don't thank me yet. And you're still benched for this interrogation."

Trent clenched his jaw, his evident temper not aiding his cause.

"Sarge, if I may make a request," Amanda began. "I'd like Trent to join me. He may make valuable observations—"

"Which he can do from in here."

"Sure. But he can't address them as they arise. As you know timing is crucial in an interrogation." Amanda wasn't going to soften what the *interview* actually was.

Both Amanda and Trent looked at Graves.

"Fine," she eventually pushed out. "But don't make me regret this decision. And know that I'll be right here the entire time."

"You won't regret it. I promise," Trent told her.

Amanda led the way into the room. Willis Merritt was

seated next to Roy Archer on the side of the table that faced the door. She dropped into the chair directly across from Roy, and Trent sat beside her.

Roy's nose was blossoming vibrant shades of blue and purple, and he was breathing through his mouth. "What the hell are you doing here? You broke my effin' nose."

"Not according to the paramedic," Trent countered.

Roy narrowed his eyes menacingly, and his mouth opened as if he were about to say something. He shut it when his lawyer put a hand on his forearm.

Amanda set the folder on the table and laid a hand over it. "Everything you say or do in this room is being recorded." She pointed out the surveillance equipment mounted in the corner of the room. "Do you acknowledge?"

"We do," Willis said on behalf of his client.

She pulled a photograph of the soles from Roy's work boots and put it in front of him. "Does this look familiar to you?"

Willis met Amanda's eye, and she knew he'd seen the potential for a trap, but it was a fair question.

"Mr. Archer," Amanda prompted.

"I guess."

She took a picture of the partial boot print near the grave site and set it beside the first photo. "I'd say they look alike. You?" She drew a pointed finger from one to the other.

"Sure, but..." He stopped speaking at the slight downward tug of her lips.

She pressed her fingertip to the second picture. "This was a print left near your wife and daughter's grave." She let silence pass for a few beats. "Could you tell us why prints from your boots were there?"

"I have no idea."

"Your question is unreasonable. How should my client know? Surely, he's not the only one who owns these boots," Willis said.

"All right, well, let me ask this," Amanda began. "Were you in Prince Park recently? More specifically, the last five days?"

"No."

She shuffled the initial photos aside and pulled photographs of Jill and Charlotte Archer from the crime scene. She pushed them across the table.

Roy shuddered at the image of his dead wife and daughter and drew back.

"Why did you kill your family, Mr. Archer? Was your wife threatening to leave you? Had she left, and you caught up with her and Charlotte?"

"I never killed them." His voice now hollow, like a broken man. And his eyes glistened with tears.

She couldn't let herself be swayed. Her job was to push him for the truth—no matter how painful or uncomfortable it might be to get there. "Say their names, Mr. Archer. Jill and Charlotte."

"Detective, this is completely unnecessary and cruel," Willis interjected. "The man has lost his wife and daughter."

"I loved them." Roy stared across the room to the door. "Why would I kill them?"

"Control, power, or maybe you had an insurance policy on her?" Trent kicked out several motives and glanced at Amanda. "We haven't looked into that yet."

"I don't have life insurance on my wife."

"So it leaves control and power. You couldn't have her, so no one could."

"No."

Trent narrowed his eyes. "Why did you delay in reporting them missing, Mr. Archer?"

"I didn't."

"You said that you came home a week ago Tuesday and they weren't there," Trent added.

"That's the truth."

"Charlotte wasn't in school since the Friday before. Monday is unaccounted for. Why wasn't Charlotte in class?" Amanda asked.

"She had the tummy flu, carried over from Sunday."

"Did you or your wife take her to see a doctor?" Trent asked.

"Why? It was just an upset stomach."

"I didn't realize you were a pediatrician," Trent replied drily.

"I'm with my partner here, Mr. Archer," Amanda said. "Your daughter was sick for two days and kept home from school for at least one."

"That's right. *Two whole days.* It's not the end of the world."

Amanda bristled. If Zoe was sick, the doctor's office would be her first stop. Let the person with the medical license determine if there was anything to worry about. "Was Charlotte still unwell on Tuesday?"

"Yep. Jill was keeping her home. So, unwell for three days then." Roy rubbed his forehead. "Can't you see that I'm hurting here? And I wasn't going to hold the gun on you. I was going to end... my life." He sniffled and turned away.

The room turned dark and solemn. Mention of suicide did that. But if he were going to kill himself, was it due to regretting what he'd done, being caught, or from overwhelming grief? Remorse certainly fit the placement of the bodies in the grave— the toy an addition for Charlotte, as if she could enjoy it in an afterlife. In this moment, she wasn't about to pass judgment. "We're sorry for your loss, Mr. Archer," Amanda said softly, cutting through the tension.

"Thank you."

"We asked before about a stuffed toy elephant." She put a picture of it on the table.

Roy barely looked at it. "I told you. I never saw her with one. She carried around"—he snapped his fingers a few times—

"a seal that Jill and I bought her at the aquarium in the summer."

Likely the one under the bed. If she was attached to the toy though, why was it secreted away? "We found the seal."

His eyes narrowed. "Where?"

"In your daughter's room, under her bed." Any glimmering compassion Amanda had started to feel for Roy was slipping away. "You say she carried it around, then what is it doing there?"

"I have no idea, but it was her favorite."

It was possible Roy didn't know his daughter that well. When Zoe was younger, she wouldn't have a moment's separation from her dog, Lucky. And if Charlotte had been attached to the seal, how did it come to be left behind in the home? But Amanda would leave that avenue for now and divert to another path. She opened her folder and took out the picture CSI Donnelly had sent over of the torn fabric found in Roy's trunk. "Does this look familiar to you?"

Roy studied the image. "Looks like it's from a sweater of Charlotte's."

"Investigators found this in the trunk of your car. Can you tell us how it might have gotten there?" Of course, Amanda had her own idea. Roy had transported his wife's and daughter's dead bodies in his vehicle and the clothing was snagged then.

"Detective, you are asking that my client speculate," Willis inserted.

Amanda was watching Roy. He was staring at the photo, his eyes shadowed. "He knows how and when. Don't you, Mr. Archer?"

Willis turned to his client. Roy broke the silence.

"Charlotte threw temper tantrums, and time-outs were the only way to calm her down." Roy swirled his fingertip on the table in the shape of a circle. Over and over. And over.

Nausea and rage rolled over Amanda, as she pieced what he

wasn't saying together. "You're telling us you'd punish your daughter by putting her in the trunk of your car?"

"It didn't hurt her. She—"

"You're a monster," Trent blurted out, beating Amanda to the same allegation. "You abused your wife and your daughter. Your wife had bruises and broken bones, but your daughter's scars were on the inside. Mental and emotional."

"Charlotte was six years old," Amanda said, feeling cold. "You shut your little girl away in a dark compartment because you couldn't handle her mood swings?" She snapped her mouth shut before she said something that jeopardized the case. And she didn't want to know how long these *time-outs* lasted.

"Abuse, Detectives? Please," Willis said, jumping on Trent's comment.

Trent flailed a hand toward Roy. "You need to talk with your client. The bruises and broken bones inflicted over months, possibly years, don't lie. Go ahead, Roy, and tell your lawyer about the animal you are."

Willis turned to Roy.

"Jill pushed my buttons," Roy snarled. "It doesn't mean I killed her or Charlotte."

Trent opened his mouth to speak, but Amanda nudged his foot.

"Let us see your hands, Mr. Archer," she said.

"Why should he?" the lawyer flipped back.

"As we told Mr. Archer before, his wife's and daughter's necks were broken. But not long prior to death they were hugged so tight it caused bruising on their backs." Amanda produced the pictures to support this. "The killer left us his handspan and finger size. So I ask again, hands," she prompted Roy.

He held them out, and Trent took the measurements.

He returned to his seat. "Both are a match."

"Oh, please." Willis sighed dramatically and threw his arms up. "You can't make it an exact match."

"Not exact, but we can determine within a measure of accuracy the size and shape that caused a bruise," she told him, though it was likely knowledge the attorney already possessed. "Mr. Archer, we have enough evidence against you to charge you with the murders of your wife and daughter. And I'd bet more will turn up to support our case against you. The search continues of your house and vehicle while we sit here."

"You're not going to find anything," Roy said nonchalantly.

"Because you hid the evidence?" Amanda countered.

"There's nothing to find."

Amanda didn't repeat her earlier words, but they already had plenty to charge him.

SEVENTEEN

"That's, as they say in basketball, a slam dunk. Great job. Both of you." Graves greeted them in the observation room with praise and a smile.

Amanda returned the expression and thanked the sergeant. It was very rare when cases were closed in under forty-eight hours, and this was one for the record books. There was a deep-rooted satisfaction that came with locking up Roy Archer, making him pay for what he had done. Darla and Irvin Meyer would have closure, and Jill and Charlotte would get justice. She tamped down the gnawing feeling in her gut that second-guessed the evidence. But it was probably because the case was closed quick, as if something had to be off due to that alone.

"Well, I won't hold you up. You both have a lot of work ahead of you." Graves left the room.

"That guy wasn't going to kill himself," Trent said. "He loves himself too much."

"I think you should let it go."

Trent's face shadowed. "He held a gun on me."

"So at one point, you were facing down his barrel?" The

fact Trent hadn't said as much in so many words made her antsy. Well, that, and Roy's claimed intention.

"Never mind."

"And after he was unarmed, you still felt threatened and justified in hitting him?"

"The guy's a douche."

"No question, and he's going to pay for killing his family. But drop the charges of assault and attempted murder against him. Please, Trent, trust me. It won't turn out well for you."

"Basically, you're saying you don't have my back."

"I can't back you up. That's why I'm telling you to leave it alone." She'd already told him she saw the gun out of reach and wasn't going to say it again.

"Fine, I'll drop the charges. But he doesn't deserve the badge."

"He's going to prison, so consider it gone."

"Cause for celebration."

There was—the killer was caught, case closed. Despite that, she found it impossible to conjure a smile.

Trent nudged her elbow. "Celebration? Just accept that sometimes justice is served with a swift hand."

She considered his words, pushed aside her niggling—not entirely sure of its source—and nodded. "You're right. We should celebrate. But first, we'll get a start on the paperwork. Then it's beers on me."

"I'm with you until the beers. I sort of have plans."

"How does someone 'sort of have plans'? Not that I want to pry." She held up her hands and plastered on a smile. He probably had a date. "It's all good."

He met her gaze, and a few awkward seconds passed. All because of that kiss there were times, like now, she wanted to sink into the earth. It had been months ago, so why couldn't she let it go?

She dipped her head and parked at her desk for the next

several hours. At five, she clocked out, ready to head home, one of the rare nights she'd be on time for Libby and Zoe. She flicked her monitor off and got up.

Sergeant Graves was in the doorway of Amanda's cubicle, her expression grim and foreboding.

Amanda lowered back into her chair, and that knot in the pit of her stomach grew. "What is it?"

"Put a hold on charging Roy Archer."

Trent popped up from his chair. "Why?" he dragged out.

"A hiker and his dog just found another grave in Prince Park."

"Don't tell me..." She closed her eyes briefly and let out a deep breath. "A mother and daughter?"

"Too soon to know, but at least one parameter fits with the Archer case. The grave's location. This time a woman's left hand was sticking out of the ground."

"Let's go." Amanda stood and started toward the parking lot. She'd call Libby on the way and see if she'd stay at the house with Zoe. Amanda would be home late tonight—if at all.

EIGHTEEN

Trent's head was spinning, not sure how to process this latest development. He was positive that Roy Archer had killed his family, but if this grave held another mother and daughter, where would that leave things? What motive would he have for killing them?

He drove to the park, foot flat to the floor, frustrated. One, he had to cancel his plans with Sydney, a nice enough woman he'd met at a bar. Tonight would have been their first date. Two, the case against Roy was left to simmer.

He and Amanda beat the medical examiner to the scene. Response officers were taking statements from those in the park and restricting access to newcomers. A man, holding the leash of a German shepherd, was talking with one of them. The only dog Trent saw around, so the man was likely the unfortunate person to stumble across the remains.

The Crime Scene truck pulled in, and two investigators got out and joined him and Amanda. One was tall and lean; the other shorter and on the squat side. They weren't often sent out to their crime scenes so introductions were made again. Tall and lean was Mary Novak. Short and squat was Glenda Rowe.

The group walked to the nearest officer, who was also moving to close the distance.

"Harry Kimbell." He pointed to the badge on his uniform.

"Detectives Steele and Stenson," Amanda said, covering both introductions in one blow.

"CSIs Novak and Rowe. The body?" Tall and Lean was obviously in a hurry to get to work.

"Ah, yeah. I'll take you to it, and then come back for the ME," Kimbell said.

They started out into the woods, just as they had the previous morning. But it was even more chilling this time. There was no morning sun heralding a new day. Rather it was twilight, signaling an end.

"It's just through here." Kimbell gestured ahead, bending his hand to indicate a quick right.

"This is quite a distance from where Jill and Charlotte were buried," Amanda said, pulling up next to Trent.

"And in the opposite direction."

No one spoke for a few moments. The only sounds were the calls of birds and other woodland creatures.

"There." Kimbell spoke solemnly and stepped back.

No further direction was needed. About ten feet away, the left hand of a female—slender fingers, long nails—reached out of the ground. As if from beyond the grave she begged to be heard, to be seen, to be avenged.

Diamonds on a wedding band she wore winked in the dying sunlight that squeezed through the tree canopy.

A gentle yet cold breeze kicked the leaves still clinging to the branches overhead. Trent shivered and zipped up his jacket to his chin.

The investigators set their cases down and got to work. Rowe took photographs of the hand and surrounding area. Novak started spouting instructions.

"Everyone needs to keep back until we've finished

processing the area." She made a brushing motion with her hands. "We'll need to know everyone who was in the area before our arrival."

"Just us, Kirk Duffy, and his dog," Kimbell said. "Obviously we can't account for any unknown passersby."

"Duffy who found her?" Novak volleyed back.

"That's right." Kimbell hoisted up his pants.

She bobbed her head and gloved up.

Trent and Amanda moved a distance away with Officer Kimbell.

"What's Duffy's story?" Amanda asked him.

"Probably what you've already heard. He was out walking his dog, which he says he does every day about this time. Rover —not an entirely original name for a dog—found her."

"You pull a background on Duffy yet?" Trent asked, his gaze distracted by one of the investigators setting an evidence marker down.

"Clean record."

"Okay. Thanks," Amanda told him. She looked at Trent. "Let's go have a chat with Duffy and see what he can tell us."

Trent followed his partner, but his mind was occupied with the Archer case and this one. What wasn't seeding well in his gut was that wedding ring. First impressions would have him conclude the victim had been married. If Roy Archer wasn't guilty, though, was there a serial killer stalking and killing women—and children—in Prince William County?

NINETEEN

Amanda and Trent stood around the grave. The CSIs, Officer Kimbell, and Sergeant Graves were with them. Hours had passed since the initial discovery. Duffy and others in the park were questioned and sent on their way. By this point, the sun had completely disappeared, and portable lights were brought out.

No one spoke a word. Likely everyone was trying to process the discovery as Amanda came to grips with it too.

The findings, heartbreaking.

Rideout and Liam had cleared out the shallow pit just moments ago. Another mother and daughter.

Their looks were painfully similar to Jill and Charlotte Archer. Both were fully clothed in sweaters, jeans, and shoes. A stuffed rabbit was buried with them. It was about the same size as the elephant entombed with the Archers.

"Was too easy," Amanda muttered. "The case being open and shut. We'll need to find out if there's any connection between them and Roy Archer."

Trent turned to her. "And if there is, he's more than an abusive man, he's a psychopath."

She simply nodded. His words said it all. And even if the killer wasn't Roy the definition of a psychopath could still apply. "You come across any other mothers and daughters reported missing when you found the Archers?"

Trent shook his head.

The answer Amanda had expected. Surely if he had, he would have said long before now. The fact no one had reported these two hurt almost as much as seeing them lying in the ground. "How long do you think they've been here?"

"The earth was more packed, and given the decomp I'm seeing, they've been dead for weeks," Rideout replied from where he was hunched next to the shared grave. "Three, possibly four. Maybe more."

It felt with these two, the time-of-death window was a moving target. "Safe to say a month?"

Rideout nodded.

"They came before the Archers." With her statement, Amanda matched eyes with Trent. His widened slightly, as hers likely did too. "Any ID?"

Liam searched the pockets and shook his head. "Nope."

She put her hands on her hips. "Cause of death?" she asked but saw faint bruising on their faces from where she stood.

"Given the angle of their heads, I suspect the same as with the Archers. Transection of their spinal cords due to broken necks," Rideout said.

Trent pointed at the woman's face, indicating a black eye. "She was beaten."

"Possible. Given coloration I'd say it predated her death by at least a week."

"So another abusive mate, or had the killer hit her?" Amanda pushed out the question, weighing the possibilities. "Guess we need to build a timeline for her and establish when she went missing."

"Uh-huh. I'd wager the killer either lives in the area or knows it well," Trent suggested.

"I'd agree. To keep coming here with his victims, the location must mean something to him."

"Roy Archer said Jill brought Charlotte here a lot," Trent said.

"Just more reason we need to question him about these two." Amanda's gaze briefly dipped to the grave. Linking all the murders to Roy Archer would be convenient. Then at least they'd have their killer. "Any bankable forensic evidence?" Amanda turned to CSI Rowe.

"We had a lot of rain going back a couple of weeks ago. It's probably what eroded the grave enough to expose the female vic's hand, but it's also destroyed evidence around the grave."

Duffy had told her and Trent he didn't regularly come through this section of the park, but it was a miracle no one else had happened on the site before now. Amanda turned to Graves. "Sarge," she prompted, and saw that she'd pulled Graves from her thoughts. "This is the second grave. Regardless of how we make out questioning Roy Archer, I'm thinking we should bring out cadaver dogs, have the entire park searched."

"I'll get it arranged. At this point, they'll likely start tomorrow, but I'll make sure that uniforms cordon off the park until the K-9 unit is finished. Do you think that Roy Archer killed them too?" Graves pointed to the bodies, while holding eye contact with Amanda.

"It is entirely possible." There was the posing of these bodies, their disposal, and the location... They were the same as with the Archers—an unlikely coincidence. "But there are enigmas that have bothered me from the start." Trent stiffened beside her, but she carried on. "The fact the Archers were hugged just moments before their necks were broken doesn't coincide with a heat-of-the-moment murder. In cases of escalated domestic violence that's expected. And there's the stuffed toy—an elephant. Roy Archer swore his daughter didn't have one and told us her favorite toy was a stuffed *seal*. Trent and I found that under Charlotte's bed."

"Now we have a stuffed rabbit," Graves said.

"Yes, about the same size as that elephant."

"Right. So if these toys don't belong to the children, where are they coming from? Of course, we're making an assumption based on the first case. The rabbit could be this girl's," Graves pointed out.

"Fair enough."

"Something else is weighing on you, Detective?"

"The method of the burial, with mother and daughter embracing, suggests affection on behalf of their killer. Possibly even regret or remorse."

"We can't ignore that Roy Archer has work boots matching a partial left next to the grave for his family. Also his handspan and finger measurements are the same as the bruising," Trent said. "We also can't dismiss the piece of fabric from Charlotte's shirt being in Roy's sedan."

"We got an explanation for that even if it wasn't what we wanted to hear." Amanda was still horrified that any father would stick his own daughter in the trunk of a car as punishment.

"You two talk with Archer, see if you can get anywhere," Graves told them. "Without an ID, it's a little tough, but mention the discovery, gauge his reaction."

Amanda nodded. "We'll make it our next stop." She might make it home in time to see Zoe off to school the next morning.

"When are you conducting the autopsies?" Graves asked Rideout.

The medical examiner glanced at his assistant and said, "It will be first thing in the morning."

"The soonest that you can do them?" Graves pushed.

Rideout placed his hands on his hips. "I could rush it

tonight, but these two deserve dignity and respect and attention to detail."

"Very well. Tomorrow morning." To Amanda and Trent, she said, "See you back at Central."

Amanda hated the thought of leaving these victims behind. But they would be in Rideout's and Liam's capable hands.

TWENTY

It was ten that night by the time Amanda had Roy Archer and his lawyer back in an interview room.

"I'm not sure why you had to drag us in here for the second time today." Willis had dark shadows under his eyes.

"There's been another discovery in Prince Park," Trent said, leveling this at Roy.

He perked up. "I'm assuming by *discovery* you mean bodies. I was in a jail cell, so I didn't do it."

"Good assumption, Mr. Archer," Amanda pushed out. "Another mother and daughter. She may have been the victim of abuse, like your wife."

"Okay... Not sure how this involves me." Roy raised his brows, popping eyes that were bloodshot.

"They were in a shallow grave, positioned the same way as your wife and daughter. They looked a lot like them too." She almost added *from what you could tell*. The decomp was far more progressed than that of Jill and Charlotte.

Willis grinned triumphantly at Roy. "Sounds to me like you've unearthed a reason to let my client go."

Amanda fought rolling her eyes at the lawyer's pun. "Do you know anything about them, Mr. Archer?"

"Nothing. I swear."

"Detective, can you connect these murders to my client? If not, you have no more reason to hold him and I suggest you release him immediately. In your own words, you describe a crime scene that is identical. That means whoever killed Jill and Charlotte Archer also murdered the two found today. That correct?"

"Yes, but here's the thing," Amanda started. "They've been dead about a month."

Roy paled. "That doesn't mean I had anything to do with—"

There was a knock on the one-way mirror. It would be Graves from the observation room.

Amanda and Trent went next door to join her.

"We've got to cut him loose," Graves said the moment they cleared the doorway.

"He killed his wife and daughter," Trent spat.

"I know you want resolution, Detective. And I appreciate you want some justice because this man beat his wife, but putting him away for murders he didn't commit isn't the way to get it."

Amanda noted the subtle flicker in the sergeant's eye.

"I believe we can all agree that the same person killed and buried both mothers and daughters?" Graves said.

"Yes, absolutely," Amanda agreed.

"It appears so," Trent chimed in.

"Then we have no choice. Since we don't have enough evidence against Archer now, cut him loose."

"We have the right to hold him," Amanda argued. "We could find evidence."

"Too much of a hunting expedition, Detective."

Trent clenched his jaw. "Archer beat his wife, abused his daughter. In the least he needs to be stripped of the badge."

Graves stiffened, blinked slowly, licked her lips. "You leave his future up to me. All right?"

"Yes, ma'am," Trent said, his facial expression relaxing.

"Detective Steele?" Graves prompted.

"I'll leave it to you." Amanda wasn't sure what the sergeant intended to do but figured it was related to the earlier look in her eye. And no doubt she'd hear of the fallout before long.

"What I like to hear."

The silence held a charged energy, as if Graves expected Amanda and Trent to leave that instant and release Roy.

Amanda's legs were weighed to the floor. "We'll give Archer the news, but there is another avenue that Trent and I never explored. You should probably know about it. Charlotte's teacher at Dumfries Elementary had noticed Jill Archer speaking with a man outside the school. The teacher didn't recognize him. Now, it might not mean anything—"

"But it might," Graves cut in and narrowed her eyes. "Why haven't I heard about this before?"

"Evidence had pointed to Roy Archer when the only victims were his wife and daughter. But now we have two more. If we're looking for someone targeting mothers and daughters, we need to consider everything."

"Agreed. Follow that up first thing in the morning. See if you can get video surveillance that shows us this guy's face and ask around the school about him."

"You got it," Amanda replied. "Would you be able to apply some pressure on the phone provider to get Jill's records? That would at least give us her communication history, even where her phone last pinged." *And where the hell is Jill's car? Yet another loose thread.*

"Absolutely. My second call after I arrange things with the K-9 unit."

"Amanda and I also discovered that Jill Archer may be a

member at New World Church," Trent said, speaking up. "We could talk with some members and see if any have something to offer the investigation."

"It sounds to me like you two have your next steps. Proceed with both avenues tomorrow morning."

"And the autopsies?" The full itinerary Graves had laid out for them left little room in their schedule.

"You leave the bodies to Rideout and his assistant. You get us some answers. Keeping the Archers' names out of the paper has been a haul, but now another mother and daughter...? The media will catch wind of this and, excuse me for saying, but it has real potential to become a shitstorm quick if the PWCPD doesn't provide answers to the public."

"I understand that." And Amanda did—quite well. Reporters and journalists crawled through the teeniest of cracks. "I know I mentioned the stuffed toys already, but I think we should have Forensics take a closer look at them. Maybe what they find will lead us closer to our killer. Don't know how but I feel it's something worth looking into."

"Sure. If you think it will help."

"Just exploring all possibilities for leads. The last thing any of us wants is more mothers and daughters being killed."

Every one of them became quiet with the stark possibility of more victims.

"Maybe we should reach out to the FBI and have them search ViCap," Amanda said. "I have a contact. Do you want me to give him a call?"

The Violent Criminal Apprehension Program was a database kept by the FBI that housed crimes from across the country that were unsolved.

"Let me sleep on that, Detective."

Amanda nodded. Most sergeants and police chiefs weren't eager to bring in the feds. But their database could show other mothers and daughters who had been found in shallow graves across the US. Tragic, for sure, but being armed with that knowledge would only help the case. A profile of the killer might emerge, preventing more death and resulting in justice. If so, asking the FBI for help was worth swallowing some pride.

TWENTY-ONE

Amanda might have squeezed Zoe a little harder than normal this morning when she woke up. It was impossible to shove aside the fact two little girls had been murdered, and she and Trent weren't anywhere close to finding out who was responsible. The mother and daughter discovered yesterday were still without names. Another check in missing persons last night hadn't proved helpful.

Currently she and Trent were in the principal's office at Dumfries Elementary School waiting to speak with Kim Brewer. While they were here, the autopsies were being conducted and cadaver dogs were scouring Prince Park. She hoped their efforts didn't turn up any more bodies. There had been enough death to last her a lifetime.

"Amanda?" Kim was walking toward her and Trent. "Is there something else you need from me? I told you everything I knew about Charlotte."

A student entered the office and reported to the secretary. Amanda asked that Kim take them to the teachers' lounge again.

Once they were there, Amanda said, "The other day you

mentioned that Jill Archer was talking with a man outside of the school, someone you didn't recognize."

"That's right. What about him?"

"There's been a development, and he is currently a person of interest." Amanda might be stretching things, but better that than dire consequences if she continued to assume he didn't matter.

Kim sat on the couch and rubbed her arms.

"If there is anything distinctive you can remember about him?" Trent's tone was warm and would encourage the teacher to speak.

"I don't really remember much about him..." She ran her bottom lip through her teeth. "Guess you could say he was good-looking."

"Hair color, build?" Amanda asked.

"He had brown hair, was scruffy-faced."

"Okay, that's good." Amanda offered the praise, though not confident the vague description would get them anywhere.

"I know it's not much, probably nothing in the grand scheme. I mean, how many men likely fit that description? Oh, he was rather tall. I'd say a few inches over six feet, judging by how he looked next to Mrs. Archer."

Trent was scribbling in his notepad, presumably recording everything Kim was saying.

"Did you see him arrive or leave? Maybe he came with someone else or he got into a vehicle?" Amanda asked.

"No, sorry, I didn't. I just saw him with Jill for the passing of a few seconds. Long enough to feel that they might have known each other."

"Right, as you mentioned yesterday." An innocent explanation for his presence remained—a kid's uncle or stepdad asked to step in that day. But then there was the fact they interacted as if they were familiar to each other. That would suggest they'd at least spoken on more than one occasion. "It would help if we could see this man for ourselves. Does the school have video surveillance outside?"

"For sure."

A rush of hope fluttered through Amanda. It was always some small clue that typically led to resolving an investigation. This footage might break this case wide open. That's if they got a clear shot of the man's face and it got them somewhere. "We'll talk to the principal about getting our hands on the footage." Kim wouldn't have the authority to give it to them.

"Yes, you'd need to. That's out of my hands."

Amanda nodded. Before they left she wanted to ask Kim about something else. If the unidentified girl from yesterday was from the area, she might have attended Dumfries Elementary. If so, they could get their identities and score a connection between the victims. She'd need to be careful how she asked though, so as not to give away that anyone had been murdered. The sergeant's words repeated in her head—*media shitstorm*. "Do you know if any other students around Charlotte's age have missed weeks of class?" She'd phrased it like this because they may be off on the estimate of the girl's age. She also might have gone to the school but wasn't in Kim's class.

Kim narrowed her eyes and studied Amanda and Trent. "None of my children. But *weeks* of missing class? I would have heard about that."

Was the unidentified little girl from outside of the county or assigned to another school in the area? Ten minutes down the road from Dumfries, Woodbridge had three. Or were mother and daughter from out of state? It might be time to call on the FBI's ViCap database, if only to help form the big picture of what they may be dealing with. But she thought of one explanation that could have students missing class that wouldn't raise concerns. "Have you had any students recently leave your class because the family moved?"

"It's just barely the start of the school year. I mean, if they were going to move, surely, for the children, parents would have done it before September. But in answer to your question, I haven't heard about any students leaving because of a recent move."

"Thank you, Kim. We appreciate your cooperation."

"Did something happen to another child?"

Trent tucked his notepad and pen away, putting it back in his pocket. Apparently, he was leaving this question for Amanda.

"We can't say anything at this time. That's probably not what you want to hear, but trust me when I say what you've told us has helped with the case." They were walking away with the knowledge that the girl from the grave yesterday likely wasn't from Dumfries.

"I didn't think I said that much, but if I was a help, good. Is that all you need from me today?"

"Just one more thing. Call me if you see that man again. I assume you still have my card?"

"I do, and I will."

"Thanks."

Kim returned to her classroom, and Amanda and Trent returned to the school's administrative office.

Amanda was debating internally whether they had enough to justify the request for the security footage to a judge if it came to that. Hopefully, the principal would save them the trouble of needing to find out. Looking at it from one angle, the mystery man may have nothing to do with the murders. But it was hard to ignore that a woman who was normally quiet and timid spoke to man in a relaxed manner. Was Jill having an affair with him—their conversation and the murders two distinct things? Or were they connected? Was that man the killer they were after? He might have gotten close to Jill, earned her trust. It certainly would make it easier to abduct her and her daughter. But how did that tie to their latest discovered victims?

"We'll talk to the principal and see if he'll give us the footage without a warrant."

"Makes sense to me."

They checked in with Flora, and she told them to go on into the principal's office. Amanda and Trent were both familiar with him. She was because Zoe went here. Trent because he'd gone with Amanda to the man for help when Zoe had been in danger last year.

"Amanda Steele, or should I say Detective Steele?" the principal said from where he was seated behind his desk. "And I'm sorry, but I can't remember your name?" He swept his gaze to Trent.

"Detective Stenson," Trent replied.

"We have a situation in which Dumfries Elementary has the opportunity to be a tremendous help to the PWCPD." Amanda set the hook. The worm was the chance for the man to be a hero.

The principal leaned forward. "Oh? And how is that?"

"We need to obtain some security footage." Amanda gave him the timeframe.

"Hmph." He sat back, swiveled. "I'd need a warrant to protect the privacy of the children and their families."

"You're likely not aware, but the case we're working involves the murder of one of your students."

His mouth gaped open, but he didn't say anything.

She'd obviously need to do more pushing and stress why he'd want to cooperate. "I can't imagine it reflecting too well on you if it leaked someone got onto school grounds and ended up killing a child and her mother. You sure there's nothing you can do?"

"Poached and abducted from here?" He swallowed roughly. "This is heartbreaking."

"So you'll get us the video footage?"

He pursed his lips and avoided eye contact. "I'm sorry,

Detective, but to hand the footage over without a warrant would require approval from the school board." There was a slight hiccup to the man's voice disclosing genuine sadness, but from what she'd seen before he was also part businessman, concerned about the reputation of his school.

That could take longer than getting the warrant. The school admins would want to meet and discuss... and discuss some more. "We'll get a warrant."

She was the first to leave his office, angry to her core. "These children—Zoe—is under this man's care and he's more concerned about image."

"Sadly, it's how the world works," Trent lamented, keeping stride with her, heading toward the department car.

"Oh, you don't need to tell me how it works. But it stinks."

"I'll call Judge Anderson."

"Thanks." While he did that, Amanda checked her emails. There was one from CSI Blair advising that she and Donnelly had assumed the lead on the second set of victims and that all the evidence collected yesterday had been passed on to them. Amanda replied to Blair.

That's excellent. Need you to look closer at the stuffed toys. Are there any similarities? Anything that might help advance the case?

Just after she hit send, her phone rang. Rideout. She answered immediately. "Detective Steele."

"It's Hans. I'm getting started on preparing the bodies for autopsy, and I have news you're going to want to hear."

He stopped there, leaving her hanging. She had a fondness for the ME, but not his flair for inserting suspense. "Which is...?"

"I know the victims' names. Connie Riggs is the mother, thirty-one. The girl was six. Name's Jodi Riggs."

Names helped and hurt. They stamped home the dire reality—lives were lost. "How did you find that?"

"I was disrobing the woman and found her driver's license in the bottom of her left sock."

"Strange place to keep it." Amanda doubted she'd walked around with it there, so had Connie Riggs hidden it or had the killer put it there? And how would the former scenario even work out? It was possible Connie had it on her person, say in a pants pocket, the killer unaware of the fact. Then she could have hidden it. Otherwise, Amanda suspected the killer would have taken her purse and she'd have no way of getting her hands on it.

Rideout continued. "When I looked her up in the system, I saw she had a daughter."

"Do you have an address?"

"Sure do. Washington."

That would explain why Kim Brewer wasn't aware of any absent children from Dumfries Elementary. But it highlighted a bigger problem. Was the killer on the move, selecting victims from different states? But if so, why were the Riggs buried in Prince Park? Their killer had to be from the Prince William County area, or in the least return occasionally. Was it just to bury his victims or did work draw him here? Another possibility was he ran into the Riggs locally, making him a resident of the county.

"Her background tells me she was married to Karl Riggs."

"Please fire the address over to me."

"The second I hang up."

"Thanks. Oh, do you know if Karl ever filed missing person reports for his family?"

"No record that I found."

Amanda thanked Rideout again and hung up. Trent was just putting his phone away too. "So?" she asked him, holding back on her news while trying to squash her temper. *Karl hadn't even reported his family missing!*

"It's a yes/no. He wants the paperwork for this before he'll give us the go-ahead."

"As if there's not enough on our plate."

"And the call?" Trent gestured toward her phone.

"Rideout. We have our ID on the other mother and daughter—Connie and Jodi Riggs. She was married, and they lived in Washington."

"Washington?" His mouth widened; his eyes became dark. "Let's go."

Her phone pinged, as if on cue, and the message was the one promised from Rideout. They had their destination to enter into the vehicle's GPS.

TWENTY-TWO

Metro PD in Washington could have handled the notification, but Amanda wasn't delegating this responsibility. The bodies were uncovered in Prince William County and similar to the Archer case. She wanted to gauge Karl's reaction to the news firsthand.

"Smart move by Connie, stashing her ID in her sock—assuming that's what happened," Amanda said to Trent as he got them on the highway to DC.

He looked over at her in the passenger seat. "This will sound morbid, but Connie must have seen her and her daughter's future. She tucked it away, so if the worst happened, at least they'd be identified."

"I can't even imagine what they suffered. But with what you're saying, it would imply Connie and her daughter spent time with the killer."

"It's just sinking in for me now, but that would have been the case for Jill and Charlotte Archer. With Roy out from under suspicion, he last saw his family on Tuesday. Time of their deaths was pegged as Friday."

"So the killer held them for three days before he killed

them." A past theory seemed to gain more credibility. "Okay, so we're looking for a man who preys on vulnerable women. Not firmed up with Connie yet, but she had bruising. We'll be able to build a timeline once we've spoken with the husband, but let's run with this theory for now: the killer abducts mothers and daughters from abusive families."

Trent nodded. "And let's say most of their injuries date back before their abductions. Does this guy view himself as a savior? He takes them in and makes them feel loved and needed, then kills them? Is he trying to make a family for himself? And, if so, what changes the status quo?"

"Good question. And then when he buries them, he does so with evidence of affection? Not regret, as we first thought? But why these two women and children, aside from our assumption they both hail from abusive households? And why children, Trent? That takes a certain kind of evil."

"I agree."

"The killer targeting these women and children, is it personal for him? Was he affected by domestic violence? And is there a connection between the families, besides their killer?" She rushed to add the latter, before he countered with sarcasm. It was also painfully obvious this stage of investigation raised a lot of questions without answers to go with them.

"Hard to see one yet. They live an hour apart."

"Doesn't mean they always have." She twisted the onboard computer so it faced her. "Let me take a quick look at their backgrounds." She did just that. "There is no crossover in previous towns."

"Then there's another connection."

"The only thing they might have in common is their killer. But did the women and children run into him at a place he regularly frequents?"

"Could have. We'll ask Karl Riggs if he knows the Archers though."

"Of course."

"You mentioned a place the killer regularly frequents. What if that is Prince Park? He seems to have some draw to it, or so burying his victims there would indicate."

"Possible." She was trying to reconcile how the Riggs from Washington ended up in the park. Did something bring Connie to the county, or even Prince Park specifically?

"I'd say most likely. Serial killers often gravitate to a certain area."

"Right. So what is it about Prince Park for this one?" A rhetorical question they had no hope of answering without more information. It didn't leave her without hypotheticals though. "Did he go as a child? Did he go as an adult...?" She stopped there, tossing that around in her mind. There were many activities that would hold appeal to an adult male offered at Prince Park. There was also the children's playground. It felt like there was something about that, lurking just at the edge of her brain, but it wasn't coming into focus.

"After the K-9 unit has finished, and the park's open again, we might want to have officers posted there in case he returns," Trent said, his mind apparently thinking along the same lines as hers. "Might be where he met the women and their daughters."

"Agreed on both counts. I'll run it past Graves. I'm sure she'll agree."

"And just thinking out loud here, but if the killer had affection for his victims, he might revisit their graves."

"Suppose it's possible, but if so—even if not—he is probably aware by this point that we've found them and are looking for more."

"So where does that leave us? He's not necessarily going to stop killing, just pick a different place to get rid of them."

Amanda hated how Trent's logical statement put the killer further out of reach. "And he might not be too happy about that."

"Just wonderful. Another killer who harbors a vendetta against us."

"I say let him come for us. It would save us the trouble of hunting." She smirked at him. Possibly putting on a tad more bravado than she really felt.

"Ah, no thanks." He returned the smile but turned serious quickly. "I'd like to know how he overlooked the ID in Connie's sock. Did he hurry the burial for the Riggs?"

"They were killed weeks before the Archers. Maybe his first set of victims?" She'd wish for that, and that there wouldn't be more bodies for them to find. "He could have killed them, then panicked. Due to that he didn't take time to look them over."

"Sloppy on his part, good for us."

She picked up on where his mind had gone. "Well, he did leave us with trace—the hairs and fibers in the Archer case."

"Likely more with the Riggs."

Amanda drew out her phone. Before tapping the contact for Graves, she said to Trent, "On another note, it might be time to ask the FBI to look in ViCap now that we know the Riggs are from DC. They could find related cases in other states."

"See what Graves says to that, but it makes sense to me we'd have them take a look."

She nodded and placed the call to Graves. The sergeant answered on the second ring, and Amanda ran through the latest information and put forth their requests. She sure hoped they'd catch this killer before any more people had to die.

TWENTY-THREE

Karl Riggs was an odd-shaped man with a rotund belly and legs like spindles. Trent and Amanda told him they were there about his wife and daughter, and he took them to his living room.

"You can give it to me straight," Karl said. "Hit me. I can handle it."

Trent didn't doubt he could; just like he *handled* a six-pack of beer every night. The man was slovenly and the house a sty. Dirty glasses hung around on the tables and an empty takeout box from a Chinese food place sat abandoned.

"Your wife, Connie, and daughter, Jodi, were found dead yesterday in Prince Park in Triangle," Amanda said, *hitting* him just as he'd asked. "Their necks were broken."

He rubbed his jaw, stared into space for a second or two, then shook his head. "Well, she brought this upon herself. I told her she wouldn't make it without me, but she left anyway."

Every part of Trent tensed like a jungle cat. "Your family is dead, and you're concerned about being right?"

"Of course, I'm upset, but I warned her the world is a scary place. She's far too trusting. Always has been."

"Just like she made the mistake of trusting you?" Trent kicked back.

Karl narrowed his eyes, shrugged.

"I'd ask why she left you, if I didn't already suspect why." Trent clenched his jaw, coaxed himself mentally to calm down. "When did you last see them?"

"When? Let's see. School had just started. Two weeks after that."

It was the last week of October, so that was four weeks ago now. "Huh, so what did you tell the school? Surely someone called asking after Jodi," Trent said.

"Yes, and I told them her and her mother were gone. Truth as I knew it."

If that was what he truly believed, then him not filing a missing person report made sense. "Where was your wife headed?"

"No idea. It's not like she has any living relatives."

Trent admired the woman's bravery in sticking up for herself and her child—especially when it would seem she was doing so on her own. But if she had no one, what had been Connie's intended destination? "Did Connie have access to money?"

"Did she?" Karl spat. "She emptied our bank account when she left. Two grand. The mortgage payment bounced. I needed to borrow against my pay to carry me over."

Good for her!

"Pardon me for saying this, but you don't seem too upset by the fact your wife and your little girl were murdered." Amanda put it far more diplomatically than Trent could have managed.

"That little girl wasn't mine. She was already two by the time me and Connie got together. As for not seeming upset, I am, but I'd just resigned myself to the fact they were gone already."

Trent met Amanda's glance briefly. How had this man released his family so easily?

"What was Jodi's favorite toy, Mr. Riggs?" Amanda asked coolly.

"She seemed to like her Barbies."

"Any stuffed toys you know of?"

"Nope." Karl shook his head to accompany his verbal response.

If what Karl was telling them held true, that meant both toys placed in the graves hadn't belonged to the girls. So as Amanda had said before, where did they come from? And only one answer seemed obvious: from the killer. But had he been known to the families? Were the families known to each other? He pulled up a photograph on his phone of Roy Archer and took it to Karl. "Do you know this man?"

He barely looked at the screen. "Nope. Never seen him before. Was Connie hooking up with him?"

Trent wasn't going to touch Karl's asinine question. He loaded a picture that showed Charlotte on Jill's lap, one they'd collected from the Meyers. Both were smiling, but in this shot, the expression didn't reach either one's eyes. Nothing more than a pose for the camera. "What about them?"

"Nope."

"Do the names Roy, Jill, or Charlotte Archer mean anything to you?" Trent persisted.

"Nope."

Trent scanned the man's eyes and believed his claim. They'd dig further, but given that the Riggs lived in Washington and the Archers in Dumfries, previously from Edgewater, it was likely they had never crossed paths. But had Connie and Jill in Prince William County? Maybe once he and Amanda received the GPS histories for their phones, they'd be able to find the link that put them together.

Amanda's phone rang, she looked at the screen, and saw herself out.

Trent stayed seated. "Did Connie have a cell phone?"

"Nope. We're not the Kennedys."

Whatever that meant... "And her car?"

Karl shook his head. "Only the one, and it's in the driveway."

Connie had either hitched a ride with a friend Karl wasn't aware of or she'd used public transit. Was it in Prince William County where she'd encountered her and her daughter's would-be killer? Or had he intercepted them along their journey and simply buried them in the county? So many questions, it could give a person a headache.

Trent stood. "Sorry for your loss." He meant it, but felt in this case it was more a token offering. Just like with Roy Archer, Karl Riggs didn't seem too broken up about his dead family. But it could be he was judging Karl too quickly. It had taken time for Roy to show some emotion, that's if he was telling the truth about intending to kill himself. But Trent wasn't buying it. He'd never forget that menacing look in Roy's eyes as he'd raised the gun.

He returned to the car and found that Amanda was still on her phone.

"Okay, well, good news so far..." Amanda explained to him. "It's the sarge. The K-9 unit hasn't found any more graves yet."

She'd dulled the shine of the good news with *so far* and *yet*. It was just after noon, and Prince Park covered a lot of ground.

"Trent and I are headed back right now." Amanda ended the call but held her phone in her lap. "Jill Archer's phone records are ready for us back at Central."

"Hopefully they shed some light. You have any interest in going back inside?" Trent gestured to the house, indicating Karl Riggs.

She shook her head. "The guy's a piece of work, much like

Roy Archer, but I believe him when he says he doesn't know the Archers."

"I do too." He pulled away from the Riggs home. "Would be nice if we pieced together one teeny bit of the puzzle. Where does the killer latch on to them? Is it a random encounter or does he build up a rapport with the mother, earn her trust? Does it play out differently each time?"

"Let's hope not. We'd need a miracle to narrow it down. To support the trust factor, there are no signs of struggle or defensive wounds. He could hold a gun on them to force their compliance."

Trent shook his head. "I'm not sure that fits with the rest of what we've discussed—the affection, for instance."

"Maybe, in the case of Jill anyway, she was having an affair. Her phone records might tell us that."

"No." He shook his head. "If she was cheating on Roy, I doubt she was in contact with the man on the phone. Connie Riggs didn't have a cell phone, and my aunt's number has now been disconnected. They weren't even trusted with their own phones. Any of these women could have a second phone their husbands didn't know about, but that would be risky. This type of man reviews their wife's activity just for the control if nothing else."

"Huh. In that case, maybe Roy Archer knows more than he told us."

Just hearing the man's full name ratcheted his temper. He might never understand what made these men the way they were. A rough childhood, following the only example they'd ever known? Shallow excuse. People repeatedly rose above adversity, proving the human spirit was strong and resilient. So what stunted these men? Addiction to substances? To power? To control? "We should know more soon without his help."

"Yep."

"You hear anything more about the toys from CSI Blair?"

"Not yet. But it's interesting that both toys can't be connected to the girls prior to their burials."

"The killer needs to be getting them from somewhere."

Amanda shifted in her seat and met his gaze. "Huh."

"What is it?" There was no doubt she'd had some sort of epiphany.

"There are at least a couple ways the killer gets the toys. He either buys them or..." She rolled her hand, begging for him to join in but he had nada. She dropped her arm. "He already had them."

"But why would he— Oh." It clicked together. "He has a family?"

"Or *had* one? Wild-card theory here, but the victims all look alike, right?"

"Right." He'd play along.

"It could be another reason they are being chosen."

"Still not sure I'm following entirely."

"The killer may be picking surrogates. Women and young girls who look like someone he knows."

"Or *knew*. Past tense," Trent tossed out, feeling a cold front move through the car. "Did our killer lose a wife and daughter of his own? But wait... Even if he did, why would he be killing people who remind him of them?"

Amanda punched her back into her seat, stared out the windshield. "No idea. Yet."

Trent would cling to *that* yet like it would be their saving grace.

TWENTY-FOUR

Amanda and Trent were back at Central. Trent was taking care of the paperwork for Judge Anderson regarding the warrant for the video from Dumfries Elementary, and Amanda was making a call to the FBI. Specifically Brandon Fisher. He was with the Behavioral Analysis Unit, but he had also been dating her best friend, Becky, for a while.

Graves had given her the go-ahead to have the FBI search ViCap out of due diligence. The fact the Riggs were from out of state probably added impetus to the request. And it was possible that this killer had more than one burial site he used.

Amanda got Brandon's cell number off Becky and placed the call.

"FBI Special Agent Fisher."

"Brandon, it's Amanda."

There was a slight pause—poor connection or he was trying to place her. "Amanda Steele. I'm Becky's friend," she added.

"Oh, yes. Is everything all right with Becky?"

"She's fine. But I'm hoping to get a little help from the FBI."

"Not often the cops admit to that." A clear attempt at being humorous.

"Don't let it go to your head. You've told me in the past if I ever needed a search done in ViCap, you'd facilitate that."

"Of course. Nadia Webber is the best."

"And she is?"

"IT and analysis. She's integral to the team, and she can handle the search."

"Great. Could I get her direct line from you?"

Brandon told her, and Amanda scribbled it down as he went.

"I'll let her know to expect your call," he said.

"Thanks."

"Don't mention it. And good—"

"Brandon." It was a man's voice, and Amanda wondered if it was Jack Harper, Brandon's boss, who she'd heard Becky mention before. It seemed he was hard on his agents but a solid man.

"Sounds like you have to go." She was smiling.

"Good luck." With that Brandon hung up, and Amanda called Nadia.

She was helpful and intelligent. She listened carefully as Amanda filled her in on the investigation details as they related to the victims and burial sites.

"This is plenty to get me started. I'll run this through ViCap, and see what comes back."

"Thank you, Nadia."

"Don't mention it."

They ended the call, and Trent was looking at Amanda.

"Brandon going to help?" he asked.

She nodded. Trent knew Brandon too.

"The paperwork's been sent to Judge Anderson. Want to look at Jill Archer's phone records?"

"You know I do."

They dug in and had a rough and dirty answer as to her last location—just which tower her phone had last pinged. No specifics. They quickly discerned Jill had been in contact with one person—Roy Archer. Either he was calling or messaging and vice versa.

Many of his texts were variations on "why aren't you answering your phone?" and "call me back ASAP." Roy had messaged her as recently as the past weekend, but then seemed to give up.

"A digital leash," Trent mumbled. "Before she went missing, it looks like there were times she didn't respond. The last time she did was a week ago Monday, confirming dinner would be ready when he got home."

"Can't imagine living like that. And quite sure that based on the time of these messages, there are also corresponding phone calls." Amanda shifted a few sheets of paper and confirmed her suspicion. "If she didn't answer, then he'd text."

"And not just once. He harassed her." Trent pointed out one string of texts—all from Roy to Jill, each message crueler than the last. No responses. "This was from the week prior to her disappearance."

"Not that he mentioned any of this to us."

"Why would he? The guy's an ass. Nothing surprises me. I still think he intended to shoot me, not himself."

Amanda didn't want to get roped into this conversation again. At least Trent was alive and employed. If he pushed things, she wasn't confident he'd walk off with his badge intact and without a mark on his record. In the strictest sense, Trent assaulted an unarmed man.

"All right, so if Roy was this obsessive about knowing his wife's every move—the phone calls and follow-up texts tell us that much—did he take things further?"

"How do you mean?"

"I wish I thought of this sooner, but there are apps that can be installed on phones that allow parents, for example, a means of tracking a child's activity and precise location. They're often loaded right on the phone. Roy could have done this to his wife's."

"He'd be just the type," Trent said.

"Again, not that he shared it with us."

"The guy was probably preoccupied with how it would make him look."

"Well, we're beyond that now. Let's go pay Roy Archer a visit."

"Oh bliss."

"That's if you think you can refrain from hitting him this time."

"I'll do my best." His face was stark serious for several seconds, but then relaxed. "I'm fine, Amanda. I can handle myself."

She wasn't sure she believed he was *fine*, but as long as he kept his temper in check and remained professional, all should go well. She clicked the button to close her email app just as one filtered in from Rideout. Then her phone lit with a text.

Just sent the early findings to your inbox.

"Just before we go, it looks like I have Rideout's autopsy results."

Trent walked around to her cubicle as she reopened the program and clicked on Rideout's message. She scanned down, focusing on the highlights. The findings for both Connie and Jodi Riggs read much the same.

Time of death: four weeks, approximate.

Cause of death: transection of spinal cord due to manual manipulation of neck.

Patterned contusions on back consistent with tight embrace.

Mother showed signs of physical abuse dating prior to her death by close to two weeks. X-rays showed previous breaks and fractures in various stages of healing.

No indication of bondage.

Both well-nourished.

Interesting difference to Archer case: Livor mortis found in bodies consistent with how each victim was positioned in the grave.

Amanda paused reading. "Could be the time of day the Riggs were killed that made a quick burial easy enough."

"Right, and with the Archers, if he killed them during the day, he'd likely have waited until nightfall to bury them."

"Could be." Amanda turned back to the email and pointed to the list of items Rideout was forwarding to the lab.

Fingernail scrapings

Wedding ring and band

Clothing

They would already have the stuffed rabbit.

"That right there too," Trent said. "Connie Riggs was buried with her wedding ring. An oversight or message? Does it mean anything at all? And what happened to Jill's band? Did she not wear one or did the killer remove it?"

"Your guess is as good as mine. Obviously monetary gain has nothing to do with his motivations or he'd have taken her rings."

"Unrelated but something else has been nagging at me on

and off. How hard did this guy have to hug them before he killed them to cause bruising? It almost strikes me that he was feeling remorseful *before* he broke their necks. Like he wanted to hold on to them, but something compelled him to take their lives."

"Are you suggesting he has multiple personalities?"

"I sure hope not."

"That makes two of us. Just one quick search and we can go." She opened Missing Persons and breathed easier when no new reports showed for mothers and daughters. She hoped Nadia Webber with the FBI wasn't finding anything either.

"I could have told you there was nothing as of twenty minutes ago. I guess I'm not the only one obsessing about this."

"Trent, we have to find this guy before more people lose their lives."

"No need to even say it."

They left the station and floored it to the Archer residence. Roy answered the door, his nose a brilliant purple where it wasn't in a splint. He leaned against the frame as if to help him stay upright.

Trent looked over at Amanda as if to say, "that wasn't me." Apparently, Roy Archer made *friends* everywhere he went.

Amanda reached out to steady him, even though there was a small part of her that wouldn't hate to see him fall and smash his broken nose. Just more of a sampling of what he'd doled out on his wife. "Mr. Archer, you're drunk."

"Ooooh"—he wriggled his hands—"someone's a detective."

"Let's get you sobered up," Trent said with authority.

Roy covered his mouth, his cheeks puffing out, followed by a large swallow that had his Adam's apple bulging. "Why would I want to do that?"

Amanda turned away. The guy spoke right in her face and reeked of bile. She made eye contact with Trent, and he guided Roy inside to the living room couch.

"Stay right there," Trent told him.

Amanda entered the kitchen in search of a glass and got Roy some tap water. "Here," she said, handing it to Roy.

"Why are you two in my house?" Even seated, his head and upper torso had a soft sway to them.

"We have questions about your wife's phone," Amanda started.

"What does it matter? She's dead. Charlotte's... dead."

"It matters because we're working to find out who did this to them. And another mother and daughter are dead too. You know this." Though given his heightened state of inebriation, she wasn't too sure he was aware of anything.

"It wasn't me." The swaying stopped, and he sparked sober for a second.

"We've been through that too," Amanda said stiffly. "Did you install a tracking app on your wife's phone?"

"Yes, I did." Roy belched, and it had Amanda stepping back.

"Why didn't you tell us before?" Trent asked, a snip to his tone. "If you had come forward with this from the start, we could have caught their killer by now."

"How would that look... me watching her every move? You were already convinced I'd killed them."

"We need to look at the tracking app, Mr. Archer," she rushed, getting in there before Trent might say or do something he'd regret.

"Sure. There's a copy loaded on the computer in the office. App's called Every Step. The password is 'ironman', one word, all lowercase."

Amanda nudged her head toward Trent, and the two of them went down the hall.

"Ironman, my ass. I'm going to squeeze the life out of..." Trent stopped speaking when she glared at him. He held up his hands. "I know, I know..."

She sat at a table being used as a computer desk and logged on to the computer. She selected the app, and a history of Jill's movements filled the screen.

Roy came to the doorway, leaned against it. "She didn't do anything exciting."

"Let us be the judge of that," Trent replied.

"Is there a way to print the activity?" Amanda would love to get out of this house and away from Roy.

"The button in the top right-hand corner."

She clicked it, and an inkjet printer thrummed to life and kicked out several pages.

Roy stumbled into the room. "Hold up. How much did you print? I'm not made of money and toner."

Trent put up his hands, and Roy stayed back.

"Just don't punch me again."

While the printer worked, Amanda scrolled through the activity, starting from the most recent at the top. She quickly noticed that repeated coordinates popped up every Sunday. She opened an internet window and searched. "Prince Park."

"I told you that Jill took Charlotte there."

Amanda bristled. "Taking her there is one thing, but doing so on a predictable schedule is another. As a cop, you should know that."

"Not a cop anymore thanks to you two!" Roy roared, spittle dripping onto his chin. "First, my family, then my job."

Might give you a chance to rethink your life... Amanda bit back the words. They were cruel, even if they held a spark of truth. It was sad that it took the loss of life for the evaluation to occur.

She turned to Trent, wanting to pick up on their findings but was struck mute for a second. His glee over Roy's loss of employment was impossible to miss. His eyes were glistening, and the start of a smile tugged at his mouth. She cleared her throat, hoping it might snap him back from his internal celebration. "The killer could have latched on to Jill and Charlotte at the park."

"Except for that's not the last place she went." Trent pointed to the screen.

He was looking at the Tuesday that Roy said they had disappeared. Amanda entered those coordinates into her phone, and it brought her to a shopping plaza in Woodbridge. A quick search told her it offered a grocery store, a bank, a hair salon, and a doctor's office. The commute from Dumfries to Woodbridge was nothing, and the latter town was larger and offered more amenities. "Do you know why Jill would have gone to Woodbridge Plaza?"

"Ah, she grocery shops there, at Corey's Grocer, and our family doctor practices out of the clinic there."

"Your doctor's name?"

"Dr. Cannon."

Amanda latched gazes with Trent. Roy had told them Charlotte had an upset stomach but had dismissed a visit to a doctor. It turned out Jill may have taken her anyway. Had the killer taken mother and daughter from the clinic or that plaza? And/or had he known them prior, possibly from the park? Did he force them to go with him, or use an established trust? Was she entirely off the mark? And did any of this tie back to the man from outside Dumfries Elementary? Amanda wished to fully dismiss him, but he was one piece of the puzzle that had yet to be sorted.

"We've been looking at your wife's phone records," Amanda said. "There were several messages from you, many one-way communications where you were looking for you wife. Couldn't you have consulted this?" She flicked a finger toward the screen, indicating the tracking app.

"She'd turn her phone off sometimes. She didn't think I knew, but I did."

This fit with what the Meyers had told them. "Seems like

she had to if she wanted to spend any time with her parents." A jab at his conscience, though she doubted he had one.

"Uh-huh."

"What about other times? Do you know where she went?" Trent asked.

"No clue."

"Guess there were limits to your digital leash," Trent pushed out.

A brief amusement toyed with the corners of Roy's mouth as if he were delighted by the terminology. It pushed anger through Amanda's bloodstream. "If she'd turn her phone off, she must have known you were tracking her."

"If she was smart enough to figure that out."

Just when it didn't seem possible Roy Archer could be more obnoxious, there was *drunk* Roy Archer. The times Roy was unable reach Jill would show as gaps in her movements. But at least the tracker gave them something to work with, like the plaza and her routine of going to Prince Park on Sundays. "Any other places your wife went regularly, Mr. Archer?" She felt a twinge of joy at not addressing him as *Officer*.

"She attended church. New World something or other."

"How nice of you to let her go alone," Trent hissed sarcastically.

"So the park, then church?" she asked.

"That's right."

Yet he had told them Jill had no friends. Did he not think to mention the church membership or intentionally decide to withhold that too? She'd confront him, but what was the point? "We're going to take this printout with us. Do you have a problem with that?" she challenged him.

Roy shook his head and lost his footing.

"May I suggest you drink some coffee," she said as she passed him, holding her breath, and she and Trent showed themselves out.

"To the doctor's office?" Trent said, turning on the car.

"You bet."

"And you've noticed that we've been led back to Prince Park? He could have met all four of his victims there. The ones we know about anyway."

She groaned. "Really? You had to go there?"

"Keeping it real. Also in that vein, there are times unaccounted for on the app. Who knows where she went then? Who knows if the plaza was her last stop?"

"You're the bearer of good news." Sarcasm through and through. The fact Jill would go offline, though, showed a spirit that defied her husband. Admirable but she likely paid for her independent streak. Amanda added, "It would be a long shot, but we could ask people at the park if they know of a mother and daughter who may have stopped going. They could be the killer's lost family if we pursue that theory."

"Or more victims."

"Would you stop? Let's think positively."

"Amen to that."

Amanda doubted God was even listening, but if Trent wanted to put faith in a Greater Being, so be it. Whatever brought a killer to justice was good with her.

TWENTY-FIVE

At least Amanda had two positive things to focus on. One, the cadaver dogs hadn't uncovered any more burial sites. And two, Amanda and Trent made it to the medical clinic by four o'clock, an hour before they closed. She was used to them cutting things much closer than that. A sign posted next to the door listed three doctors —two general physicians and one psychiatrist. Inside, the space was clean and bright, but minimally decorated. A few patients sat in chairs and a smiling nurse greeted them at the front desk.

Amanda flashed her badge, tucked it away. "We're with the Prince William County PD. We're investigating the disappearance of two of your patients."

"Oh my." The woman was edging toward sixty, and the news had her mouth gaping open.

"Can you tell us if Mrs. Jill Archer brought her daughter, Charlotte, in for a visit Tuesday last week?" Amanda asked.

"I'm not sure I'm permitted to say." She spoke softly and her gaze darted at the waiting patients, then over her shoulder.

"If you could just verify that, it might help. We're talking about a mother and her daughter here..." Amanda hoped stressing the girl would soften the woman just enough to loosen her lips.

"I see..." She worried her bottom lip.

"We're trying to figure out their last steps." Amanda side-stepped so as not to lie completely.

The woman leaned in closer to them, stretching over her desk. "They were here." Almost in a whisper. "Charlotte had a mild tummy ache. But I can't say more than that."

"The flu?" Amanda countered, though the nurse's words implied there was more to say.

"I've probably said too much already."

This woman wasn't quiet because she didn't know. She'd be responsible for filing the patient's records and could read them. Rather, Amanda took the woman's guarded statements to mean Charlotte had more than a tummy ache. She could be reading this wrong—the woman just protecting confidentiality. Regardless, Amanda had firsthand knowledge that emotional and mental trauma manifested in physical ailments. She'd been through it when dealing with the loss of her family. Phantom pains in her abdomen and gut. Doctors put her through a battery of tests involving several ultrasounds and lots of poking and prodding. It wasn't a stretch to imagine that Charlotte suffered from mental and emotional issues from witnessing her mother's abuse, and being locked in the trunk of a car herself. "May we talk with Dr. Cannon?"

"I'm sorry, but he's booked solid with patients today."

Amanda considered their next course of action. While speaking to the doctor might shed some light on Charlotte's ailment, he might refuse to discuss her medical condition. And would a conversation with him get them any closer to finding their killer? Unlikely, but she was curious. "Did Charlotte and her mother ever speak with Dr. Wood?" He was listed as the psychiatrist.

The woman shook her head. "Dr. Wood specializes in treating military veterans."

And there went that lead...

In the lot, Amanda zipped her jacket to her chin. There was a definite fall chill in the air today. She turned to Trent. "They were here the Tuesday they disappeared. Were they taken from here or...?" She looked down the plaza at the different businesses.

"Hard to know, especially with Jill's habit of turning her phone off."

"We work with what we have. Let's canvass the businesses here. If luck's on our side at all we'll find a witness who saw her and her daughter on the Tuesday, possibly even leaving with someone."

"It's worth a try, but remember we have another lead to follow. It also might take us to a person Jill confided in." He peered into her eyes until his point hit home.

"New World Church." The address was one that came up on the tracking app on a fairly routine basis right after Prince Park.

"More specifically the priest or father there. Do we know the denomination? But this person might help fill some gaps in Jill's travels."

"Let's go." Amanda beat Trent back to the car. It's true they were already at the plaza, but they might have more success speaking with those at the church, who had actually known Jill and Charlotte. They could always come back here if it was deemed necessary. "Hopefully, we can find someone around." It may be a long shot given that it was a Thursday afternoon, but often there were living quarters attached to churches for the head honcho, whatever the title for this religion.

Trent took them to the church, and the parking lot was empty except for one sedan parked in the shadow of the towering steeple, complete with cross.

"We'll try there." She pointed out a door on the side of the building that had a mailbox next to it.

Trent knocked, and footsteps padded toward the door.

It swung open, and a sixty-something man with bright blue eyes was looking out at them. "Children of God, to what do I owe the pleasure?"

His words at face value were sickly, over the top, but his delivery struck Amanda as sincere. She pulled her badge. "Prince William County PD."

"Well, bless you for your work within the community." He flashed a smile.

His compliment threw her off some. "Ah, thank you." She made the formal introductions and got his name—Galen Walsh. His title was priest. "We'd like to ask about one of your parishioners."

"Certainly. Who would that be?"

"Jill Archer."

"Oooh, that dear child. Please come in." Galen held the door for Amanda and Trent to enter.

The space was basic, what some expected for a professed man of God. She never viewed an oath of poverty as evidence of a person's spirituality. There was a couch and chairs right near the door. They both took a seat.

Galen remained standing. "Would you like a tea?" he asked while on the move to the galley-style kitchen at the rear of the apartment.

"Sure. That would be nice." Amanda would play along. Accepting offers of hospitality often led to people opening up, but her first choice was never tea. Her parents had ruined it for her with the daily ritual of two a day—at four in the afternoon and again with the evening news. She'd drank all the tea she'd ever need while growing up.

"Or would you prefer coffee, Detective?" The priest leveled

his gaze at her, and chills danced down her arms as if he'd read her mind.

"Only if it's no bother."

"None. Black?"

"That's right."

"Me too, please," Trent said, speaking up.

Galen returned to the living area a moment later. "Pod one is in the thingy." He smiled, giving away that he tolerated modern invention for its convenience.

"Thank you," Trent said.

"Police want to talk about Jill Archer," Galen began. "Something is obviously wrong."

Amanda would have preferred the priest to be sitting before she delivered the news, but she proceeded anyhow. "Sadly, both she and her daughter, Charlotte, were found murdered earlier this week."

"Oh, dear heavens me." Galen dropped onto the arm of the couch. "I read the news of dead bodies being found in Prince Park, and I had a horrible, sinking feeling." He was shaking his head and tsking. "But they will be rewarded in heaven." He glanced up now as if to pay tribute to his deity.

At least Graves's efforts to keep the Archers' names from the media were working. But one thing gnawing at her was that he'd had this *horrible, sinking feeling*. Was there more to that? "You mean you suspected something had happened to them? How is that?"

"Ah, the spirit knows everything." He put his palms together in front of his chest and opened them as if mimicking a blossoming flower.

This church may have a cross, but she was wagering it was a blend of traditional and new-age beliefs that accepted mysticism and mind-reading. "You need to realize that I don't share your beliefs. How did you know about their deaths?"

"Please don't read too much into my words, Detective. I'm

what you might call an oracle. I see things, know things, *sense* things. So when I saw the news, I had a flash of insight, or a vision, you might call it. But now with you here—two detectives, asking about Jill Archer—I don't think one needs to be clairvoyant to piece together they have moved on to the next plane of existence." Galen popped up. "The first coffee should be ready." He disappeared into the kitchen and returned shortly after with a steaming mug, which he handed to Amanda. "Next is on its way," he said to Trent.

"Were Jill and Charlotte regular in attendance?" The tracking app put her phone here on Sundays, but Amanda asked anyway.

"Every Sunday. Well, except this last one and the one before."

The Sunday Charlotte had felt ill...

Galen went on. "Their absence was another reason I suspected something was wrong. There was much pain in her. Both of them, truly."

Hearing him say this saddened Amanda. For all the people orbiting Jill's and Charlotte's lives—even knowing what was going on—not one did anything to help them. And for a priest who *knew things*, why hadn't he stepped in to aid Jill and Charlotte?

"Then you knew about the abuse?" Trent spoke quietly, as if he'd revered the man for his position but was wounded by his lack of action.

"That she was oppressed? Yes, and I tried to help her."

"Oppressed?" Trent spat. "She was beaten and raped by her own husband."

The priest's cheeks reddened, and he glanced at Amanda.

"You must understand our frustration. We've found that many people were aware of what was going on in the Archer home yet did nothing to save Jill or Charlotte." It took all her reserve of self-control to say that calmly.

Just the slightest glimmer of a smile on the priest's lips. "The thing is, dear child, a person needs to want to help themselves."

Amanda sipped her coffee, mostly to occupy her mouth so she didn't say something she'd regret. She hated being addressed as "dear child." The inference being she belonged to God. But there was no way. The loss of her family had squashed any faith she had in a Greater Being. Even though she was happy these days, forgiveness for a mysterious deity remained too tall an order. On another note, Galen's phrasing angered her, as if the victims of abuse were to blame. She lowered her cup, the coffee hot and with a smooth finish.

"As I told you, I see things," Galen said. "Call them visions, if you will. There was lots of darkness surrounding them, but there was also love. Warped, but love nonetheless."

"I don't get what you're trying to say," Trent said.

Galen looked at him, a subtle smirk on his lips. "The darkness could represent the abuse, but they were seen out of this world with a blessing." He steepled his hands.

Her hackles shot up. His words smacked close to what people had said when she'd lost Kevin and Lindsey—"they're with God now" or "God needed another angel." "What do you mean a blessing?"

"I don't know exactly, but I do sense their passing was met with tears."

Shivers raked down Amanda's spine. The posing of their bodies, the doll. They had suspected the killer felt regret, remorse, even affection. If the priest was innocent, he'd have no way of knowing that. He told them when he'd last seen them at church, but that didn't mean he hadn't run into them outside these walls. "When did you last see Jill and Charlotte?"

"Three Sundays ago."

Amanda nodded. "And where were you Tuesday of last week?"

"I was here, in deep meditation."

"All day?" Trent asked, skepticism plain to read.

"Yes."

Amanda would poke her eyes out after five minutes. "Did you notice if any men hung around Jill or her daughter? New friends or otherwise?"

"What you are really interested in, Detective, is if I know who may have posed a threat to them."

She didn't respond to that, not appreciating how he'd trampled on her question. She just waved a hand for him to continue.

"Besides her husband, and whoever killed them, no. Someone you may want to speak with is Morgan Costa."

"And who is she?" Trent asked.

"Another congregant. I originally asked Morgan if she'd take Jill and Charlotte under her wing, as it were, but they became fast friends."

Finally, a lead that wasn't some hocus-pocus nonsense. "Do you have a number for Ms. Costa or know where she lives?"

"Absolutely. One moment, dear child." Galen left in the direction of a hallway.

This man, this place, gave her the heebie-jeebies. She was all too happy to leave a few moments later armed with Morgan's information.

TWENTY-SIX

The address for Morgan Costa led Amanda and Trent to a two-story townhouse in Dumfries. The clock on the dash announced it was close to five. She might be a little late getting home to have dinner with Zoe, but hopefully she'd be able to salvage the evening. Then again, that was dependent on their visit with Morgan Costa and whether she had insights to help the case. Obviously if she did, Amanda would be further delayed in getting home.

"I never even got one sip of my coffee," Trent griped from beside her.

"It wasn't anything special." She wouldn't tell him it was close to as good as the stuff from Hannah's Diner.

"I'm not sad that we had to leave that guy though."

"Makes two of us." She knocked on Morgan's door, and it cracked open a few seconds later.

"Hello?" A woman's nose and eye appeared in the slit.

"Morgan Costa?" Amanda asked, holding up her badge.

"That's me." Morgan stepped back and opened the door, allowing Amanda and Trent a view inside the home.

"We're Detectives Steele and Stenson. We're here to talk about Jill and Charlotte Archer. Could we come in?"

"Ah, sure." Morgan stopped in the entry and turned to them.

"Somewhere to sit would be better for this conversation," Amanda said.

Morgan stiffened but took them to a living room where she sat on the couch. Amanda and Trent dropped into chairs.

"What about Jill and Charlotte?" Morgan nudged out her chin, and her eyes were full of tears.

Morgan hadn't made any claims to having the "gift" Galen had. There was no talk of mind-reading or visions—though it was early yet. But she wouldn't need to be psychic to sense something was wrong. Two detectives were at her door, and presumably she hadn't seen Jill and Charlotte for a couple of weeks. Both would have been a tip-off. "Sorry to inform you of this, Ms. Costa, but Jill and Charlotte were found dead on Tuesday morning."

"No. No, this can't be." Tears fell. "In Prince Park? I read in the news that bodies were found there."

"I'm afraid so," Amanda said.

"I'd really hoped that Jill had finally taken Charlotte and left town."

"We spoke with Father Walsh, and he told us he asked you to watch over Jill."

"As if she were assigned to me like a job? No. Not like that. Jill and Charlotte weren't an assignment. I loved them." She walked across the room and took a framed photograph from a table. She handed it to Amanda. "Taken this summer at a church barbecue."

Amanda held the picture for Trent to see. Jill, Charlotte, and Morgan were bunched together—all of them with bright smiles. There was no evidence of the timidity described by

Charlotte's teacher. Both she and her mother looked extremely comfortable with Morgan. Even at home with her. "How long did you know them?"

"Most of a year."

"Since they moved into town then?" Amanda asked.

"Sounds right."

"So you two were close," Amanda started. "Did you see each other outside of church?"

Morgan nodded. "We usually met up once a week, just to talk and hang out. She was supposed to come here last Wednesday."

Amanda thought back to the call logs. "There was no record you tried reaching her to see where she was."

"No, of course not. You probably know this by now, but Roy isn't a good man. He never would have tolerated Jill having friends. I was to be kept a secret. She was allowed to go to church, the grocery store, bank, doctor's. Oh, and to drop Charlotte off at school. Other than that, she was to be straight home."

"She also took Charlotte to Prince Park," Trent inserted.

"Yes, that's right." Morgan flailed a hand. "How could I forget?"

Amanda figured the shock of the news she'd just received had something to do with it.

"But, yeah, she took Charlotte every Sunday before church to let the girl burn off some energy before she'd be asked to sit for two hours. Jill would bring along a change of clothes for her."

"Smart," Amanda admitted.

A small smile. "Jill was smart, and she deserved far better than Roy. But she wouldn't divorce him, couldn't even seem to leave him. Said God frowned on marriage that ended in divorce."

Amanda kept her mouth shut. So people were supposed to

stay imprisoned in unhappy wedlock until death? How outdated and ridiculous. Humans took the liberty of saying too much on God's behalf—talk about an act of reading minds. "Did you ever go to the park with them?"

"Not me. I'm not an early riser. I'm doing good to make it to mass for nine."

It had been too much to hope that Morgan saw someone at the park who stood out to her.

"I tried to get her to leave him, take Charlotte and run. Just separate. I would have welcomed them here for as long as they needed. She wasn't having that. But I think she looked into Brighter Horizons at one point, just never made the leap."

"Brighter Horizons?" Trent asked.

"It's a woman's shelter in Woodbridge."

Trent looked over at Amanda and slightly widened his eyes. She got his message. They needed to sort out where the killer connected with or latched on to the women and children. A shelter was a strong possibility.

"Do you know of anywhere Jill liked to go besides the places you mentioned?" Amanda asked. "Her husband tracked her whereabouts through her phone but sometimes it blacked out."

Morgan grinned. "That was one thing she did that showed gumption and made me proud."

"So where would she go off the grid?" Amanda repeated.

"Well, she couldn't be offline for long. Roy would have beat her unconscious." With the admission, Morgan's chin quivered, and she rubbed her arms. "Sometimes she'd treat Charlotte to ice cream. I'd give her some cash so Roy wouldn't know her every second. That man really doesn't deserve to draw breath. Did he do this to them?" Her gaze was cool, as was her tone.

"He's been cleared." Amanda's mind drifted to the Riggs—no connection there or motive. But it left her and Trent, and

Prince William County, with a more horrifying possibility: a serial killer. "You ever see a man watching Jill and/or Charlotte, possibly lingering around the church? Or were there any new male members of the congregation?"

"Not that I'm aware of."

"We have been told about a man she was speaking with outside Dumfries Elementary. A good-looking man, brown hair and eyes." Amanda wished she had something more descriptive to share. They needed to follow up on that video.

"I can tell you she wasn't cheating on Roy, but no one would blame her if she did."

"Did she have a male friend, even if it wasn't an affair?" Trent asked.

"You must be kidding. If Roy ever found out..."

"Okay, thank you for your time." Amanda got up and handed Morgan her business card. "And we're very sorry for your loss."

"Thank you."

Amanda's steps were heavy as she returned to the department car. Based on that one photograph of the trio smiling, Jill had found a place she and her daughter belonged. Still, it hadn't saved her. She did up the seat belt and turned to Trent. "I didn't miss what you said to me in there, by the way."

"What I said to you? I'm confused."

"Not *said* exactly, but you made intentional eye contact. I read your mind." She smiled, appreciating the irony in light of the priest.

"Huh. If you're so smart, hit me."

"It was to do with the women's shelter. Brighter Horizons. You think it might lead to the killer."

He held on to the steering wheel with his left hand and faced her. "Why not? Karl Riggs made a point of saying his wife had nowhere to run. I was wondering where she would have gone. A women's shelter could make sense."

"Why wouldn't Connie Riggs have gone to one in Washington?"

"Too close to home? We just know that Jill Archer stopped by Brighter Horizons in Woodbridge. But it's entirely possible that Connie and her daughter had too, or that they were even staying there. This could be the connection between the women and/or the killer we've been looking for."

"I'd hope if they had been staying there, the place would have reported them missing." A knot formed in her chest again. It felt like everyone had let these women and girls down. "Let's check out this angle, but first thing tomorrow morning? Fresh start and fresh minds."

He backed out of Morgan's driveway. "That's a smart move."

Is it? As much as she looked forward to hugging Zoe, could she justify bowing out for the night? There were other families who didn't have their daughters to tuck in tonight. And what if while she was home enjoying time with her daughter another mother and her child were suffering? Would she ever forgive herself? "You know what? Let's go over there now. I'll just have to call Libby."

"Tomorrow should be fine. We can't save everyone, and your daughter needs you too."

"But what if...?"

"What if there are other victims out there right now?" he tossed back, reading her mind. "You can't save everyone."

"Never said I could."

He angled his head. "You never had to. You think you can, and it's what drives you. But spend time with Zoe. With a case like this one, she must be foremost on your mind."

"That she is."

"Besides, as you've told me before, sometimes a fresh start is exactly what a case needs."

She took a deep breath. "I just hope I don't live to regret it." *Or that people die because I took a break...*

As Trent drove them to Central, she couldn't shake this bad feeling that the killer had his next two victims. She only hoped if she was right, she and Trent wouldn't be too late to save them. Was Brighter Horizons the connection and the lead they were looking for?

TWENTY-SEVEN

Days had passed, and Leanne was no closer to a solution on how to get her and Gracie out of their prison. The man barely spoke and whatever he did say was often gibberish or meaningless to her. Any attempts to connect or pleas for release were met with grunts or the latching of the deadbolts. And she rarely heard the dog. Just when she'd wonder if something had happened to it, she'd hear it bark.

One positive was the man hadn't yet laid a hand on them, but that didn't mean he wouldn't. And his moods were growing increasingly sullen. He mumbled a lot when he came in to see them.

Tonight was no different when he brought in plated roast beef with potatoes and carrots.

"Your favorite," he said to Leanne.

But he had her confused with someone—possibly the Holly or Cheryl he'd mentioned a number of times now. Whoever they were. As for Leanne, she was a vegetarian, a fact she'd reiterated several times, but it never seemed to penetrate. In fact, even the smell of cooked meat sent her stomach tossing.

"Eat." He waved at them to consume what he'd prepared.

"Let us go, I beg of you," Leanne pleaded.

In response, he loaded Gracie's fork with potato and took it to her mouth as an airplane headed for the hanger.

Gracie looked at Leanne, and she nodded at her daughter. It was best to keep him happy. When he was pleased, he treated them kindly. If something triggered his temper, he'd slam the door and bolt all the locks.

"Open the hangar," he told Gracie, who still hadn't complied.

"Gracie," one word from Leanne, and the girl opened her mouth.

Leanne fought off tears. What if he'd poisoned their food? He had drugged them to get their compliance after ice cream. And the last time they'd seen him, he was quaking with rage. He'd called Gracie his little girl, and she refused to call him *Daddy*.

He leveled a glare at Leanne. "Why are you calling her Gracie? She's Holly."

"Spit it out, Gracie! Now!" Leanne yelled.

Gracie did as she was told, as Leanne bolted to her feet and hurled her daughter's serving across the room. The mashed potatoes clung to the wallpaper and the beef and carrots landed on the carpet.

"What have you done?" More pain than anger was present in his eyes as he looked at Leanne. "I worked on that for hours. For you. Your favorite meal."

"It's not my favorite meal," she spat. Her entire body was vibrating. She'd reached the end of her rope. Enough was enough.

She brandished the steak knife and motioned for her daughter to move behind her. "Stay back, or I swear I'll—"

He came at her so quickly she had no chance to react. His fist caught her in the jaw and sent her flying to the floor. Pain flashed her vision white, but she mustered her strength and drew up again. She'd kept her hold on the knife and thrust it toward him. She nicked him in the arm, blood staining his shirt-sleeve red, but he gave no indication that he'd even felt the blade.

His eyes were pinpointed and cold—a hardened stare that pierced right through her.

She lunged out to slash him again. But he intercepted.

His hand gripped her wrist and he squeezed so hard, she dropped the knife. But he kept his hold fast until the bones in her wrist popped loudly.

Everything went white. The pain excruciating.

She wailed as her daughter cowered in a corner, crying.

"Leave us alone!" Leanne screamed.

"I can't do that. You know that. Please, Cheryl." The pendulum swung back. He was calm again. The quick and massive shift in mood sent shivers racing through her. The unpredictability was far more frightening than facing down the devil.

She drew up, peacocking her posture. "I'm not Cheryl. She's not Holly!"

He blinked, and when his eyes opened, the light in them had dimmed. He'd returned from whatever peaceful place he'd visited. In place of calm was anger again. He looked at the mess she'd made. "Clean that up."

She stood there cradling her hand as he saw himself out of the room. At the sound of the third lock being turned, she hurried to her daughter and lowered to the floor beside her.

"I will get us out of here somehow. I promise, baby."

"He hurt you." Gracie kissed her fingertips and pressed them to the back of Leanne's hand that cradled her injured wrist.

"He did, but I'll be all right." She'd been through hell before, survived broken bones and sprains. The wound he'd inflicted was flesh and blood, but the spirit was stronger than both put together. This thought compelled her back to her feet, and she went to the window.

It was nighttime and there wasn't much to see—until the door to the small barn opened and a light was turned on. It made it possible for her to see inside. There was a workbench with assorted tools hanging above it, and she spotted the fender of a white car just before he shut the door behind him.

She sank against the window frame, and Gracie came over and hugged into her mother's side.

"I'm hungry, Mommy, and I want to go home."

"I know, sweetie." She ran her good hand through her daughter's hair, wishing that she was a stronger person, someone for Gracie to look up to. It took Bill raising a hand to Gracie before Leanne had done anything. At least she'd been able to intervene before he struck the girl. One right move as a mother. The fact it had gone that far, though, nipped at her soul. And with it, his taunting words wreaked havoc again. Maybe he'd hit the mark when he'd said she was a stupid, good-for-nothing waste of skin.

Warm tears trickled down her face, but she let them be.

She'd just wanted to prove him wrong, prove *everyone* wrong, and let them see she was capable of forging ahead on her own and caring for Gracie. She still wanted that so badly, but it was over. Time to admit defeat.

Leanne started to close her eyes, but her gaze landed on the steak knife a few feet away. Had she actually secured a way out for her and her daughter?

She got up, retrieved the knife and returned to the window. Using her good hand, she dipped the tip of the blade into the rotting wood of the sill and dug some out. It might take a while, but if she chipped away, she might be able to pry the bars from the window. Step one.

Step two was making it safely to the ground.

She was looking over the room, and her eyes landed on the beds. Maybe if she tied the sheets together, they'd provide just enough length.

The vision of hope had her working fast. They might get out of here and away from that man after all.

TWENTY-EIGHT

Brighter Horizons was next to a building that housed community offices for municipal services such as water and electrical, dog registration, driver licensing, and financial aid for war veterans.

Amanda rang the shelter's doorbell early on Friday morning.

"Hello? Do you have an appointment?" The voice was coming over an intercom.

"We're detectives with the Prince William County PD," she replied, wondering how far that would get her.

"You may enter, but the other detective needs to stay outside."

Amanda turned to Trent and understood. As a man, he might make the residents uneasy. But if men weren't allowed in the shelter, how could it be the hinge point where the killer encountered his victims?

"Understood," Amanda said, and the door buzzed. She said to Trent, "I'll be back as soon as I can."

"Don't rush on my account."

Amanda signed a registry before they buzzed her through

another set of doors. Inside, a woman even taller than Sergeant Graves greeted her; she must have been over six feet.

"Detective...?" The woman fished for Amanda's name.

"Steele. I have some questions about a woman and her daughter I believe you may have helped here."

"Whatever I can do to help. I'm Sadie Kerr, the administrator here. If you'd like to come with me."

Amanda followed Sadie into a modest office with a few visitor chairs positioned across from a desk.

"Make yourself comfortable. Who is it you have questions about?" Sadie leaned forward and clasped her hands.

"Are the names Jill or Charlotte Archer familiar to you?" Amanda was banking on visitors' names being put in the system. Considering the security measures she had just jumped through, she figured there was a good chance.

"Off the top, no." She clicked on a keyboard and squinted at the screen. "Hmm. Well, neither name is in our system." Sadie narrowed her eyes and angled her head.

"Mrs. Archer apparently looked at the facilities, but didn't check in. That type of thing isn't documented?"

"We don't track people who don't check in so as not to violate anyone's confidentiality. We want to encourage a haven of trust, which in this case means anonymity."

Amanda wasn't sure she backed that policy given the purpose of the shelter. The more this investigation wore on, it felt increasingly like these abused women and children were just out there, flitting about on their own. She pulled up a photograph of Jill and Charlotte Archer and showed it to the administrator. "Ever see them around?"

"They do look familiar, and I believe they looked around." She drew back, settling into her chair.

"Any idea when?"

"About two, maybe three weeks ago."

The Riggs would have already been dead at that point. Still, she asked about them. "Do the names Connie and Jodi Riggs mean anything to you?"

"Connie and her daughter stayed here a few days. Then she was off. Don't know if she followed through but she spoke a lot about heading out to the east coast. She never shared what was drawing her there besides getting far away from her husband. Did something happen to them?" Sadie's bottom lip quivered just subtly, as she was visibly fighting for dominance over her emotions.

There would be no more putting it off. "Unfortunately, they were murdered. As were Jill and Charlotte Archer."

"Oh my goodness. Do you know who could have done this? I'm guessing you're not looking at the husbands." A pinch in her forehead had her skin veeing down between her eyes.

"It's an open investigation. When did you last see Connie and Jodi?"

"As I said they only stayed a few days, and that was about a month ago."

The Archers and the Riggs had the shelter in common, but the timeline made it impossible for the women to cross paths here. "And I assume at that point, Connie Riggs checked out?"

Sadie's face became shadowed. "She just wasn't here one day."

Amanda stiffened. "Did you call the police or report them missing?"

A gentle shake of her head. "Women up and leave all the time around here. Some go back to their abusive mates, justifying that course of action in all sorts of ways. We try to help these women discover their inner power. We offer programs for building self-esteem along with others that teach skills for returning to the workplace. Many of these women haven't worked in many years. Sadly, all our training and best intentions don't always stick."

"But when children are involved, they are at risk. Do you report such cases to Child Protective Services?"

"We do, but what's done after that is with them."

Amanda was sickened by how society failed women and children in abusive homes. The buck of responsibility kept getting pushed down the line.

Sadie said, "I know this will sound like a lame excuse, but we're doing all we can."

Amanda's fight wasn't with the administrator but the system in general. There were too many holes for victims to fall through. "They have to want to help themselves," she parroted what she'd heard repeated too many times in this case. And though she realized the truthfulness of the statement, it didn't make it sting less.

"Sad, but true. When it boils down, we're not a jail and can't force them to stay."

Amanda wondered how often the administrator chanted that before bed so she could sleep. "Have you recently had any mothers with a young daughter up and leave?"

"Connie and Jodi were the last, but a few months before that, we had an Abigail Cohen and her six-year-old daughter, Mia."

A labor shortage and bureaucratic red tape might limit Sadie's actions, but she obviously cared about the women and children who stayed at the shelter. She didn't even look at her computer. "You just remember them off the top?"

"I had an extra soft spot for Abigail. She came here with a fresh black eye and a broken rib. Her husband used her as a punching bag because he didn't get the promotion he wanted at work. Her injuries were bad enough that, at least, he brought her to the hospital in Manassas. A nurse there—heaven-sent— got Abigail alone. From there, she arranged for Abigail and her daughter to ditch him and get in here."

This nurse did sound like an angel on earth. "But Abigail didn't stay?"

Sadie shook her head. "Nope."

"You said this happened a few months ago?"

"About four, but that's right."

"Do you know if she went back to her husband?"

"Honestly, I have no idea."

"Would you know the nurse's name who referred her here?" She might not factor into the investigation, but it was always better to be armed with more than not enough.

"Summer Freeman. She's incredible. She's gotten a lot of women in here actually. She saves lives at the hospital and outside of it too."

"Was she, by chance, who brought Connie and Jodi Riggs here?"

"No. Connie came from Washington if I remember right."

"Thank you for your help." Amanda gave the woman her card and added, "Please call if you think of any other mothers and daughters who left here in recent months. Also if any more suddenly do."

Sadie nodded and took Amanda's card. "I will, Detective."

"Thank you."

Amanda saw herself out and found Trent in the car listening to country music—and singing along. It wasn't the first time she'd busted him belting out some tune.

He stopped singing and turned the radio off when she slipped into the passenger seat.

"Don't stop on my account." She tried to smile, but the expression failed. Being in that building had been depressing. While they helped abuse victims, the need for the shelter's existence prickled. That, and the fact these women were really on their own.

"What did you find out?"

"Got a lead. Another mother and daughter to follow up on."

"Oh, no."

"An Abigail and Mia Cohen. They stayed for a while four months ago but were just gone one day. Guess it happens here."

"Huh."

"That basically sums up how I feel about it. It was never confirmed that they returned home, and the parameters fit. Six-year-old daughter and the mother was abused. She'd checked into Brighter Horizons with a black eye and a broken rib. A nurse at the medical center in Manassas, a Summer Freeman, brought her in. Apparently she does this sometimes."

"Hopefully, she didn't go back to that bastard."

"Let's hope mother and daughter are both safe and alive."

"We can call around the family home, see if they're there."

"I think we should. Also, I'd like to talk to that nurse."

"All right. Well, I'm not without leads either. I received an email while you were in there. The footage from Dumfries Elementary is in."

"Okay, we'll look, hopefully get a clear view of Mystery Man's face. We don't recognize him, we'll be able to run it through facial rec databases."

"Yep, and we'll have a face to show and ask around about. Speaking of, we still need to return to Prince Park and see what we might be able to find from people there."

"One hundred percent." While Amanda was pleased that they had next steps, she was left with a bittersweet taste in her mouth. How often did this abusive cycle repeat every day in America, in the world?

TWENTY-NINE

Trent respected why he had to sit in the car while Amanda went inside Brighter Horizons, but that didn't mean he had to like it. He was a cop, and he had vowed to serve and protect.

He was in his cubicle with Amanda, and they were watching the video from Dumfries Elementary. He forwarded to the timeframe in which the teacher had mentioned seeing Jill Archer speaking with the mystery man and found them on the edge of the school's property rather quickly. "Her body language reads like she knows the guy," he said.

"Agreed."

"She's relaxed and smiling. So is he." The man certainly didn't strike Trent as the type to kill mothers and daughters, but what exactly did *the type* look like? Trent strained to look closer, as if something telling for the case would magically appear.

"Can you zoom in?"

"Let me give it a go." He wasn't a techie, but he could get by. It didn't hurt that one of his sisters was savvy with computers and shared some of her knowledge with him. He tried something—and it worked.

"Just as Ms. Brewer said. Good-looking, dark hair, average build."

"An average Joe Schmo all around." Even his clothing appeared to be of department store quality. He wore a stylish fall jacket, the zipper undone, exposing a white shirt with a rounded collar, pressed jeans, and boots. Trent pointed out the latter.

"Not taking a leap into the rabbit hole because the guy's wearing boots."

Trent held up his hands. "I know, but we are interested in finding out more about this mystery man. I was just sayin'..."

"Search for a clear image of his face."

He nodded and let the video move forward in slow motion. "There, just for a second, he turns his body." He reversed the footage, and they were looking at him face on. The man had his hands in his pockets and wore a silver-chain necklace.

"No one I've seen before," Amanda said. "But send a copy to our phones so we can take it with us. Also forward it to the CSIs to run through facial recognition databases."

"You got it." Trent did as she'd asked.

"Steele?" It was Graves coming toward them. "And Stenson," she added once she reached the doorway to Trent's cubicle. "Where are we with things?"

Amanda told her about the shelter and Abigail and Mia.

Graves let out an enormous sigh. "Follow that up yesterday. The last thing we need is more deaths."

"You got it," Trent replied, reading grief off the sergeant. She'd likely taken the lack of additional shallow graves in Prince Park to mean no more victims. But for Trent, it had been a tentative acceptance. He'd been proven wrong before.

Graves left, and Trent brought up a report on Abigail Cohen. "Abigail is thirty-three. Married to Jeremy Cohen. Address is in Woodbridge."

"Let's hit the road."

. . .

Trent pushed on the gas a little harder than normal, but he wasn't good with suspense. He was hoping desperately that they would find Abigail and Mia alive and well, though well was debatable if they'd returned to an abusive household. Then again, the mother and daughter could have left that sorry excuse for a man. With that came other worries. Were they out there doing well or dead somewhere? It was crazy how the mind worked, daisy-chaining one thought to the next and then the next.

He pulled to a stop in front of the Cohen residence, a brick bungalow, in record time.

Trent knocked, and a burly man answered the door.

"What is it?" He traced his beady eyes over Trent and Amanda. "I have no interest in finding religion."

Trent held up a hand to stop him from closing the door. "Are you Jeremy Cohen?"

"What's it to you?"

Charmer all around... Trent held up his badge. "We're Detectives Stenson and Steele with the Prince William County PD."

"Hey, congratulations."

Trent took a few seconds to shake his temper. "We'd like to speak with your wife, Abigail." Somehow he delivered the request coolly and calmly.

"Good luck. She ain't here."

"When will she be back?"

"Now, ain't that a good question." Jeremy leaned against the doorframe and ogled Amanda.

"You don't know where your wife is?" His question was designed to insult him, the implication being he was less a man if he were in the dark.

"Oh, I'd know if I wanted to, but ya see, I don't."

"She left you." Just stating that brought a smile of satisfaction to Trent's face.

"Yep. Turns out I'm better off without her."

"And your daughter?"

"Who even knows if she was my kid?"

Trent stepped forward but eased back again with one side-glance from Amanda. "When did you last see her?"

"Four months ago."

Just after you gave her a black eye and had her fleeing to the shelter...

"Do you have a phone number for her?" Amanda asked.

"Nope. She left me, and I had her number disconnected."

If thoughts of his aunt's well-being weren't haunting him before, just the mention of a disconnected line had him tail-spinning again. "Did your daughter have a favorite stuffed toy, Mr. Cohen?" They still didn't know where the killer was getting the dolls. It was possible if he got to Abigail and Mia before the Riggs, the rabbit and/or the elephant was Mia's toy.

"No idea. She had a bunch of stuffies." He shrugged. "That's what the girl called them."

"Any rabbits or elephants, about this big?" Trent mimed the size.

"Don't think so."

Trent handed Jeremy his business card. "Take this. If she comes back around, have her call me." He turned toward the road.

"I won't be needing this."

Trent looked over a shoulder and saw Jeremy flick his card into the hedges near the door.

Amanda leaned into Trent's ear. "Just ignore him."

"Easier said than done." He took a deep, heaving breath. "And what if Abigail and Mia didn't leave of their own free will? What if somewhere between the shelter and plans to return here, our killer got to them?"

"*What if...?* You'll go crazy fast thinking that way."

"I know. I just hate not having the answers." He slid behind the wheel, becoming paralyzed by his dark thoughts.

She got into the vehicle and closed the door. "Makes two of us. Like where the toys came from. That one's eating away at me."

"Me too. Did they come from other little girls we don't know about?"

"Well, we're not doing any good sitting here, spinning. Let's go talk with Nurse Freeman. She helped Abigail and Mia once. It's possible that Abigail returned to her. She might know where they are or have a way to reach them."

"That's a glimmer of hope." He put the car into gear and got them on the road.

THIRTY

Amanda hated hospitals for the reason they rarely brought good news. While she'd given birth to Lindsey in one, she'd faced far more heartbreak than celebration within their walls.

She breathed shallow, as if by not inhaling the smells intrinsic with a hospital, she'd be guarded from the emotional repercussions. No such luck. Not only did the corridors bring back the loss of her family, but her memory of being told Scott Malone had a brain tumor. For a minute or two there, it had been touch and go as to whether he'd survive.

At the nurses' station, she asked for Summer Freeman.

"What's this regarding?"

Amanda showed her badge. "Police business."

The woman hesitated, reaching for the phone, drawing her hand back. Eventually she picked up the receiver and paged Nurse Freeman. "I'm sure she'll be here as soon as she can."

"Thank you." Amanda tucked her badge away and did her best to block out anyone who wasn't Trent. If she let her gaze wander past him, she took in the sick—those being pushed around in wheelchairs or walking with portable IV machines. In the one corner, a couple sat hugging, and the woman was crying.

Amanda turned away. She'd lived through enough heartbreak and grief to feel their pain. Either someone they loved had died or faced the near possibility of death.

"Yes? You paged me?" A woman of solid build with a buzz cut and arms the size of Amanda's calves tapped the front counter. She had directed what she'd said to her colleague there.

"Police." The station nurse bobbed her head toward Amanda and Trent.

"Summer Freeman?" Amanda asked.

"I am. And you are?" Summer crossed her arms.

"Detective Amanda Steele, and this is Detective Trent Stenson. We'd like to ask you about a patient of yours." Technically Abigail was a former patient, but Amanda figured going with the present tense might elicit more urgency.

"What about them?"

"We're trying to locate her."

It seemed with the mention of *her*, any defensive guard surrounding the nurse dropped. "Her name?"

"Abigail Cohen. She came here about four months ago seeking treatment for a black eye and a broken rib."

Summer's mouth set in a thin, straight line, as she glanced at the nurse at the desk. "I remember Abigail well. Why are you trying to find her?" Summer briefly let her gaze travel over to Trent, but returned her focus to Amanda. "Is she in trouble?"

"We honestly don't know, but you may have heard on the news about the shallow graves found at Prince Park?" Amanda asked.

"I read about it online." Her voice was leery, hesitant.

"Abigail and her daughter were not victims," Amanda rushed to say, thinking it was best to ease the nurse's concern. "But the ones who were came from similar home conditions."

Amanda had probably said too much now. Shockingly, the media hadn't yet caught wind the graves held mothers and daughters, and she didn't want to be the reason they did.

"Oh." Summer walked across the area and dropped into a chair.

Amanda sat next to her, Trent beside Amanda.

Summer rubbed her forehead. "I get so many women in here who are abused. The husbands break their bones and then bring them in for treatment. They try to pass it off as—"

"A fall down the stairs," Trent cut in. "Or tell you that the women are clumsy. It's always the woman's fault..."

Summer narrowed her eyes at him. "That's right. And I sense you're familiar with the scenario. You know someone who is abused?"

"My aunt."

"Sorry to hear that. You've probably tried all you can."

Trent nodded, and Amanda sensed his pain, empathizing how hard it would be to accept his hands were tied.

Summer continued. "These guys hover over their wives for fear if they let them out of sight for a minute, someone will talk sense into them."

"Which you do," Trent said softly.

Summer met his gaze and nodded. "I try. Lord knows, every single time, I try. On rare occasions my efforts pay off. I've just treated so many women and many have been here repeatedly. Each time, they tell me they lost their footing or some other such rubbish. You know the husband pushed them or hit them. I do my best to help these women find the courage to use their voice, but I can't make them. And you know as the police you can't charge the men unless the women push for it."

Amanda nodded, thinking that law should be changed.

"Now, that's different when we're talking about children who are abused. We have the immediate right to call in Child

Protective Services. But then it's a matter of what they do from there."

"You were able to get Abigail and her daughter into Brighter Horizons," Amanda said.

A slight smile. "Guessing you've been talking with Sadie Kerr?"

"I did."

"Then you probably also know that Abigail left the shelter."

"One reason we're here talking to you," Amanda began. "Do you have a current address for her or a way to reach her?"

Summer turned away, rubbed her arms.

"Please, if you know..."

"I gave her some money and told her to use it to get out of town."

Amanda thought back on Sadie's description of the nurse being heaven-sent. She agreed. Gifting cash from her own pocket was above and beyond.

"Did she have a car?" Trent asked.

"If you want to call it that. It was a jalopy, but she assured me it would get her and Mia from point A to B."

Amanda hoped they had made it to point B. "Do you know where she went?" She'd try again.

"She didn't tell me, and I didn't ask. Best that I don't know anyway in case that lunatic of a husband ever comes after me."

Amanda didn't say as much, but she didn't think the nurse needed to worry about Jeremy Cohen. He seemed resolved to his wife and daughter being out of his life. "Do you have a way of reaching Abigail or are you still in contact?" Amanda would be crossing fingers and toes—if it altered the result.

"I gave her a burner phone. Ya know, for in case of emergencies. I haven't heard from her."

"You ever try to reach her?" Trent asked.

"Sure, but never got through. And that's fine, really. As I said, it's best I don't know where they went."

Mother and daughter could be perfectly fine and happy somewhere, but the opposite was equally possible. "Would you give us her number? I assure you we won't share it with anyone."

"Certainly not her husband," Trent interjected with force.

"I'm not sure if I should..."

Amanda let silence fill the space between them, hoping that Summer would feel the need to volunteer the number.

"I'll give it to you." Summer rattled off the digits from memory, as Trent scribbled them in his notepad.

"If you reach her, tell her to call me, just quick."

"We will. Just a few more questions, and we'll be out of your way. Did you ever treat a Jill Archer?"

"Hmm. The name rings a bell. I can check patient registration."

"We'd appreciate that." The Cohens and Archers had the shelter in common, but did they also have Nurse Freeman? And while the administrator at the shelter didn't think the nurse treated the Riggs, it didn't hurt to ask the source. "And what about a Connie Riggs?"

"One minute." Summer headed to the station desk and dropped into a chair next to the other nurse. She pulled a set of glasses from a pocket in her shirt and slipped them on before clicking on a keyboard. A few moments later, she said, "No Connie Riggs, but Jill Archer?"

"That's right."

"She came in with a broken arm six months ago... Actually, I remember her now. Wasn't her husband a cop? I seem to remember a uniform."

"He was with the Dumfries PD," Trent said. "I'm pleased to say he isn't anymore."

"I see." Summer perched her glasses on her head.

"There's something I'd like to show you." Amanda took her phone out and brought up the image of the mystery man.

She held her screen toward the nurse. "Do you recognize him?"

She reached out for Amanda's phone. "Could I?"

"Sure."

Summer pulled her glasses down and studied the picture. "He looks kind of familiar. Why or where from, I can't say." She gave Amanda her phone back. "Then again, he is rather nondescript, isn't he? Could be anyone."

"Well, if it comes back to you who he is or where you saw him, call us." Amanda gave the nurse her card.

She and Trent were a few steps away when Summer called them back.

"Who is he? I mean, it's obvious you don't have a name, but why are the police interested in him?"

"I'm sorry, but we can't say." Amanda turned to leave again.

"You said that Abigail fit the profile of the victims found in that park...?"

The lingering question had Amanda returning to Summer. "That's right." She could be misreading the nurse, but she sensed Summer's motivation wasn't to poke her nose into the investigation but rather that she had something to contribute.

"These women came from abusive homes. Did they have children?"

"Young daughters." Amanda felt safe in admitting that. She wasn't saying the children were in the grave with their mothers.

"Huh. Like Mia?"

"That's right."

Summer paled. "In that case," she said, "there's someone I'm worried about."

The skin tightened on the back of Amanda's neck. "Who and why?" She best not get ahead of herself.

"Her name's Leanne Reilly. She's early thirties and has a daughter named Gracie."

"And why are you worried about them?" Trent stood next to

Amanda, inadvertently bumping her elbow and drawing back with a mumbled apology.

"She came in here a few days ago with a sprained ankle. Monday, I believe. Said she twisted it on an uneven rug but that was a clear lie. Her husband was hovering and wouldn't let go of the daughter's hand. I got the mother alone, and she admitted her husband had caused her injury. She was afraid he might hurt Gracie if she didn't leave him. Before she checked out, she seemed real determined to leave him but kept saying the timing wasn't right. I called to talk to her yesterday, and her deadbeat man answered the phone. He said Leanne and Gracie were gone. He actually added 'good riddance.'"

"It sounds like she built up the courage to leave him." Amanda wanted to believe that, but there was this niggling starting in her gut.

Summer was shaking her head. "I don't think so. As I told you I've treated a lot of women who were beaten by their husbands. You get to know the ones who are ready to claim their power, and the ones who are afraid to just yet. Leanne wasn't giving me any signs she was ready to leave him. But he told me that Leanne had ditched her car, and it was going to cost him a fortune to get it out of the impound lot. Why would she have done that? The car would have been their best shot of getting away from here."

"And a means the husband could use to track her." Amanda hoped that was the explanation.

"Maybe, but I don't know. Just a feeling right here." Summer put a fist over her gut. "You will follow up on this and talk to the husband?"

Amanda glanced at Trent, and his body language and energy said he was ready to move on it. "We will. If you have her address, phone number, to give us, that would be a big help."

"Sure." Summer gave both to them and said, "Hopefully I'm wrong and they're fine."

"Hopefully," Amanda parroted, and Summer excused herself saying she needed to get back to work.

"We can't ignore the similarities," Trent said. "The abusive households, the fact Jill Archer was also treated by Nurse Freeman, even if months apart. And where are Abigail and Mia Cohen?"

"We'll try to reach her using the burner."

"And Leanne's car was impounded. Did she ditch it to shake her husband? He'd just need to report it stolen, and she could have been dragged back to him."

"I think you and I both know we need to follow this up. We pop by, check in, and go from there." Amanda was ready for some good news, but she feared she'd be waiting a while longer.

THIRTY-ONE

Leanne had worked all night on chipping away at the window frame and had just managed to loosen the bars. Her injured wrist throbbed even though she used her other hand.

The first deadbolt clunked.

She slipped the knife between the mattress and box spring as the door opened.

"I told you to clean this up," he snarled, pointing to last night's meal that was now hardened to the wall and the carpet. "Do it before I see you next."

"I'm sorry. I'll get it right now." She made a move toward it, but he held up his hand. Gracie ran to Leanne's side and wrapped her arms around her legs.

"Not now. After I leave, but when I come back it better be—"

"It will be cleaned up. I promise." Tremors ran through Leanne, but with any luck, when he returned they'd be gone.

"I see you ate some."

Leanne had picked at the potatoes and carrots during the night, finally surrendering to her body's needs, but there had been no protein to complement the vegetables. She refused to put the flesh of a once-living being into her mouth.

He turned his gaze to Gracie, and Leanne's insides burned. She hated it when he looked at her. A protective instinct bubbled within her. Who knew what perverted thoughts danced through that warped mind of his? He was obviously some sort of deviant—that much was clear simply because he was holding them prisoner.

"We have people who will be looking for us." Leanne puffed out her chest to be convincing, but even she didn't buy her words and posture.

"No. You have *me*." He said nothing more as he gathered the plates and cutlery and left.

Leanne let out a deep breath. He hadn't noticed the missing knife.

Gracie tugged on her shirt. "Mommy? When can we go home?"

Her daughter's tiny voice pierced her heart, and Leanne sniffled and blinked back tears. "Soon." She got onto her haunches and hugged her daughter, tighter than she had in her life. She'd only concocted a half-ass plan, brought about on the wings of hope. Well, hope let you down more than half the time.

There was the rumble of his truck coming to life.

She hurried to the window and watched as the two-tone blue Ford 150 disappeared into the distance, the tires kicking up plumes of dust from the gravel drive.

Maybe luck was finally on their side. They had daylight to put to use, and the man was gone. Only for how long? They had to hurry.

Leanne turned her focus to the immediate area beneath the window. A garbage and recycling bin—the kind that were tipped by specialized trucks—were down there. They were about four-and-a-half feet tall. Nothing to offset a straight descent.

But, surely, this wasn't the way it was supposed to end for her and Gracie.

Herself maybe. She had made so many stupid choices in life, starting with marrying Bill. Then they seemed to build from there. But little Gracie had done nothing wrong. She was innocent, blameless.

Why are you doing this? She yelled the question, directed at the man, in her head, not wanting to startle her daughter.

She had to be strong for her, protect her, rescue her. She pulled the bars from the window and set them on the floor, leaning them against the wall. Her injured wrist was throbbing.

"What are you...?" The rest of the question dried on Gracie's lips.

"Mommy just needs to think, baby." Last night she'd had the hare-brained scheme to tie the bedsheets together and slip out. There was too much chance for things to go wrong. With a direct fall, they'd be lucky if all they broke was an arm or a leg. And how was she going to manage rappelling with an injured wrist and ankle? Would the sheets even be strong enough to hold her suspended weight?

She opened the window and clawed out the screen, then stuck her head through the opening. The bedroom was at the end of the house, and there was a downspout less than a foot to the right.

She could shimmy down and go for help. But leaving Gracie here—even for a second—wasn't acceptable. And this escape plan was one for the movies. She was no hero.

The thought pinched her heart, and an ache burrowed into her chest. But she squeezed out the self-judgment. She had to at least try to get them out of here—and now was the time for action.

There was no way Gracie could manage on the spout though. It would be tough enough for Leanne with her injuries.

Leanne rushed to the beds and yanked off the bedding. She rolled the four sheets like cigars and tied the ends together. She laid them out in the room, getting a feel for the length, and how this would work.

Now, what to secure the sheets to...?

The leg of a bed might be the best option, but the nearest one would eat up too much length. "Can you help Mommy move the bed?"

"Uh-huh."

The frame was heavy with the box spring and mattress. Her vision flashed white a few times from pulsating aches in her wrist and ankle. "You're doing a great job, baby," she winced through gritted teeth, trying to bite back the pain.

They eventually got the bed against the wall beneath the window, and Leanne tied the sheets to a leg. She then stood back, lowered herself to her daughter's height. She fingered a wisp of her hair and tucked it behind an ear. "You're a brave girl, and you'll need to pull on that. Okay?"

"Okay." Gracie's cheeks were red, and her eyes glistened.

"We're going to slip out the window and down the side—"

"I don't like heights."

Leanne wasn't a fan of heights either, nor did she look forward to taxing her existing injuries, but the end justified the means. "I know, baby. But this is very important, Gracie. It's our only way out."

Gracie pointed to the door.

"I can't get past the locks. We must be brave. Repeat after me—I am bravery, I am courage." The words were a mantra she'd recently adopted to help her when she faced Bill's fits of rage.

"I am bravery. I am courage."

"You are. All right, I'm going first. I'll be using the downspout, but you will use the sheets." She had no doubt they'd support her daughter's weight. But it was a gamble determining which order would be the best. Leaving Gracie in the room made it possible the man would return and she'd still be captive, but if Gracie slipped, Leanne may be able to catch her.

Gracie nodded.

Leanne threw the sheets over the sill and looked out after them. They ended only about a foot from the ground. She tugged on the fabric, and the knot on the bed leg seemed to hold strong. "When I reach the ground, then you go." She didn't wait for Gracie to reply and hoisted herself out the window and shimmied over to the downspout. Her wrist and ankle screamed for mercy, but she squeezed out the pain—as she was so used to doing whenever Bill took his fists to her body.

The air was cold, a breeze circled around her. She was only wearing a long-sleeved shirt and pants. He'd taken their coats and shoes, and she didn't know where he'd put them.

The cold from the siding cut through her socks, turning her toes to ice. She counted off the inches that eventually amassed to feet. After a bit, she was farther from the window than she was to the ground.

As her feet touched earth, Leanne let out a breath. "Okay, your turn."

Gracie filled the window and then turned, coming out.

"You've got this." Leanne coached her the entire way down, filling her daughter's mind with confidence.

A few feet from the ground, Leanne scooped Gracie into her arms and kissed her forehead.

"I did it." Gracie grinned at her.

"You did. Now, we need to—" *Leave* dried on her tongue. The distinct rumble of the man's truck getting ever closer sent ice through her veins. She ran, holding Gracie in her arms—her additional weight and injuries moot as adrenaline fueled her system.

Leanne kept running, headed toward the barn. The grass along its sides had been left to grow wild. At easily five feet tall and dense, hopefully it would work to conceal them. She tucked close to the barn and went around the back.

She set Gracie down and held a finger to her lips, telling her daughter to keep quiet. But as she did that, her eyes caught two wooden crosses. One was adorned with a fresh floral wreath.

"Stay here." She walked toward them, feeling drawn to investigate. A glance over her shoulder revealed Gracie hadn't listened. "Go back."

"No." Gracie shook her head.

Leanne took her daughter's hand and crept to the crosses, even as the engine's noise grew louder. Both graves were unmarked, but there was a small card attached to the wreath. In handwriting, it read,

Cheryl and Holly, I will love you always.

Cheryl and Holly? Isn't that what he called them? Dread crept over her shoulders, laced down her arms, lifting the hairs as the flesh became goosebumps.

Tires crunched loudly over the gravel, and the vehicle's engine cut out. Then a door opened, slammed shut.

She ducked down in the tall grass, and Gracie did too. Leanne closed her eyes, putting all her focus into listening.

His boots kicked stones—he was pacing in the driveway. He would have noticed the sheets and open window the moment he pulled up.

"Cheryl!" he yelled.

Shivers tore through her. Gracie was nestled tightly into her side, and her palm was wet in Leanne's hand.

"Cheryl," he called out, his voice drawing closer, but his tone was less threatening. It was like a husband playing hide-and-seek with his family.

Leanne needed Gracie to get as far away from here as possible. She lowered to her haunches to speak with her. Talking in a whisper, she said, "Mommy needs you to run."

"No. I can't leave you."

"You need to. When I say, head in the direction of the road, but don't go up the driveway. Go through there." Leanne indicated the surrounding field, which was high with crops. "Understand?"

"Uh-huh."

"Then you go to the nearest house and call the police. But don't move until you know the man's back in the house."

Gracie nodded, and Leanne tapped a kiss to her daughter's forehead, not wanting to leave. "Remember, go once he's in the house."

"Okay."

Leanne crept back to the barn, keeping low to the ground and putting distance between herself and her daughter's hiding spot. She then stepped out and walked along the side to meet her fate. "I'm right here. I just needed fresh air." She was aware her heart kept an even rhythm though it felt like she was circling above and watching from out of body.

"Where's Holly?"

The name sent shivers coursing through her. Had Cheryl and Holly been his wife and daughter or were they previous victims? But she knew he referred to Gracie. She nudged out her chin and said, "She's gone."

His face became shadows, his gaze briefly flicking to the fields before he yanked on her arm and dragged her back to the house.

Run, Gracie, run like the wind!

THIRTY-TWO

If plugging her ears and closing her eyes worked to keep the evil out, Amanda would give it a go. But she knew better. The darkness was right there, lurking ever closer, and ready to pounce. They tried Abigail Cohen's burner, and it was out of service. It was impossible to know what her and her daughter's fate had become. But they'd focus on Leanne and Gracie for now. "Is it too much to hope that they're all right wherever they are?" She referred to both the Cohens and the Reillys.

"Not at all." Trent looked over at her. "That's exactly what I'm doing."

The Reilly home was in Woodbridge, so Gracie would attend one of the three public schools there. Amanda had been right not to attach certainty to Kim Brewer's assurance that no other students were missing class at Dumfries Elementary.

They found Bill Reilly at home. He was a good-looking man, but his overbearing personality overshadowed any redeemable attributes. Not to mention he was an abusive man. He hung on the doorframe like they were having a casual visit, not discussing his family's whereabouts. "Why are you looking for Leanne? She do something illegal?" He snickered a laugh.

"We just have some questions for her," Amanda said.

"You know she hurt her ankle all by herself. She tripped on the rug."

"I'm sure she did." This from Trent, entirely sardonic.

"And you can't take me in unless she's pressing charges."

"We're not here about that," Amanda said coolly.

"So you don't believe me. I don't care. Now scram." It was as if he hadn't heard a single word from their mouths. Bill started to close the door, but Amanda stepped forward, and it had him halting his movements. "What do you want?"

She drew up her height. "Where is your wife, Mr. Reilly?"

"Beats me. Quite sure she left me, but she'll be back. She can't take care of herself."

Amanda's hackles rose, but she swallowed her temper. "When did you see her last?"

"Tuesday morning before I left for work, but I didn't see her after that."

A Tuesday, just like with the Archers. They'd been killed on the Friday, three days later. Today marked the third day for Leanne's and Gracie's whereabouts being unknown. If they were the killer's latest targets, she and Trent were quickly running out of time to save them. That's if they weren't already too late.

"You try reaching her?"

"Of course I did," he spat. "Her phone kept ringing through to voicemail though. Now it's off. But whatever. I'll be fine. And she'll probably come back, tail between her legs, begging me to forgive her."

I highly doubt that! The thought fired through that Leanne might not even have the option. "When did you last try reaching her?"

"Wednesday."

"That's two days ago," Trent pushed out.

"So?"

"You track your wife's phone, Mr. Reilly?" Amanda asked, hoping to cool Trent some, though she felt somewhat hypocritical given her rising temper.

"No. Better things to do."

Either he released the leash a bit more than Roy Archer had or was lying to them. But they couldn't force him to admit to tracking his wife's movements.

Bill added, "Besides, she'll be back. What's she gonna do out there all by herself?"

"It's not just your wife who's missing, Mr. Reilly. Aren't you worried for your daughter, Gracie?" Marriages fell apart every day, but how a person could write off a kid was beyond her.

"What am I supposed to do?"

"Did you even file a missing person report?" Trent asked.

"Why? She'll be back."

Trent stepped forward, and Amanda put out an arm, and only lowered it when she was confident he was staying put.

"Does your wife have money of her own?" Amanda asked.

"Nope."

"Kind of hard to get anywhere without money," Amanda pushed back.

"Exactly, so she'll be back. I dunno what else to say."

"Does she have a car?" She figured it best to make it sound as if they had no foreknowledge of this, just in case it set Bill's sights on Nurse Freeman.

"Listen, I don't know why Prince William County police detectives are so interested in Leanne, but leave me out of it."

"Answer Detective Steele's question," Trent seethed.

Bill stared blankly at Trent, then said, "She did, but it was impounded."

"We're going to need to know where."

"What's it to you?"

"For us to know," Amanda seethed.

Bill squinted and looked at them, then retreated into the

house. "I'll be right back," he called out.

Trent stepped close to Amanda and spoke quietly, "I'm a few seconds away from punching his face."

"Get in line."

"Here it is." He handed Trent a slip of paper with handwriting on it.

"Thank you for your cooperation," Amanda said stiffly.

"Say, you don't think something happened to them, do you?" For the first time since they'd graced his doorstep, he showed a crumb of concern.

Trent turned toward the car and mumbled, "What would it matter to you?"

Bill glanced at Amanda—Trent's question had been cold and cutting, but she understood where it came from. The man hadn't given them any indication that he cared his wife and child were gone.

"Open investigation." She'd hide behind that because she was with Trent on his decision to leave Bill completely in the dark, as cold-hearted as that might sound.

She joined her partner in the car. "We need to have Leanne Reilly's phone traced immediately, though it's probably long dead by this point." She paused there, hindered by her word choice. *Dead.*

"That's where this is different from Jill Archer. Leanne's phone wasn't off right away. He said it rang to voicemail."

"Not sure what that's telling us, but something else is bugging me. It might be nothing. But Jill was last seen on a Tuesday morning and now Leanne. Is that a coincidence?"

"Hard to say. Were both women taken from the same place, somewhere the killer frequents on Tuesdays?"

"We know that Jill Archer was at the doctor's office with Charlotte on Tuesday. From there? Somewhere else in the plaza or its lot? Finding out where Leanne Reilly's car was impounded might be a good start."

"Agreed."

Trent got them moving, and Amanda pulled out her phone and updated Graves. Her next call was to Judge Anderson for verbal approval to trace Leanne Reilly's phone and to collect her car.

She no sooner hung up with him than she called CSI Blair.

"Amanda, we're working as fast as we can over here."

"I know, but I need you to run something for us. Top of the pile."

"Hit me."

"We have a number we need you to trace. Could you do that right away and call me back?"

"Just for you."

"Thanks." Amanda gave her the information and ended the call, still a bit in shock at the transition in their relationship. Apparently the value of talking things through was underestimated. She filled Trent in on where they were.

"Any updates on forensics?"

"Not yet." She hadn't put her phone in her pocket yet as she debated following up with Nadia Webber at the FBI. She ended up doing that.

"I was just about to call you," Nadia said after Amanda identified herself. The analyst continued. "Good news is I'm not seeing any other unsolved cases that appear to be connected with yours."

"Thank you for looking."

"Anytime. Good luck finding the unsub." *Unidentified subject...*

"Thanks again." Amanda ended the call and informed Trent.

"Hey, that's good news."

"It is." But Amanda wasn't celebrating just yet. The news didn't mean Leanne and Gracie were safe.

THIRTY-THREE

Trent had taken them through a drive-thru for a bite to eat. He scarfed down a messy cheeseburger while driving. Somehow he managed not to wear it.

He pulled into the impound lot, and he and Amanda were greeted by two barking Dobermans when they got out of the car. Thankfully they were on the other side of a chain-link fence. Their fuss didn't bring anyone out to investigate, so he and Amanda went into the office, which smelled heavily of motor oil and gasoline.

Amanda pushed the bell on the counter two times in quick succession.

They gave it a few seconds before splitting up and calling out, "Hello?"

"Hold on. I'm coming." A man in stained coveralls, with a round belly, stepped out from an office across the room.

"Prince William County PD," Trent announced.

"Whatever you're after, I'll need a warrant."

"And we have one," Amanda told him.

The man held out a meaty hand covered in black grease.

"It's a verbal, but I can get the judge on the line."

"Do that." The man walked over, panting from the twenty-foot journey.

"Your name?"

"Casper."

Trent's gaze snapped to the man, and he laughed.

"That's what my buddies call me. Real name's Tommy Hooper."

"It will be one minute," Amanda said and placed the call. A few seconds later, she said, "Here you go. Judge Anderson."

Tommy got on the line and handed the phone back to Amanda. She confirmed the judge was no longer on the other end and returned the phone to her pocket.

"A car registered to William Reilly..." Tommy was clicking on the keyboard. "Here it is. Right, it's that real piece of crap I picked up. Thought it was going to fall apart when I hooked it to the truck. It's a ten-year-old Volvo S60."

Apparently Abigail Cohen wasn't the only one with a beater. "Where did you hook it up?"

"Woodbridge Plaza. A Brad Stevens, manager at Corey's Grocer, called us in."

Trent glanced at Amanda and found her already looking at him. This placed Leanne in the same plaza as Jill Archer's last known location.

"Do you know what made him call it in?" Amanda asked.

"Besides wanting it out of his lot, I don't know."

Trent considered how long it would have probably taken the manager to even notice a car abandoned in his lot, and his mind kicked back at least twenty-four hours. "And you picked it up when?"

"Wednesday afternoon."

Leanne and Gracie Reilly had likely been in the plaza lot on Tuesday then. "A team from the crime lab will be retrieving the vehicle, but could we take a look at it now?"

"Don't see why not. Just let me chain up the dogs, so you're not dinner." Tommy flashed a smile, showing off a few gaps in his teeth, and took off into the lot.

"We'll wait," Trent said.

Amanda had her phone to an ear again. "Emma?" she said into it. "I appreciate you might not have finished the trace... Yeah? Oh? You're sure?... You're right. I should know if you say it, you are. Thanks. We're there now."

Trent perked up. *Was the phone in the car?*

Amanda continued, talking into her phone. "I didn't want to mention it until we had confirmation, but we need someone from your office to collect a ten-year-old Volvo S60 from that impound lot. We are going to see it now. If we find the phone, we'll bag it and leave it with an officer for you. Okay..."

There was a lengthy pause, and Trent was curious what Blair was telling Amanda.

"Thanks. Bye." Amanda stuffed her phone into her jacket pocket.

"What did she say?"

"Apparently, Leanne's phone was last active *here* up until Wednesday evening, when it went offline."

"The battery ran dry," Trent said.

"Guess we'll know if we can put our hands on the phone. It's probably in the Volvo, but if it's not, the people around here have some answering to do."

"Huh, so did Leanne sense danger and conceal it?"

"In that case, why not try to hide it on her person? All of this raises another anomaly to the Archer case. Jill's vehicle hasn't been found, so presumably the killer hid it somewhere."

"So why leave the Volvo behind?"

"Here we go with the questions again." She smirked at him.

It was a sort of standing complaint with every investigation but somehow acknowledging it lessened the frustration. It reminded them each case had a cycle, and if they followed the leads, eventually and possibly God-willing, they'd find resolution and justice.

"We haven't discussed this before, but we need to think about the logistics. Does he have transportation of his own that he takes to the locations where he targets women? If so, what happens to his vehicle? If he left it behind for too long, it would be towed like Leanne's Volvo."

"He sometimes works with a partner, like with Jill Archer?" Trent volleyed back. "He carted her and Charlotte in her vehicle, and someone else drove him back to pick up his?"

"I don't want to leap to a partnership just yet."

"All right, alternatives? He took a taxi back to retrieve his vehicle or he... *he* lives within walking distance." Trent snapped his fingers. "Lance Crane. He called in the fire. He takes his dog to Prince Park every day. Why? Just because it's convenient or does it carry a special meaning for him, as we think it might for our killer."

"Maybe we should revisit that guy and really dig into him. See where it gets us."

"Okay, folks, if you want to follow me." Tommy stuck his head through a side door and waved them over.

As they stepped into the impound lot, Trent had one thought tormenting him. Had they messed up in releasing Lance Crane from suspicion?

THIRTY-FOUR

Amanda gloved up and so did Trent. Their main goal was to see if there were signs of foul play. Had Leanne and Gracie left of their own volition or had they been coerced?

"This is it." Tommy waved toward a rust bucket.

The metal-eating virus had rotted away the wheel wells and was working its way along the sides. The Reillys had obviously never bothered with yearly rustproofing.

"And the keys?" Trent asked the man.

"We don't have 'em, but the doors are unlocked. I'll leave you to it. When your friends arrive, I'll let them back."

"Thank you," Amanda told him.

Tommy responded by waving an arm overhead while he retreated toward the office.

Trent opened the driver's door and stuck his head inside but quickly retreated. "Whoa, that's ripe." He fanned a hand in front of his nose.

She caught a whiff feet back. "Smells like a rotting carcass. Pop the trunk." She headed to the tail of the car.

He popped the clasp and joined her. They both moved back from the stench.

There were seven bulging cloth grocery bags.

She took shallow breaths. "My guess is there's meat somewhere in there that's gone bad."

"No arguing with that reek."

Neither of them moved toward the source of the odor.

"You know what this is telling us?" Amanda asked.

"Not to leave your groceries in the car?"

She understood his desire to delay acknowledging what this find told them. But she wasn't going to sugarcoat it. "Leanne wouldn't have grocery shopped and then took off of her own free will. They were taken," she said, resolved. "We need to save them, Trent. That's if we're not already too late."

"We'll do all we can."

"I'm sure you agree it seems likely Leanne was loading the trunk when she was interrupted by the killer."

"Yep."

"So did she toss her phone in the vehicle or did the killer? We might get his prints off it." The spark of hope burned bright, even for a second. "Hate to say it, but we need to dig." She nudged her head to indicate the bags.

"Guess we're going in." He took the lead.

She rummaged in a bag next to the one he was going through. "Nothing here." She buried her hand in another and came out with it wrapped around a cell phone. It served as a bittersweet discovery. She held it up for Trent to see, then turned it over in her hand. She tried to wake the screen, but the battery was indeed dead. "We'll get this bagged and hand it over to a uniformed officer. He can give it to CSI Blair. Let's hope there are prints on it that get us somewhere. You and I are going over to Corey's Grocer. Maybe they'll have video surveillance and we'll get something to go on."

"If they don't, I'd bet one of the places in that plaza do."

Amanda refused to raise her hopes too high. Hope was a best friend that sometimes stabbed you in the back.

. . .

The cashier at Corey's Grocer paged Brad Stevens to the front, and Amanda thanked her.

"You're welcome. But if you could just stand over there..." She swept a hand to indicate the area at the end of her till.

"Sure thing." Amanda turned to leave the lane, but an older woman who was unloading her items onto the belt grumbled. "If I could just get by you."

Reluctantly the woman moved out of the way.

"Thank you."

Amanda joined Trent where he was standing next to the gossip magazines. To his credit, he wasn't even scanning the headlines.

"As you heard, the manager's been paged," she told him.

"I did hear." He smiled, and she realized how rarely she'd seen his smile of late. She'd ask if he found out any more about his aunt and her disconnected number, but now wasn't the time.

"Brenda?" A man's voice had Amanda turning, and the cashier who had paged him pointed to Amanda.

She stepped over to him. "Brad Stevens?"

"That's me. What can I do for you?" He was bright-eyed and eager, late twenties, and held obvious pride in his position.

Amanda tapped her badge, clipped to her waistband. "Detective Steele, and this is Detective Stenson." She gestured to Trent. "We're with the Prince William County PD. Do you have somewhere private we could go to talk?"

"Ah, sure. This way." He took them up a set of back stairs to an office. It had a window that looked out over the store, and a desk and computer, as well as multiple stacks of printouts. A chair for visitors was against a wall but heaped with paper.

Brad sat at the desk, and she and Trent stood in front of him.

"You called to have a vehicle towed from your lot on Wednesday afternoon," she began.

"I remember. It had been here overnight. I don't like to call on people right away, but there are signs posted. Parking is for customers with a two-hour limit, which is generous."

"You keep a close eye on your lot?" Trent asked.

"Somewhat."

"Did you notice anything unusual on Tuesday?" Amanda realized how vague that question was and the room it left open. She added, "The reason I ask is that my partner and I believe that a mother and daughter may have been abducted from here."

"What? No. Well, nothing that I noticed anyhow. Wow." Brad's previous bubbly personality dulled to a fizz.

"Does the store have security video, or should we contact the plaza owner?" Often surveillance and towing landed on the shoulders of property management.

"The management for each store is responsible for their own monitoring and even the install of cameras."

That might make it easier to obtain the footage than going through some corporation. She'd assume the same went for towing unwanted vehicles, as Brad had made the call to Tommy.

He added, "And we do have cameras, just not dedicated staff to watch the feeds all day."

"Yet you seemed confident that Volvo had stayed in your lot overnight," she pointed out.

"I'm always the last to leave and first to arrive and happened to notice it there."

"Fair enough. We'll need to see your video feed from Tuesday as soon as possible." With the request, it struck that while they were at the Archers' grave, another woman and her daughter were taken.

"I might need a warrant?" More question than statement, and Brad looked at them as if for permission.

"It depends on the store's policy," Amanda said. "But you should know that your video could help save two lives."

Brad paled. "Let me call the owner."

"Whatever makes you comfortable." Amanda was pulling from a deep-seated patience and doing her best to be diplomatic. But her head and heart were screaming for things to move along faster. This close yet so far away. Any delay risked death.

While Brad made the call Amanda passed the time rehashing all the ugly possibilities.

It was Friday. Three days after the abduction. Did the killer adhere to some sort of timetable? If so, and it followed the pattern of the Archers, that meant Leanne and Gracie would be murdered today. Possibly while she and Trent were standing around here. She felt pressure closing in on her. "I can talk to the owner if it would help."

Brad lowered the receiver on the landline. "He says it's fine."

"Great." Amanda's chest expanded with a full breath again. "We'd like to watch it right now. And take a copy of the entire day with us." She was thinking again about the killer's logistics. It was quite plausible that somewhere on that feed, they might find his vehicle. All they'd need would be a plate to track him. But how many vehicles passed through the lot in a day? Likely quite a few, and they had no means of truly narrowing it down. Then her thoughts gelled. If Jill and Charlotte Archer also went missing from this plaza's parking lot, she and Trent could confine their interest in vehicles that showed on both days. Go from there. They might even end up seeing two abductions. "We'd be interested in getting Tuesday from the week before too."

"Just follow me." Brad led them to a smaller room with

another computer station. He directed Amanda to sit and leaned over her shoulder and worked the mouse.

He clicked on a folder labeled with this past Tuesday's date. "Do you know what time specifically you're interested in?"

"Not exactly. Whereabouts was the Volvo parked? That's the field of interest."

He minimized the folder, letting the live feed populate the monitor on the right. He pointed to a spot toward the back of the lot. "It was right there."

"Thanks. That's a big help. I think we have it from here." This surveillance system looked a lot like one she'd accessed in a coffee shop for a past case.

"Okay. I'll leave you to it." Brad left the room, and Trent stepped in behind Amanda to view the screen.

She hit the play button and forwarded in slow motion, locking her gaze on the parking space Brad had pointed out.

At 10:33 AM, the Volvo pulled into the spot, and the trunk was popped.

Leanne got out of the car, slightly hobbling, and met her daughter, Gracie, at the trunk and grabbed cloth bags from there before shutting the lid.

The video continued to play out, showing the Reillys headed toward the grocery store.

"Watch for anyone who might be noticing them," she told Trent.

"You know I am."

She scanned the people in the background and the far edges of the feed. No one was showing the mother and daughter any interest. It didn't mean their killer wasn't out there, just that he'd been wise enough to keep out of the camera's line of sight. Well, that or he'd show up later. "You see anything?"

"Nope."

"I'm going to forward until they come out. We know they were taken after they finished shopping."

She forwarded in slow motion until she saw Leanne's and Gracie's backs to the camera. It was just over an hour after they'd entered the store. Leanne was pushing a cart and holding her daughter's hand. Witnessing that small act of love had Amanda's heart swelling. There was also something to the way Leanne tugged the girl close. Almost protective. Was she already uneasy for some reason?

Leanne let go of her daughter's hand and opened the trunk with a key. She started loading the groceries into the back.

Nothing exciting until— "Look." Amanda shimmied straighter in the chair and pointed to the screen.

A man entered from the right side—dark hair and casually dressed. He approached with his hands in his pockets, a nonthreatening stance.

"Could be the man who was talking with Jill outside Dumfries Elementary," Trent said. "Right size and coloring, anyway. And isn't that the same jacket?"

"Shit. I think you're right." She pulled out her phone and brought up the photograph of their mystery man and held her screen toward Trent. "I'll be."

"So the same guy...?"

"Might be. We don't see his face. He could just as easily be Lance Crane, honestly. Ever since we brought his name up again, he's been on my mind. But look at Leanne's body language," she said to Trent. "She tensed and drew back from him."

"And just so subtly moved so her daughter was behind her more."

Amanda nodded. "She's certainly uneasy. Her shoulders are back, her head slightly angled. I'd guess he said something to her."

"If only we knew what."

No expert lip-reader could do it from the back of a person's head—and that's the view they had. Amanda watched the interaction play out. A few seconds later, Leanne was smiling and gesturing. Relaxed.

"She knows him," Trent concluded.

"Huh."

The man was closer to Leanne now, and Gracie peeked out around her mother's legs and was smiling at him.

"He's charming," Trent shared his observations, mirroring her own.

"Yep. He's able to set the women at ease and get their guards down." It pained Amanda to watch. She wanted to scream for Leanne and Gracie to run, but her warnings would come far too late. "I do suspect, though, that Leanne and Gracie knew him, or at least were familiar with him."

Leanne was laughing now, but Amanda's gaze drifted to her hands, and ever so smoothly Leanne tossed her phone into the grocery bag. Next she was closing the trunk and she and her daughter were walking away with the man.

"What the...?" Trent said.

"Is she running away with him?" Amanda shook her head in answer to her own question and paused the video. "But that makes little sense given her initial reaction, which was hesitancy and fear."

"She might have wanted to avoid answering her husband's calls for an hour or so while she spent time with the man... whoever he is."

"Possible. It would seem Leanne and Gracie went with the man willingly. Who is he to them? If Leanne had sensed any danger, wouldn't she have brought her phone with her? Obviously we won't need to check it for the man's prints now, but was she leaving her husband for that guy?"

"Hmm. I don't know about that. Why bother shopping if that's the case? Why not just rendezvous in the lot and leave with him?"

"Okay, keep talking."

"Just before she ditched her phone, she was laughing. Didn't seem forced, but what if he told her to in order to make it seem genuine—like he knew about the camera—and leaving the phone had been at his direction?"

"Her laughing would give the impression that Leanne took her daughter and left her husband willingly. It would give any cop watching the video pause—it could be an affair or abduction. But as we said, the affair angle doesn't feel right with the timing. On another note, he might not have known she left her phone behind." Amanda faced the monitor again and hit play. The trio exited off the right side of the screen.

"Is he aware of where the cameras are placed and trying to avoid them?"

"Too soon to leap there. Besides, it looks like the grocery store just has the one outside. Suppose other units in the plaza could have their own. Either way, we need to show this man to Brad Stevens and see if he knows him."

"Here, do you recognize this guy from the back of his head?"

"Very funny. He might recognize the man's build and clothing. We can also show him the man's face from the Dumfries Elementary video."

"Let's watch from two Tuesdays ago and then get him?" Trent raised his brows as if asking.

"Let's." She opened the folder and started the feed. They weren't armed with where Jill Archer had parked, just the make and model of her vehicle.

Jill's Chevy sedan entered the lot around ten thirty and went off-screen to the right.

"We know she took Charlotte to the doctor's office, and they are at that end of the plaza," Amanda said. "We need to see if there are any other cameras on the lot that will show that section."

"Yeah, considering that's also the direction the Reillys went with the man. Did the man have actual business at the plaza besides selecting his next victims? Could he have been here for the clinic even? As you said, it's at the end of the plaza."

"We'll go talk to the people at the doctor's office again. Show them our mystery guy's picture." She hated the room for error as the man from outside the school might not be the one they'd just seen on the video with the Reillys. They had similar build and wore the same jacket, but they didn't have an image of the latter man's face.

"Let's do it. Right now. We'll come back for the video."

THIRTY-FIVE

Leanne felt like a rag doll as the man dragged her up the stairs to her prison.

"Why couldn't you leave well enough alone?" He pulled the sheets from the window and bunched them in his arms. Then he collected the comforters from the floor. He left with all of them.

The three deadbolts were thrown.

She screamed out and cried, destroyed. Broken. But her little girl was safe. She had to be.

That had been hours ago. The time passed painfully slow as she watched the sun move across the sky. She guessed it was at least mid-to-late afternoon now. But no matter her own fate, as long as Gracie got away free and clear.

Chills ran through her, and she got off the bed. Her boredom had sparked a curiosity she could no longer ignore. She slipped her hand tentatively between the mattress and box spring and found the knife she'd stored away. Grabbing its handle, she pulled it free and went across the room to the closet.

The door was sealed by two screws on the handle side—one top, one bottom. Rising on her tiptoes, she pushed through the pain in her ankle and stuck the blade's tip into the slot on the top screw. And twisted. It gave way.

Leanne picked up speed, spinning the knife and loosening the screw. A few moments later, it popped free and dropped to the carpet.

Next, she repeated the process with the bottom screw.

She hesitated. It might be best to leave the space unexplored. Her imagination was serving up hellish concoctions that had her wanting to draw back. Instead, she took a deep breath, twisted the handle and pulled.

It was a closet, stacked full of plastic totes. She pulled one out and cracked the lid, not wanting to think what he'd do to her if he found her invading his privacy.

But at least she was armed. She had the knife.

She set the lid on the carpet next to her and peered inside.

Children's clothing.

She continued digging in the box, looking for anything that might help her connect with the man and understand him—something to wield to her advantage as leverage.

Leanne's hands landed on a framed photograph. It showed the man with a woman and young girl. He had his arm around the woman, and the girl was front and center between them. They were standing in front of a lit Christmas tree, all of them smiling.

The man was in military uniform with dog tags dangling from a silver chain.

Leanne interpreted the photo as him returning from active duty just in time to celebrate the holidays.

But what happened to his family? Did the answer have something to do with that cross adorned with a floral wreath.

Cheryl and Holly?

The totes revealed no concrete answers. But having all this memorabilia shut away and sealed in a closet had to say something. If his family had died, wouldn't he cherish these items? But it was almost as if he wanted to push their memory away.

She closed the totes and put them back. As she set the last one in place, she noticed something on the shelf. It barely hung over the ledge—a belt or a strap... She reached for it and pulled it down.

A beige purse.

She was trembling as she opened it and looked inside. A sunglass case, a comb, a nail file, a plastic sleeve of tissue, a wallet.

She opened it, expecting to see the woman from the photographs on the ID. It turned out to be someone named Abigail Cohen, a person of similar appearance to the woman in the family photo with the man. The resemblance was eerie. But she clued into something else now. Both women also looked a lot like her.

She removed wallet-sized photos of a young girl. Her breath froze. She looked like Gracie and that child in the photo with the man. The pictures fluttered from her hands to the floor.

"Holy shit."

She stuffed the photos back in the purse and returned it to the shelf. But there was something behind that wouldn't allow her to push it back. Rising on to her toes, she eyed another purse. She brought it down.

What the hell is going on...?

Leanne fished in the bag and found the contents were similar to Abigail Cohen's. She opened the wallet, seeking the driver's license. *Jill Archer.* Photos in her purse showed a young girl too.

Again, it was like Leanne was seeing her and Gracie. The entire lot of them looked like that woman and child with the man.

The possibility clicking into place was terrifying. Had the

man killed his own family? And what about these other women and their daughters?

She swallowed roughly, a large lump forming in her throat. *Is he selecting replacements?*

He'd called her Cheryl, and Gracie, Holly.

No, no, this has to be a nightmare. I'll wake up soon.

But just in case this was her reality, she tossed both purses onto the shelf, letting them settle wherever. She didn't want to see anything else in this closet of horrors. She hurried to seal the door again. Once finished, she lowered to the floor and drew her knees to her chest.

Maybe the only reason he hadn't beaten her when he'd caught her escaping was because he still saw her as Cheryl. Maybe the secret to her freedom relied on her assuming the identity of Cheryl. But she wasn't a therapist. Would that enrage him or appease him? Would it buy her time in case help was on its way?

If only she had visions of the future as her mother had. But she had died a lonely, bitter woman in a home for the clinically insane while muttering away her last days, claiming she had a "gift." Maybe mental illness ran in the family. It might explain Leanne's tolerance of Bill's mistreatment of her. But she couldn't make it on her own. She was too stupid to make the right decisions.

All that nonsense the nurse had filled her mind with was lies. She wasn't strong or powerful. And a divine being? Ludicrous. Leanne was a maggot clinging to any carcass she could to stay alive.

The nurse had also tried to convince her there was good in the world, but how was Leanne to accept that belief? She'd only known suffering, and that's all she would know.

She bunched the fabric of her shirt at her bosom and cried until the tears ran dry. The entire time she muttered a prayer to a god she wasn't even sure existed that her little girl be safe. *Please, please, let her be...*

The deadbolts were unlocked. One by one. Before she could stand, the door flung open.

The man was back, but he wasn't alone.

THIRTY-SIX

Amanda's phone rang, and she answered on the move.

"Sorry it's taken so long to get back to you with some forensic findings," CSI Blair began.

"Hey, you're calling us now." She'd had her mind set on asking the people in the doctor's office if they recognized the mystery man. But it would have to wait. Amanda motioned for Trent to follow her. She stepped to the side of the plaza, out of earshot of people, and put the call on speaker. "Trent's here too. What do you have?"

"I took a closer look at the stuffed dolls—the elephant and the rabbit. Both are made by the same manufacturer and in rather new condition once you get past the dirt. I left a message for the distribution manager of the company to tell me where they retail these items in the area. I'll let you know once I hear back. Moving on, hairs were pulled from the toys. No human DNA exemplars, but I have canine."

Trent leaned into Amanda's phone. "Do you know which breed?"

"A black Lab."

Amanda lowered her phone. "Lance Crane," she said to

Trent. He wasn't the mystery man from Dumfries Elementary, but he could be the man on the plaza video, as they'd discussed. Was the fact he had a black Lab a coincidence or a clue?

"Hello?"

It was the sound of Blair's beckoning that had Amanda lifting her phone again. "Sorry about that."

"You said 'Lance Crane?'"

"He's the man who called in about the fire. He said he was walking his dog. A black Lab," she stressed.

"Huh. Rather early to be out walking. I'd say the guy deserves a second look."

"Agreed." And she did more than ever.

"On another note, that photo of the man you sent me didn't get us anywhere in facial recognition databases."

"It always feels like a long shot," Trent said.

"Well, I think we're getting closer now, and we need to move." Amanda took her phone off speaker and told Blair about Leanne and Gracie Reilly as she huffed it to the department car. Trent kept pace with her.

"Good luck to both of you," Blair said before hanging up.

Amanda palmed her phone and turned to Trent. "News about a black Lab trumps the doctor's office for now. We need to go to Lance Crane's. If he is our killer, he could have Leanne and Gracie right now."

"All right."

They both got into the department car.

"Let's pull some information on Crane, then I'll update Graves. We'll go from there." She bounced her leg, impatient, ready to move.

"You know, Crane lives in a small residential neighborhood," he said as he logged on to the onboard computer. "If he held any of these women and their daughters hostage in his home, someone would've seen something."

"We have theorized about a partnership before. Lance and

his partner take the women and girls somewhere else. His partner's home?"

"Could be."

"We also tossed out the idea that our killer lost a woman and child in his life. Was Crane ever married? And maybe we should dig into his employment history, talk with his friends, get a real feel for the guy."

"Also compare the size of his handspan and fingers to what CSI Blair has determined."

"All of it. Lance Crane makes for a good suspect. Even if he's working alone. Does he own or have access to other properties? Possibly something more isolated or rural."

"I'll check."

"Before we go, do you want to grab that security video?"

She considered. Time was of the essence, especially if Lance was holding Leanne and Gracie Reilly. All the same, Trent needed to get some background on Lance before she called Graves and they headed over to Lance Crane's. "Ah, yeah, but I'll be quick. You work fast too." She jumped out of the car and headed to the grocery store.

She set out in search of Brad and found him pacing at the bottom of the back stairs.

Brad spun at the sound of her saying his name. "Did you find everything you needed?"

A small bob of her head. "We just need copies to take with us."

"No problem. I'll get that now." Brad headed up the stairs and Amanda bounded behind him.

"There's something else I need your help with."

"Name it."

The manager's eagerness to please was respectable, but she suspected his enthusiasm would dull with her next words. "Does the name Lance Crane mean anything to you?" It was a thin possibility, but their killer could have intentionally parked out of view of Corey's surveillance cameras.

"Lance, Lance, Lance..." Brad prattled off the name as if trying to summon a memory. "Actually I think we had a Lance Crane who worked here once."

"When was this?"

"He was one of my first hires as manager. So that would've been, say, three years ago... Somewhere in there." Brad entered the security office and put a USB drive into the computer.

"And what did he do for Corey's Grocer?"

"Stock person. He would also face the shelves after closing."

"Face the shelves?"

"It's a term given to pulling product forward so it's flush to the front edge. Looks organized and is easily accessible for customers." Brad copied the file from two Tuesdays ago.

"I see, and why did he leave?"

"He got a better paying job. I think it was with some plumbing fixtures company, something like that."

"So he worked here for how long?"

"Just under a year." He grabbed the next file and copied it over.

"Would Mr. Crane ever have reason to see the security video?"

"Every new hire is given a tour of the entire facilities, including this room. Nothing top secret about it. The cameras are only here for two purposes—to catch shoplifters and for insurance."

"Insurance?"

"In cases of injury and lawsuits against the store."

"And you said cameras plural?"

"Just the one on the lot but several inside."

"To confirm then, Mr. Crane would know what cameras covered what?"

"No question, unless he had his eyes closed." Brad took the drive out of the computer and handed it to Amanda.

"Thanks. Ah, just one more thing." Amanda took out her phone and brought up Mystery Man's face. "Do you recognize him?"

"Quite sure I've seen him in the store before."

Amanda gave her card to Brad. "If this man turns up, call me immediately. Number's on there."

Brad nodded, confirming her message got through, and she hurried from the store.

Had they let a killer slip through their fingers right from the start?

THIRTY-SEVEN

Amanda's legs weren't moving as fast as she'd like. She was armed with another mark against Lance Crane to share with Trent. She slipped into the department car, and Trent was hunched forward and working on the onboard computer. Maybe he should go first. "Talk to me."

He barely looked up, so she spoke, the words quickly spilling over each other.

"Lance Crane is a former employee of Corey's Grocer, and he had access to the video room. That means he knows what the exterior camera covers of the lot and what it doesn't."

He sat back and looked over at her. "You had far more success than me. From his background, Lance has never been married and has no children. I can't see that he owns any properties or has access to any besides where we've already been. He doesn't fit the profile of our killer."

"Beg to differ. What I just told you, but he also has a fondness for Prince Park. He walks his black Lab there every day." She didn't know which point to stress over the other. "We need to watch the videos in their entirety for the two Tuesdays in question—when the Archers were last here and the one the

Reillys were—and see if we can tie him or his vehicle to the plaza's lot."

"Which could be a coincidence. But, trust me, I'm with you. We need to at least question this guy."

She nodded. "I'm going to call Sergeant Graves and bring her up to speed. You get us headed to Crane's house."

"Yes, ma'am." Trent saluted her, a smirk tugging at his lips.

"Uh-huh, always a smart ass." Amanda placed the call, and the sergeant answered before the second ring. Amanda filled her in on their plans, and Graves said she'd arrange for officers to meet them outside Crane's place. She was also sending officers to the other stores in the plaza to see if any of them had surveillance cameras that would cover the entire lot. "Also, have officers show a picture to everyone who works in those places. I'll send it over when I hang up. The man's also a suspect."

"Someone besides Crane?"

"Yes. It's the man we told you was seen talking to Jill Archer outside Dumfries Elementary. He could fit the man on the plaza video too. Without a clear shot of his face, it's hard to tell."

"All right... Could the man outside the school be Lance Crane?"

"Definitely not. Trent and I would recognize him. But we need to focus on the man we have on the video with the Reillys."

A few seconds passed in silence.

"I'll take care of everything. Keep me posted on Crane. Bring him in, question him here. We all know the power of an interview room."

"Will do."

The sergeant held the line for a few seconds, and Amanda thought she was going to add something else. All she said was "goodbye" and "thank you for bringing me up to speed."

"The sarge wants us to bring Crane to Central for questioning."

"Suits me just fine."

The time on the dash read four fifty-five. *Zoe...* Sometimes she felt like a total failure as a mother. And it was often paired with making progress on an investigation. Amanda called Libby to let her know she'd be late.

"It's really no problem, Amanda. Zoe's got some friends over and from what I hear, she sounds pretty happy."

Amanda would have to take Libby's word for it, but she conjured the sound of Zoe's laughter and it put a smile on her face. But that was the girl's superpower. "You're the best."

"Remember that at Christmas."

Amanda laughed. Libby had a love for the holiday that went above and beyond reason. Every corner of the house she shared with her partner was decked with garland and twinkly lights during the season. The display put Amanda's decorating skills to shame. She was proud of herself when she got a tree up.

Amanda ended her call with Libby just as Trent was pulling up in front of Crane's house. A police cruiser was headed down the street toward them. Graves hadn't wasted any time getting their backup. Good thing because Amanda was ready to move.

She beat Trent to the door and knocked hard.

The pup answered right away. She barked and tapped her paws against the back of the door.

"Well, the dog's home. Crane's vehicle is in the driveway..." He could be inside breaking Leanne's and Gracie's necks right this minute. She pounded on the door in a successive rapping pattern for several seconds.

The dog responded in kind, its barking intensifying. Its nails now scurrying on the entry floor.

Lance should have answered by now. The thought he was ignoring them didn't give her a good feeling. "Where the hell is this guy?"

The dog silenced, and the door opened. Lance had the pup

in his arms and was stroking its head and soothing it with, "It's all right, girl."

"I'm sorry to inform you, Mr. Crane, but everything is far from all right." Amanda stiffened her posture and made solid eye contact with the man.

"Okay," he dragged out. He looked past them to the road where the police cruiser would be. "What's going on?"

"Are you home alone, Mr. Crane?" she asked, stiffening.

"Just me and this girl."

"Would a search of your house confirm you are telling the truth?" They didn't have a legal right to enter and search his home, but she served that to gauge a reaction.

"Yes." His voice was shrill.

She scanned his eyes and strained to listen. Heard nothing. That might not be a good thing. Leanne and Gracie could be hidden inside the home and gagged—or worse, already dead. "My partner and I need you to come down to Central Station with us."

"Like I'm some sort of criminal?"

"Not saying that just yet, but we have questions you need to answer." The interview could give them a basis to obtain search and arrest warrants.

Lance stepped back just a few inches. "I answered all your questions the other day when you were here. I have nothing more to say. I saw a fire, and I called it in. That is all. You said some woman and her child were found? That has nothing to do with me."

"Then you should have no problem accompanying us to Central." Her words weren't giving Lance any chance to negotiate.

"Fine, I'll go with you, but you're looking at the wrong person. I never knew about them until you came to my door."

"Mr. Crane, we'll talk about all this momentarily. If you

could grab your shoes and your coat..." Amanda gestured inside the house hoping to prompt him to get moving.

"Sure. Just let me get this one sorted away."

Amanda's gaze fell over the pup, and she reached out and pet her. The action had Lance pausing all movement for a few seconds. He was obviously surprised by the affection she'd shown the dog, but she'd done so for a purpose.

"I'll be right back."

"And we'll be here."

Lance left, and she looked at her hand. *Mission accomplished.* She held her palm out for Trent to see. Hairs from the black Lab were clinging to it and her fingers. Forensics testing would confirm if these hairs matched the canine ones plucked from the dolls.

Trent nodded, getting the meaning. "Slick move."

More an action born of necessity. If Lance Crane was their killer, she wanted a strong case against him. Though her immediate priority was finding Leanne and Gracie Reilly.

Lance returned and declared himself ready to go.

Amanda led him to the cruiser and the uniformed officer.

"You're not expecting me to go in that. Are you?"

"We'll meet you at the station," she said to the officer, ignoring Lance. She wanted to impress upon Lance the severity of the situation in which he found himself.

THIRTY-EIGHT

Leanne's next breath froze in her chest. If she'd been standing, she would have collapsed.

Her baby, Gracie, was standing next to that man. Just when she'd thought she had gotten away. She should have known better than to think good luck would be on her side. And obviously Gracie had inherited the ability to attract the darkness as well.

"Please, just leave her alone," Leanne begged.

He released Gracie's hand, and she ran toward her.

Leanne hugged her, and tears fell down both their faces.

"You should be happy for all I've provided you. I've given you shelter and food, and how do you repay me? You try to run away. Why? What have I done, Cheryl?"

She recoiled at the name, her thoughts transporting back to that closet full of memories. Leanne stood, gestured for Gracie to sit on one bed, and faced their captor. She held the steak knife behind her, at the small of her back.

"I'm sorry. I don't know what I was thinking." She reached out to caress his cheek gently, playing a role and hoping the sign of affection would work in her and Gracie's favor. But his face became shadows, and his brows arched downward. From sadness or anger, it was hard to tell.

"That's because you weren't thinking about me and how I'd feel. You were just thinking of yourselves." He let his gaze travel to Gracie, but it only stayed there briefly. "You know I love both of you. Right?"

It was taking every bit of strength she had to keep up this facade as Cheryl. Would doing so tear down his defenses and bring him closer? She needed him weakened and to afford her an opening. "We both know that. And you know we love you too, right?" Bile rose in her throat at the words, and she swallowed it back down.

"I know you do your best around here, Cheryl. And you've had to spend a lot of time on your own raising Holly. Don't think for one minute I don't appreciate that." He was looking through her as if observing someone else.

Shivers laced through her as her mind turned to ghosts and apparitions. She talked herself back from the ledge of fear and distracted herself with mental chattering. Why was Cheryl often left alone? Was it because he served in the military as the uniform in that picture had suggested? And did it matter? They just needed out of here! If that meant playing a character, so be it. She drew herself up. "Thank you."

"No. You deserve better." He dipped his head as if experiencing great sorrow, but he didn't keep it lowered for long. He met her gaze. "I only go where and when they tell me. I know you understand my need to serve our country."

She studied the man before her, trying to make sense of the puzzle. Was his military service to blame for his wild mood swings? He obviously took his duty seriously, even sacrificing time from his family. Had something happened during a mission, possibly abroad, that warped him? So many soldiers returned home suffering from post-traumatic stress.

"Cheryl, aren't you going to say anything?" he prompted.

His softened approach certainly contrasted her image of a tough military man, but maybe he wasn't that tough. He was obviously suffering from a mental issue and likely grief. "You know I respect what you do. Just the fact that you serve your country."

Now it was him who reached out to caress her cheek. It took all her willpower not to recoil under his touch and stab him. But the timing was crucial.

He continued. "They're not going to send me back. I'm officially done now. I can be here for you and Holly, and be the father I should have always been."

How to react? With his delusions, was he here in the present or living in the past? Did his words mean he planned to keep her and Gracie in this room forever? And what about those other women and girls? Where were they? Had he killed them as she'd thought before? Possibly they'd displeased him, and he'd abducted her and Gracie to take their place.

"Now, I do need to leave for a bit. Please promise me you won't run away again."

"I promise." The easiest lie she'd ever pulled off. "How long will you be gone? Just so we can look forward to your return," she added quickly.

"Just a few hours, and I'll be back with dinner. It will be another of your favorites, so please eat it."

"Sounds delicious." Not that she could eat; her stomach was a tight knot.

He turned for the door, and Leanne lunged forward, brandishing the knife. She sunk it into the meat of his shoulder, and he howled in pain and arched back.

Leanne pulled out the blade and held it, squaring her stance like a boxer—something she'd seen on TV.

The man stared at her, his eyes blank, his hand over the wound. He pulled his hand back and looked at the blood coating his palm.

Her heart pounded in her ears, as time stood still.

Is he going to make a move or just stand there?

She let her guard down for a second.

He swatted her, and she fell in a heap. He'd moved so fast that she had no time to react.

"Mommy!" Gracie yelled.

Leanne wanted to tell her daughter to stay back, but her head swam, blinded by white light.

Three clunks rang out as each deadbolt was secured.

He'd let her live, and Gracie too. But for how long?

She tried to focus, determined to clear her vision. There was no sign of the knife. He must have taken it with him.

"Mommy, are you okay?" Gracie's voice was small, angelic.

"Don't worry about me, baby."

"Why does he keep calling you Cheryl? And me, Holly?"

"It will be all right." She stroked her daughter's hair, not wanting to burden her with what she feared was the truth. If he'd suffered a psychotic break, he was capable of anything.

Her eyelids became heavy, and she lost the battle to keep them open any longer.

THIRTY-NINE

Amanda and Trent set Lance Crane up in an interview room.

"Should I be getting myself a lawyer?"

"Only if you've done something wrong." Amanda gave it two beats. "Did you?"

She was seated across the table from Lance, Trent next to her.

"I don't think so."

"We can play this one of two ways, Mr. Crane," Amanda began. "One, you cooperate and we finish up here quick—which I suggest. Or two, you act coy, don't answer questions and things become more complicated."

"One, of course." He splayed his palms open on the table, gesturing to that effect.

Normally she'd start from the beginning. She'd set up the interview by establishing the base of the conversation, asking questions, going from there. But if Lance was their killer, and he had Leanne and Gracie out there somewhere, she needed to get to them sooner than later. She reached into a file she'd brought in with her and pulled out a photograph of Leanne and Gracie. She pushed it across the table in front of Lance. "Do you know these people?"

Lance hesitated then relented, taking a look at the picture. He immediately shook his head. "I've never seen them before."

"Is that your final answer?"

"It is." The way he said it almost made it sound like he doubted himself.

Amanda took out a photo of Jill and Charlotte Archer. She put that in front of Lance. "What about them?"

"Nope. I've never seen them before either."

"And them?" She presented a photo of the Riggs.

"No."

"Then can you tell us how hairs from your black Lab got onto stuffed toys buried with them?" Amanda fudged the truth. His pup's hairs hadn't even been submitted for testing yet. But she had to shake him to get the answers she needed—and fast. She refused to accept she and Trent were too late, and Leanne and Gracie Reilly were already in a grave or awaiting burial.

Lance opened his mouth, shut it, swallowed roughly as if he were going to be sick. Even his complexion paled.

"You chose option one, Lance. Talk," she pushed.

"I... I have no idea. I can't even speculate. Maybe I should get that lawyer?"

"Again that's up to you, Mr. Crane. But if you talk to us, we could work that in your favor with the judge."

"Whoa, hold on there. Just to be crystal clear, what do you even think I did?"

"We think you killed these four." She pointed to the pictures of the Archers and Riggs. "And that you may have them." She jabbed her finger toward the Reillys. "We need to know what you've done with them."

"What I've— I haven't done anything with them. As I said, I've never seen them before."

Amanda studied his face and his body language, and she

read nervousness and anxiousness. It was tricky to decide whether he was covering guilt or not. "So if we searched your house we wouldn't find any trace of them?"

"Absolutely not. And I'm tiring of these accusations. You want me to level with you, you level with me." Lance, who struck Amanda as a rather quiet man, had been cornered and was pushing back.

She played the video from Corey's Grocer showing the man approaching Leanne and Gracie Reilly. She paused it. "Do you know that man?"

"I can't see his face."

"Is that you, Mr. Crane?" she countered.

"No. I've never seen them, and I don't know that guy either."

His expression seemed sincere. His body language wasn't defensive, and she believed him. Was he just skilled at hiding the truth? She took a photograph of the mystery man as captured on the Dumfries Elementary surveillance video. "Do you know him?"

Lance sighed loudly. "Please, what do you want from me?"

Amanda tapped the photograph and didn't say a word.

"No, I've never seen him before."

"So if we spoke to any of your neighbors they'll never have seen him around your place before or going inside your house?"

"I'd certainly hope not."

"All right, I'll lay it out for you." She leaned back and did just that in a cool, detached manner. "The Archers you know about. You probably heard about a second set of remains found in Prince Park."

"I did. But I'm guessing these two are missing?" He pointed to the photo of the Reillys.

"That's why we've been asking you where they are."

A few beats of silence.

Amanda continued. "The man on the video walking away

with them looks like it could be you." Again, a bit of a stretch without seeing the face.

"So he's a doppelganger? As sad and horrifying as this all is, I have nothing to do with this. Please believe me."

Honestly, Amanda was thinking they had the wrong person. She turned to Trent. "Detective, could we talk in the hall for a moment?"

She and Trent headed for the door.

"Oh, please, don't just leave me here. Talk to me. Can I go?"

"One minute, Mr. Crane." Amanda got the door and held it open for Trent. She shut it behind him and said, "I don't think he did this."

"That makes two of us. But we can't just cut him loose because of a feeling."

"We certainly don't have enough to pursue a warrant for his handspan or his finger size. I have dog hair, but it still needs to run through the lab."

"I know." Trent bit on his bottom lip. "This is frustrating as hell. Guess all we can do is ask if he'll volunteer his DNA, let me measure his handspan and finger length, width. See where it takes us."

"Let's." Amanda led the way back into the room, and they sat back down. "You claim you're an innocent man, Mr. Crane. Would you do something for us?"

"If it gets me out of here."

Trent took the measurements they were after. Neither was a match. He next swabbed Lance's mouth for DNA, just for due diligence.

"You are free to go, Mr. Crane," Trent told him. "For now."

"Thank you." Lance made haste leaving the room.

She wanted to punch something. Frustrating didn't begin to touch how she felt. "While we're busy banging our heads against a wall, Leanne's and Gracie's lives are on the line."

"We're doing the best we can." He said it in such a confident and assuring manner, Amanda faced him.

For a few seconds, a moment passed between them that catapulted her back to her kitchen a few months ago. She turned away before her thoughts derailed her. Only one thing deserved her focus right now—getting to Leanne and Gracie. That's if they were still out there to save.

FORTY

Amanda's stomach had been growling the entire time she was with Lance Crane. How she could have an appetite at a time like this was beyond her. She and Trent were back in their respective cubicles talking over the partition.

"Just think of it this way, we're down one suspect," Trent said.

"And not up any. Unless you count any number of people who may have been employed at Corey's Grocer or still are."

"Hmph. Way to deflate a man."

"And if I didn't tell you already, Brad Stevens recognized our mystery man. But he just said he'd seen him as a customer in the store."

"You didn't tell me that, and I forgot to ask."

"I think we need to give ourselves some forgiveness. There's a lot weighing on us."

"Namely Leanne and Gracie Reilly. I know I'm not the only one wondering how they are... whether they're still..."

"Alive?" Amanda finished, and Trent nodded. "I can't stop thinking about them." While Trent hadn't said much about it today, she bet he was doing a lot of thinking about his aunt too.

"Detectives," Graves called out and hurried toward their cubicles holding her cell. "Bring me up to speed. I missed the interrogation. This thing has been ringing"—she held up her phone—"and I've been trying to do damage control."

"Regarding what?" Amanda asked, sorry she had the second the question left her lips. The sergeant's mouth turned downward into a scowl.

"Word about Leanne and Gracie Reilly has reached the media. Now every news outlet in a hundred-mile radius wants to know what PWCPD is doing to bring them home."

"Not that returning them home would be any sort of rescue," Trent inserted.

"You know my point," Graves said drily. "They're calling me. Ronald Topez from the department's Public Information Office is too, needing direction on handling the inquiries."

"How did they hear about it?" Amanda hated that the possibility existed for a leak with every person they spoke to along the way. Even being careful about who they mentioned names to wasn't always enough.

"Does it matter? The damage is done."

"And it's not like any of those reporters are going to name names. They protect their sources," Trent said.

"Bingo." Graves pointed her now-ringing phone at Trent. She looked at the screen, slid a finger across it, then leveled her gaze at Amanda. "The interview with Lance Crane. How did that go?"

"His handspan and finger size aren't a match to the bruising impressions on the victims," Amanda said.

"But those were provided as an estimate. Could still be him."

"Except we're not seeing it after speaking with him," Amanda said firmly. "And Lance Crane doesn't have access to any properties where he could hold the victims. We suspect our killer has somewhere isolated and rural."

"And that he has an affinity for Prince Park? The same place Lance walks his dog regularly."

Amanda didn't remember specifically mentioning the affinity aspect to the sergeant. But with so many balls to juggle it was hard to know what she told anyone. "We assume so given two graves were there."

Graves's phone rang again. She shook her head but glanced at her phone. Another finger swipe. Amanda suspected another call was sent to voicemail purgatory. But the sergeant did something else on her screen. "There. It's silenced. I should have done that a long time ago." She pushed her phone into a pocket and crossed her arms.

"I don't think I mentioned the change in the killer's behavior with the Reillys. With the Riggs and Archers, he seemed to take precautions. He took Jill Archer's car, or in the least did something with it. The Riggs didn't have one. He just left Reilly's behind."

"The killer also didn't leave Jill Archer's phone for us to find, like he did with Leanne Reilly," Trent interjected.

"And with Leanne, he let himself get caught on camera," Amanda added.

"I didn't think we had a clear shot of his face."

It was feeling like the sergeant was fighting forward movement. "We don't, but he approached Leanne and Gracie within its view. Then again, maybe he didn't even consider the cameras." Amanda was spinning and second-guessing herself now.

"Are you able to tell from the video what vehicle the Reillys were taken in?"

"That might be a tall order, but we're going to watch all the video from Corey's Grocer. We'll cross reference any vehicles that show up this past Tuesday and the one from two weeks ago," Amanda said.

"Good way of narrowing down the possibilities," Trent said.

"It might help." She wasn't getting too attached to a positive outcome though.

"Are we even sure that this Leanne Reilly went with the man under duress?" Graves asked. "You told me she seemed to know him. And why leave her phone behind? If she was in trouble, why not take it along and call for help when she got a chance? We could be jumping the gun. This man could be her lover and someone she was leaving her husband for."

"Trent and I debated that, but it doesn't explain why she shopped first."

Graves worried her bottom lip. "Hmm."

"I'm curious if his behavioral changes tell us he wants to be stopped?" Trent said. "He might not have known about her phone, but he left her car behind."

"I don't know... That may be stretching things," Graves said.

"I'm not saying consciously, but—"

"Detective." Just one word, and Graves shut down that theory. "If he wanted to stop killing, he would."

Apparently, their sergeant didn't buy into the mind being a mysterious universe. "Whatever the case, Sarge, I'm quite certain the Reillys need our help." Enough talk. Time for more action.

"Another reason I came over here is to give you an update. Officers spoke with staff working in the plaza, apart from the clinic. We missed them. They were closed and open again on Monday. No more cameras to afford you more coverage of the parking lot. No one recognized that man." Graves nodded toward Amanda, indicating the mystery man from outside of Dumfries Elementary. "So next steps? Do we have any other potential suspects?"

"We've just have that man from the plaza surveillance," Trent said.

Graves glanced at him. "Well, watch it in full. Let me know

if you find anything. Maybe you'll get lucky and his face will be buried in there somewhere."

"Will do." Amanda's stomach rumbled loud enough that Graves stepped back and looked at her wide-eyed.

"Might be time to grab something to eat?"

Amanda stiffened. "Doesn't feel important right now."

"Suit yourself." With that, the sergeant left, pulling her phone from her pocket. Amanda just had time to think she was turning the volume back on when it rang.

"The sarge is right."

She met Trent's eyes. "About…?"

"You should eat something. If only to make it quieter around here."

"Ha-ha. Very funny." As if to talk back, her gut growled. "Fine. But it's going to be something from the vending machine. Load up the video. When I get back, I want to start watching."

"Hey, I've got no plans for my Friday night."

That admission had her lost for how to react or respond. She gave him a smile and put her back to him as fast as possible. She didn't want to give one thought to his dating life.

FORTY-ONE

Amanda woke up the next morning, missing Zoe. She'd surrendered at eight last night and called Libby to have Zoe sleep over with her. It turned out to be a wise decision, as Amanda and Trent didn't call it quits until 3 AM. They watched the video covering the Tuesday Jill and Charlotte were taken. They'd fast-forwarded some to cut down on time. Since the camera from Corey's Grocer covered the entrance to the lot, they noted every vehicle as it entered, recording make and model and license plate numbers. They'd compare this list to what they found on the footage from this previous Tuesday— when the Reillys were abducted.

One gem they'd uncovered was Jill's Chevy Malibu leaving the lot at eleven thirty with a man in the driver's seat. There wasn't any shot of his face, but the build was unmistakably male.

Amanda had only gone home when her eyes became cross-eyed and fuzzy and a piercing headache jabbed her skull. Even if they had discovered a solid lead then, she wouldn't have been able to act on it.

It was twenty to eight in the morning when she parked in

the lot for Hannah's Diner. She did a double take when she saw Graves's Mercedes parked where it had been the last time. Graves was behind the wheel and staring at the building.

Amanda followed the direction of her gaze and saw May through the glass, moving around behind the counter. *Is she watching May?*

She had half a mind to rap on the car's window and ask what was going on. *But it's not my monkeys, not my circus...* A catchy phrase her older brother would sometimes say.

Amanda entered the coffee shop, the bell chiming over the door, and May perked up at the sight of her. Eight at night or eight in the morning, May was always there. Amanda hoped to have that kind of energy when she reached her sixties.

May tapped the counter. "Extra-large black coming right up."

"Make it two."

"Going into work with that partner of yours on a Saturday morning?"

"Yep. All fun and games."

May set about pouring the coffees, while Amanda brewed with frustration. Was it too much to ask for one solid lead? And were Leanne and Gracie even still alive? She had to believe they were. Saving them served as stronger motivation than simply capturing this killer.

Her tired mind was also obsessing about the sergeant's recent behavior. She hadn't been skulking outside the diner for months or Amanda would have noticed long before now, as Hannah's was her regular haunt. To think of it, she hadn't seen Graves here before Jill and Charlotte Archer had been found.

Is there a link between the investigation and Graves lurking?

"Here ya go, hon." May handed Amanda the to-go cups in a tray.

"Thanks." She should just take them and go, but her legs weren't moving. "Whose Mercedes is that?" Amanda jacked a thumb behind her. She'd play dumb. May had told her she never met the new sergeant, but for a woman who noticed everything surely she'd seen the car.

"It's interesting that you ask." May braced both her hands on the counter. "It's here pretty near every day. I'm just too busy to check on it."

"Every day?"

"For at least a week, anyway."

As she'd thought, around the start of the case... "The person ever come in?"

"Nah. I'd have noticed. But you know what..." May rounded the counter and beelined for the front door. The moment she opened it, Graves pulled out of the lot. May swept a hand in gesture of *good riddance* and faced Amanda. "Maybe you would look into that for me? Seems a little creepy that someone is watching me."

Amanda knew the stalker's identity, and it was creepy—strange for certain. "I'll do what I can."

"Thanks, dearie, I know you will. Though I'm sure you have your hands full with more important matters."

"Why's that? Just because I'm working on a weekend?"

"I'm guessing you're caught up with the bodies found in the park, and now that it's hit the news..." May returned behind the counter, pulled a newspaper from a shelf there, and plunked it on top. "I haven't read it yet, but the title says enough."

Amanda read the headline: "Local Mother and Daughter Missing, Suspected Victims of a Serial Killer."

Amanda set the tray of coffees down and picked up the paper. It would seem despite Graves's efforts to deter reporters and their ilk, the story made it to print.

She dropped onto a stool.

"Mandy, are you working this case?"

"Yeah, I..." She let her words trail off, glancing over the article.

"Is there a serial killer active in Prince William County? If there is, I tell ya, you're the best the department's got. You'll get them."

Amanda appreciated the woman's confidence but didn't feel it herself right now. Especially when she and Trent were so desperate for leads. She didn't respond to May but started reading. The article exposed names: the Archers, the Riggs, giving the public faces to go with the unnamed victims earlier reported as being found in Prince Park. It also mentioned the Reillys. This article wasn't designed to just give the news, it was a slander piece against the PWCPD and Sergeant Graves. The reporter had even dug into her personal history.

Katherine Graves took over the post of sergeant for the PWCPD Homicide Unit back in March. A transplant from the NYPD, Graves has a dark past closely relating to this investigation. The victims were women who were allegedly abused by their husbands. It's believed Connie Riggs was trying to get away from her husband when the killer targeted her. We can only hope that Sergeant Graves's experience as a child in an abusive household will serve as strong motivation to push her team into action and get some resolution.

"Mandy, everything all right?" May's voice cut through the chatter in her mind.

Dark past... abusive household... That might explain the cooperation they'd received from Graves with this case and potentially explain her behavioral changes.

"Thanks, May. I've gotta go." Amanda popped up and rushed out the door. She turned back when she realized she'd forgotten the coffee.

"Be careful out there," May called after her.

She waved a hand over her head in acknowledgment. She drove to Central, her mind more preoccupied than before she'd stopped at Hannah's Diner. What was in Graves's past? Did it factor into her move from New York City? Did it have anything to do with her basically stalking May Byrd?

She held her breath on that last question as the words were bare and pointed. What had the sergeant watching the older woman? Graves haled from the Big Apple with no history in Prince William County that Amanda was aware of. And maybe that was the key point. Amanda didn't know a lot about the woman's past or present.

She turned into the station's lot and saw protesters clustered together, holding signs and waving them up and down en masse.

Bring Leanne and Gracie home

PWCPD work for us

Catch the killer!

Their chants made their way through the glass and metal of Amanda's Honda Civic. "Save them! Save them!"

There wasn't one officer in sight working to corral them and get them off the property. No one from crowd control dressed up in their armor and shields ready to withstand pepper spray and paint bombs either. While the protest seemed rather peaceful at the moment, that could change in a flash.

She pulled around back, through the lot that was used for department vehicles.

Some members of the crowd turned their heads in her direction but thankfully never pursued her. She parked and got out.

The sound of a vehicle pulling up behind her had her turning quickly.

Diana Wesson stepped out of a PWC News van and smoothed her skirt.

Amanda had run-ins with this reporter before and didn't want a repeat experience. She held up a hand, not that it persuaded the woman to back off.

Once her cameraman caught up, Diana put the microphone in Amanda's face. "Where are Leanne and Gracie Reilly? Do you have any leads on their whereabouts?"

"No comment." Amanda pivoted and carried on her way despite the cries of the reporter to give her just one minute of her time. She had nothing to say, and this reporter knew the drill. Statements from the department came from the Public Information Office.

Amanda went into the station and headed directly for the sergeant's office. She found Graves behind the desk. "They all need to go." She doubted she'd need to clarify who *they* were.

Graves sat up straighter, nudged out her chin. "Good morning to you too, Detective Steele."

"Did you hear me?"

"I'm not hard of hearing, so, yes, I heard you."

"Then?"

"We make a move on them, this will turn ugly fast."

"It's already ugly. Diana Wesson, a reporter with PWC News, is now out there. We don't need the pressure, but how might this affect the man who has the Reillys? He could do something rash." She was desperate, wanting to save them but so powerless.

Graves spoke slowly and methodically. "This isn't about us —you or me."

"Seems to be some about you," Amanda slapped back, and was sorry the moment she had. The one time she failed to do the countdown in her head before speaking. "I'm sorry, I..."

"You saw the article?"

"I did."

"Well, as I said, this isn't about either of us. We do our jobs. And, please, tell me you have a lead."

"I disagree." Amanda peacocked her stance. "Those pick-eters and the press are outside because they think your past does affect the case."

Graves scowled, and she spoke through clenched teeth. "My past never should have been mentioned. It has nothing to do with this case." The sergeant's eye contact challenged Amanda to contest her.

There hadn't been a reason to link the sergeant with the victims or the killer, but they could have missed something. A possible clue intended for Graves. But surely if she'd seen it, she would have mentioned it. Failure to do so didn't reconcile with Graves's sincere interest in resolving the case. Still, Amanda had to ask. "Is there any way someone in your past, maybe from your time with the NYPD, could be messing with you or calling you out?"

"No, Amanda." Graves sighed and massaged her temple.

The sergeant rarely, if ever, pulled out her first name. Amanda nodded.

"Tell me you and Trent have something."

"Wish I could." Amanda filled her in on what she and Trent had done last night and how late they hung around.

"Still nowhere. This is unbelievable. There must be something we're missing."

"Trent and I plan to watch the video from the day the Reillys were taken. It seems possible our killer may go to this plaza on Tuesdays—basing this on when the Archers and Reillys disappeared. Too soon to know for sure until we make the vehicle comparisons though."

"Guess that's the best we've got at this point." There was silence, then Graves added, "God help us."

Amanda bit her tongue on a reply. The sergeant didn't put faith in the science of psychology, rather in an invisible all-powerful being. They'd never fully see eye to eye. "We'll get started immediately."

"Keep me posted." Graves shuffled papers on her desk, and her cell phone started ringing in unison with the one on her desk.

Amanda left her to it, not envying the sergeant her position in this shitstorm. She also observed that Graves had given no indication she'd seen Amanda at Hannah's this morning when she would have. But that was a riddle to solve another day. Just like Graves's mysterious, abusive past. The priority now was finding Leanne and Gracie Reilly.

FORTY-TWO

Trent was happy to see Amanda had made it safely past the picketing outside. He'd been watching it grow since he'd arrived at seven. The plan had been to meet at eight, but he didn't have anything else productive to do, so he set out for an early start. He had driven past his aunt's house on the way in and talked himself into backing away again. He'd funnel his energy into rescuing Leanne and Gracie, as if that would redeem him—if only to his own conscience.

Amanda entered his cubicle and held out a tray with two coffees. "One's for you."

He hit pause and wasted no time plucking one for himself. "Thank you."

"Don't mention it." She pointed to his screen. "Early start?"

"Yeah. Figured what the heck."

"The video from this past Tuesday?"

"That's right. Making a list of vehicles. We'll compare later, hopefully find a lead in this mess somewhere." He ruffled the edge of his notepad on which he'd written all the vehicle information.

She tore the top on her lid back and took a draw. From the

looks of it, a long one, and he followed her lead. He'd drunk one at home, another at his desk, but what the heck? He'd drink all the caffeine he got his hands on today.

"You find any that are a match yet?" She held her coffee in front of her chest, as if it were a defensive barrier warding off bad news.

"Nothing yet. But I'm just up to nine thirty in the morning. I haven't gotten that far." Maybe if he hadn't wasted time outside his aunt's place torturing himself, he would have been further along.

She wheeled her chair next to his. "All right. We keep going."

He started the video, and he stopped it when the timestamp in the bottom read 10:15 AM. "That two-tone blue truck right there looks familiar to me." He consulted the list and tapped a finger on the page. "Same plate. It was on the video from two Tuesdays ago about the same time too." He looked closer at the screen. "You can make out one figure. I'd guess male."

"All right, but let's not get too ahead of ourselves. Where does he park each time?"

He let the video play, and the truck went right, leaving the camera's view. Next, he brought up the feed from two Tuesdays ago and forwarded to the time he'd indexed on his notepad. "Heading in the same direction, to the end of the plaza. We can only assume he parks down there."

"Huh. All right, so for at least two Tuesdays in a row, that truck pulls into the lot around ten fifteen."

"A standing appointment? There's a hair salon there, but it's also where the doctor's clinic is located. Seeing as he's not an elderly woman trying to fill his social calendar..." He latched his gaze with hers.

"He's going to the clinic. That's where he might have run into Jill and Charlotte Archer."

"Or he met them before that?" Trent shrugged. "We've

already said the man leaving with the Reillys could be the one outside the school talking with Jill."

"Right, so what was he doing there?" She waved a hand of dismissal. "We can fill all the pieces in later. Let's bring up his plate info, get a name."

She didn't need to ask him twice. He typed as fast as his fingers would cooperate. "Plate is registered to a Cheryl Brock of Gainesville. That's rural." It was a town about fifty minutes north of Woodbridge, but it was still part of Prince William County.

"A woman? You're sure? We'd pegged our killer as a man. The size of handspan, finger length, width, the partial work boot print near the Archers' grave all point to our killer being a man." Amanda's phone rang, and Trent jumped.

"Detective Steele," she answered. "Oh, yeah? Okay. Good to know. Trent and I just got our best lead yet." She ended the call but held on to her phone, remained speechless.

"Who was that?"

"CSI Blair. She got a call back from the manufacturer of those stuffed dolls."

"On a Saturday? Hey, not that I'm complaining, just somewhat surprised."

"They distribute those specific dolls to dollar stores. One of these is One Hundred Pennies in Woodbridge."

"We might be able to place this Cheryl Brock at the store. We'll try to confirm that. Ask them about her." His mind was spinning in a million directions.

She held up her hand and shook her head. "We have a man walking away with the Reillys, and a man in the truck with plates registered to a woman. We hit the address, feel it out, see if Leanne and Gracie are there."

"We also discussed a partnership," Trent volleyed back. "A man—who is behind the truck's wheel—picks up the women and their daughters, murders them. But what's not to say the woman, Cheryl Brock, helps take care of them for a time and that she also gets them the toys?"

"But why? For what purpose?" Amanda shook her head and glanced up at the ceiling, frustrated. "And maybe we're latching on to the wrong vehicle? Can we forward until it leaves the lot this past Tuesday? We could see, for instance, if two more figures are with him—namely Leanne and Gracie Reilly."

Trent forwarded the video at slow motion. The Ford F150 was leaving the lot at 11:40 AM. He froze the image.

"Crap. There's no way we can tell anything from this. Not with that dark tint."

"Do we know when the truck left two Tuesdays ago?"

Trent referred to his handwritten list. "Unfortunately not. It must be sometime the next day."

"Footage we don't have. Sergeant Graves might want more before we move in, even to have a casual conversation with this woman. And I'm back to that... a woman? Is she married?"

He brought up a background on Cheryl Brock. "Uh-huh. Spouse's name is Joshua Brock. He might have been driving her truck. But are they working at this together? Does she know what he's done?"

"Wouldn't be the first time a husband and wife abducted and killed. Is there any record on him?"

Trent did the background pull and seconds later had their answer. "None."

"Do they have a child? Any records to that effect?"

"One second... Ah, yeah, a daughter. Holly." He clicked on Joshua's DMV photo. "Holy shit."

"Say that again."

They were looking at the man's face from the Dumfries Elementary video. He was also likely the same man who had walked off with Leanne and Gracie Reilly.

"We need to talk to the sarge and move on this immediately." Trent might receive that redemption he longed for after all.

FORTY-THREE

"Let's just step back a minute," Graves said, standing behind her chair, clasping its back with her hands. "Joshua Brock is the man in both videos?"

"We believe so. Circumstances line up," Amanda said.

"Except for you told me before you can't see the man's face on the plaza video. Is that right?"

"Yes, but—" Amanda stopped there at Graves shaking her head. She had planned to elaborate on the *circumstances*—the timing of his arrival at the plaza and the unmistakable resemblance to the man outside Dumfries Elementary for starters.

"No. We can't risk jumping ahead and mucking everything up."

Amanda bristled. "What we can't risk is a little girl and her mother getting killed while we're jumping through bureaucratic hoops."

"Whether you like it or not, Detective, we have procedures to follow. We get justifiable cause, then we move in. You have a pickup truck going into a plaza at the same time on a Tuesday, but you can't prove it left with more people than the driver it arrived with. That right?"

"Yes, but we have Jill Archer's car leaving the lot with a man in the driver's seat."

"Who could be anyone."

Amanda's anger was reaching the boiling point. "We have enough to question the Brocks. Just let Trent and I get boots on the ground, feel them out, then go from there."

Graves sighed and dropped into her chair. "I want more before I even agree to that. Get me something."

"A mother and her daughter are out there, and the longer we take—"

"Detective Steele, I'm well aware of the repercussions."

Trent nudged Amanda's forearm, and it had her looking at him. "What?" Spoken with a touch too much attitude, but her nerves were shot.

"Sarge, we just got another lead before here," Trent stepped in. "It might help us get that justifiable cause you mentioned."

"By all means..." Graves gestured for Trent to continue.

Trent told her about the toys possibly linking back to the dollar store in Woodbridge.

"Okay, now that might be something we can use. Go there, see if the staff recognize him or his wife. Could get so lucky as to confirm they purchased the stuffed elephant and rabbit."

"While we're doing that..." Amanda closed her mouth, abhorred the sergeant was aware of the risks in delaying, but she was still willing to take them. "We'll go right now."

"The second you get anything, report back."

In her mind, Amanda was already behind the wheel of the department car and on the move. Her legs and feet had yet to get her there. When she did, she kicked the front driver's-side tire.

"Unfreakin' believable!" She shook her head, raging inside. The more they hemmed and hawed, the more likely they'd be finding corpses than rescuing anyone.

The news reporter lady started over for her, and Amanda hustled to the driver's door. Trent intercepted.

"Let me drive. You're impaired by anger."

"And you're not?"

"I didn't kick an innocent tire."

"Fine. Hurry. We're about to get railroaded."

"We already have," he mumbled.

Amanda rushed around the other side and ducked inside, narrowly escaping the reporter. Diana Wesson would never know how lucky she was dodging *this* bullet—that being Amanda and her foul mood. "How can she not at least let us go question them? This is ridiculous."

"I agree, but let's just get what she's after as fast as possible. There's no changing the sarge's mind once it's made up."

"Isn't that the truth."

Trent took them out of the lot, bypassing the protesters, and she found watching them scurry out of their path somewhat comical.

"Come on, Trent. Don't you know each one is a thousand dollars a head?"

He smiled. "Don't laugh, you'll cry, huh?"

"Pretty much. But like you said, we get what she wants—hopefully anyway, go from there." She shoved back into her seat and replayed what they'd uncovered and the conversation with Graves. "Gainesville..."

"What?"

"Gainesville. That's where you said the Brocks live?"

"That's right."

"Well, their daughter would attend Haymarket Elementary out there."

"All right, so what was he doing outside Dumfries Elementary? We know it was him comparing the video to his driver's license photo."

"Right, but we don't know for absolute certainty he's who

walked off with the Reillys. We can only connect Joshua Brock
to a lighthearted conversation outside a school. Maybe Graves
had a right to push back like she did. We need more."

Trent made a right into the parking lot for One Hundred
Pennies, joining a couple other vehicles in the lot.

"Not exactly rush hour here," Trent said.

"And that's a good thing."

They left the car and went inside the store.

The two of them beelined to the cashier, and Amanda
requested the manager. It was best they speak to them before
questioning their employees.

"Yes?" A friendly looking woman came over wearing a half
apron, tattooed with sales stickers. Apparently some items were
two for a buck.

Amanda held up her badge. "Detectives Steele and Stenson
with the Prince William County PD. We need to ask you and
your staff if you recognize someone."

"We'll do what we can." The woman glanced at the cashier.

Trent got their names while Amanda pulled up Joshua
Brock's photo. Usually, they'd approach something like this
with a spread of photos—their person of interest and others who
looked similar. Then when the case went to trial, and assuming
it was against Joshua Brock, they wouldn't be giving a defense
attorney ammunition to dismiss based on prejudicing witnesses.
Amanda would be sure to let the staff feed her and Trent information—assuming they had any.

"Here. This man. Do either of you recognize him?" She
held her screen for them to view.

The cashier and manager leaned in. The latter drew back,
shaking her head.

"I've seen him in here a few times." The cashier's green eyes
met Amanda's. "Don't know his name, but it was sad about his
wife and daughter."

"Sad?"

"Well, he used to come in here the odd time with them."

"What happened to them?" Amanda put it out there in a conversational manner.

"He told me they left him, but honestly, I got the feeling something terrible had happened, like they might have died. He never used to be so moody."

Amanda glanced at Trent. One of their earlier theories—that the killer had lost a wife and daughter. But how and when? And Trent said nothing about her being deceased. And how could a dead woman hold a valid license registration? Goosebumps traced down Amanda's arms. "When was the last time you saw his family?"

"Several months ago."

"And him?" Amanda asked.

"Earlier this week."

"Did he buy anything?"

"Anytime he's here, he buys the same type of thing. The plush animals." The cashier pointed to an aisle marked 2.

Trent walked down there and returned with an elephant and rabbit.

"Yep, those are the ones."

"And he bought one earlier this week?"

"Yeah. An elephant."

"You never found it odd considering his family left him?" Trent asked.

"Hey, not for me to worry about. Figured it was for his daughter or some other young person he had in his life."

Amanda turned to the manager. "Does the store have video surveillance?"

"Inside and out," the manager told her.

"We will probably be back for that. Right now, we've got to go. Thanks!" Amanda led the way to the car. She called Graves on speaker, and she answered before the third ring. Amanda ran through what they'd just learned.

"All right. Go over to the house. Feel it out. Maybe ask for the wife, see what sort of read you get from him."

"Consider it done."

Trent was already driving them toward the Brock residence in Gainesville.

Graves added, "Do not go into his house without invitation or cross any lines. Call once you have a feel for things, and we'll go from there."

"Fine." Amanda hung up. What Sergeant Graves didn't know was Amanda's fingers and toes were crossed.

FORTY-FOUR

Amanda took in their surroundings as Trent drove down a long driveway and around the side of a red-sided, two-story house. The two-tone blue F150 was parked at the back. No other vehicles in sight, but the barn about a hundred feet from the house could have stored more.

"Just keep your eyes open," she told him.

"Always. Unless I'm sleeping." He smiled at her.

She couldn't return it, feeling the crushing weight of this case on her shoulders.

"We'll get to them in time."

"But you don't know that."

"No, but it's what I choose to believe."

She held eye contact with him for a few moments, then nodded. "Oh, just before we go. Check something out for me?" She pointed to the onboard computer. "Are there any previous addresses linked to the Brocks?"

"Ah, you're thinking about why he'd be outside Dumfries Elementary?"

"I am. I mean, say if his wife did leave him, it could be seen as a death in its own way. I suppose being at the school could serve as a trip down memory lane for him."

"Let me see..." Trent pecked on the keyboard and seconds later had an answer. "Yep. They lived in Dumfries three years ago."

If Holly had been six when she'd left her father, she would have been in junior kindergarten. "Okay. Good to know. Not entirely sure how everything fits yet, but hopefully we'll find out."

They both got out of the department car and walked to the back door. It appeared to serve as the main entrance, suggested by the two potted plants on the step.

Amanda knocked. A dog barked in response. Otherwise silence. But she wasn't leaving until she spoke with the Brocks.

Trent stepped up and took over. He banged on the door without mercy. He must have felt the same as her.

The dog barked more earnestly, and a man yelled for him to shut up. He still didn't come to the door.

She knocked again. This time it swung open. Joshua Brock was standing there—in the flesh—a black Lab at his side.

"Joshua Brock?" she said, though there was no mistaking the man's identity.

"That's me. What can I do for you, Officer?"

"*Detectives.* Steele and Stenson," she clarified, feeling adrenaline wash over her. "We'd like to speak with you and your wife, if you have a minute." She wanted to see into the house, but his frame blocked the view.

He offered a pleasant smile, but it didn't touch his eyes. "Sure, come on in." He backed up, allowing them to enter.

Amanda passed Trent a subtle glance, just a reminder about keeping his eyes open. In the least, they could place this man with Jill Archer. But it was hard to ignore the striking similarities to the man who had spoken with the Reillys. Add the purchase of the stuffed toys and it felt like case shut. She'd keep calm though and not tip her hand. To do so wouldn't advance their goal of saving Leanne and Gracie.

They passed through the meager entry with its mat for shoes and a few hooks on the wall for coats. One hanging there was a visual match to both videos—the school and the plaza. No sign of work boots, but they could be anywhere. And there weren't any pairs of shoes belonging to a woman or child.

The living room was off to the right, a staircase straight ahead tucked behind a half wall. Joshua put the dog in a room off the kitchen and closed the door, then sat at a dining table to the side of the kitchen. He invited them to join him there.

"Your wife, Cheryl, Mr. Brock?" Amanda prompted. "We'd like for her to speak with us too."

There was a slight pause, then, "I'm sorry, but she's not home."

"That's fine. We can wait until she returns."

"I don't know when that will be. How can I help you?"

"Just a few questions. We won't keep you long." Amanda pressed on a smile, hoping it carried. The truth was she had a tightness in her chest from being here and sitting across from this man. "I'm sure you've seen the news—the tragic deaths. We're trying to get as much background on the victims as we can, talking to anyone who knew them, if only in passing. We believe you knew Jill Archer?"

"Yes. Nice lady."

Bold. He wasn't even denying knowing her. "How did you know each other?"

"My daughter Holly goes to Dumfries Elementary, like Jill's daughter."

Amanda resisted the urge to glance at Trent. "Oh, I didn't know the school district reached out this far."

"Doesn't really. Holly liked the kids there so after we moved out here, Cheryl and I would take turns driving her in."

"I see." And Amanda did *see* that he was lying.

"Where is Holly, by the way?" Trent made a show of looking around.

"With her mother." A tight smile sent chills running through Amanda.

"How well did you know Jill?" Amanda asked.

He offered another strange smile that started off as a twitch. "Just in passing, as you say. We'd say hello when we dropped the kids off at school—that kind of thing."

He was definitely lying. "What about Connie and Jodi Riggs?" She brought up a photo of them on her phone and held it for Joshua to look at.

He barely glanced at the screen. "Uh, yeah, Jodi played with Holly at the park sometimes."

"Oh? What park is that?" Amanda asked.

"Prince Park." Joshua was avoiding eye contact, but his gaze was shifting about the room. Anxious.

Amanda recalled an earlier theory they had... the one that had the killer targeting women and children to serve as surrogates for what they had lost. The cashier at the dollar store seemed to think Joshua's family had died. But both were showing as very much alive in the system.

"And had you seen either the Riggs or the Archers recently?"

"I don't think so. Maybe Jill at the grocery store?" That shifting gaze again.

All her instincts were telling her to back off—for now. She pulled her business card. "Thank you for your time today, Mr. Brock. Sorry we missed your wife and daughter."

"No problem. Honored to help the law when and where I can." He ran his fingers along the chain on his neck and the tops of pendants peeked above the rounded scoop of his collar.

Only they weren't pendants just anyone would have; they were dog tags. Her mind flashed back to the doctor's office in the plaza, specifically Dr. Wood, a therapist who specialized in treating military veterans. Was it appointments with him that had Joshua going into that plaza's lot on Tuesdays at ten fifteen?

Joshua saw Amanda and Trent out and remained watching them from the stoop.

"Is he going to stand there until we leave?" Trent asked her.

"I think he is. Just delay for a bit. Pretend you're on the phone." She was watching Joshua from her peripheral while Trent took out his phone and began playing out the ruse. She couldn't keep her leg still—every part of her was sparked to life. Joshua Brock was the man they'd been hunting. "He's our killer, Trent. He has to be holding Leanne and Gracie somewhere on this property."

"He didn't deny knowing the victims. I noticed you never asked specifically about the Reillys."

"I didn't want to alert him, make him feel under scrutiny. But did you notice the dog tags?"

"Oh... *Oh.*" Trent's eyes widened. "Dr. Wood from that clinic in the plaza."

"Yep. How much you want to bet that Joshua Brock is a patient of his?"

"I think we can both agree that Brock needs help."

"We can indeed. Well, the dog tags alone tell us he's active or former military. But if he's seeing Dr. Wood, he obviously has baggage to offload."

"Post-traumatic stress."

"Just one possibility. Those who suffer from it can also have severe and rapid mood swings that turn violent. His wife might have left him if he posed a danger to her and the girl."

"*Might have* being the keywords. Either way, he may feel responsible for their departure from his life, maybe for what he put them through. That's why he seeks women with abusive husbands."

"Surrogates, supported by how similar in looks the victims

are. I haven't seen a picture of Cheryl Brock yet, but I bet she looks like our murdered women and Leanne Reilly."

"It might explain why he doesn't abuse the women and children he abducts and takes care of them—at least for a while."

Joshua Brock waved and withdrew into the house.

Amanda returned the wave and shuddered. "That guy just gives me the creeps."

"All-American hero turned serial killer? That *is* creepy." Trent quickly brought up a photo of Cheryl Brock from the driver's licensing office. "What do you think?"

"Cheryl could be these women's sister. We need the search and arrest warrants yesterday."

Trent pulled the car into a spot to turn around. He'd probably rather navigate the long driveway back to the road nose first. Just as he was reversing, her eyes caught something.

"Stop right here."

He applied the brakes. "What is it?"

She narrowed her eyes, focused on the field in front of them. *Am I seeing things?* But she could swear when the long strands of grass swayed just right, there were two wooden crosses just off to the rear of the barn. "Look." She pointed them out to Trent and blanched as she faced him. "What if Cheryl and Holly are dead? Just no one knows yet."

"Are you suggesting that he killed his own family?"

"It might explain why there are no records of their deaths. He could have buried them right there." She gestured specifically to the marker adorned with a floral wreath.

"If he did, I'd say this guy is sicker than we thought. So he returned home, suffering with PTS, and killed his family?"

"Possible. Something snapped for him and had him reliving something that happened during his time in a war zone?"

"Okay, so he deeply regretted killing his family, and a part of his psyche tries to soothe itself by taking other women and their daughters?"

"Specifically ones who weren't being looked after right. Like he's trying to make up for what he did to his own. But then something snaps again..."

"Yep. We're already looking at four victims. Let's stop it here if we can."

FORTY-FIVE

Every day Leanne watched the sun come up outside the window, bitterness washed over. This hellhole was sucking her optimism dry that a new day would bring positive change. They were prisoners of a madman trapped in his own mind, in the past.

Dinner had been roasted chicken last night, another of Cheryl's favorites, but thankfully it was served with heaps of vegetables. Leanne wondered if the man had heard her, or whether it was still a preference of Cheryl's. She didn't miss that every time he looked at her or Gracie, his eyes glazed over, like he wasn't truly present.

Yet so far, her ruse to play along seemed to be working. They were still alive. She supposed as long as they drew breath, there was room for hope.

Knocks sounded on the main door, and the dog started barking.

Leanne looked out the window. A man and woman were on the step. Given their posture, they were cops. Had to be. The car they drove was unmarked, but it could belong to detectives.

Oh, please, help us! She screamed those words in her head, terrified that if she did so out loud, he'd come and silence her forever. But she could crack open the window. It made some noise as it slid up in its frame that might alert the visitors. Nothing the man would hear. She could hope.

One deadbolt clunked.

Then the other two.

"Get away from that window. Now. Both of you in the bathroom, shut the door, and stay quiet. If you make one peep, you're dead. Understand me?"

Leanne stood, paralyzed in place. Torn. Those people could be her and Gracie's ticket out of here.

More knocks on the door downstairs.

"Move!" the man urged, waving his arms around wildly.

Gracie tucked into Leanne's side, and they went into the bathroom.

"And stay perfectly still. I will hear you if you leave this room. If you talk or scream, I will kill the girl first, then you. Understood?"

Tears spilled down Gracie's cheeks, and Leanne hugged her daughter tight. "You're a freaking monster, asshole," Leanne seethed.

He grimaced, the expression extinguishing all light from his eyes, as if he were the walking dead. He closed the door on them.

Three deadbolts thunked into place.

The man said he'd hear them if they moved or left the room. The house was older and had its inherent creaks and groans, and she'd become familiar with them during their days in captivity. She refused to let this opportunity pass. It might be the last chance they had to get out of here.

"Sweetie, don't move, just like he said. But Mommy needs to do something."

"No." Gracie tugged on Leanne's hand trying to hold her back.

Leanne took a few steadying breaths. She'd never forgive herself if she slipped up and this man killed her daughter. Never.

Something had brought the cops to the door, and she could only hope they were on to him. Didn't police bring backup and move in heavily armed on a suspect in a case like this? But she'd only seen the two...

This acidic feeling bloomed in her chest telling her they were running out of time. She had to take a chance and try something.

"I shouldn't be long." She pried her hand free of her daughter's.

Leanne slowly cracked open the bathroom door, and headed toward the window, creeping along methodically. She needed to avoid hitting any floorboards that would give her position away.

She stopped moving at the sound of the door downstairs opening and voices that filtered upstairs. They were asking cop-like questions. They'd arrest him and rescue her and Gracie.

We're saved!

She wanted to scream to let them know they were there. But what if the cops didn't respond fast enough, and the man killed them? She'd have signed her and Gracie's death certificates.

Leanne resumed her path toward the window, figuring her best shot might be catching their attention somehow on their way out.

She hunkered down, her eyes and the top of her head all that would be visible from outside. She was ready when they were.

Minutes passed with nothing but more conversation, then the door opened.

She peeked out, and the man and woman got back into their car. Beneath the room, the man stood at the back door watching them. She couldn't risk opening the window with him there.

Leanne stood to full height. *Please look up here!*

She waved her arms, hoping to catch the eyes of the female cop who was on the side facing the house. At one point, Leanne could swear she was looking right at her, but she turned away.

Leanne's heart sank. The sun's reflection on the glass could make seeing her impossible.

Their car started, but they didn't move for a while.

Had the cop seen her after all? Just as hope was worming in, it was gone.

The car was in motion. The driver had pulled into a spot to turn around.

This is it. Gracie and I are dead.

But they weren't moving. They were idling in place. Had they seen something that had them hesitating?

In her mind, Leanne followed what would be in their line of sight. She felt hoping rising back into her soul. They just might have seen the wooden crosses.

Please, get us out of here!

FORTY-SIX

"No way we're going anywhere now. It's just this feeling I have." Amanda's eyes were fixed on the swaying grass and the cross with the wreath beyond it.

"We have no right to go traipsing around on his property."

"Here's what's going to happen. You're going to call Sergeant Graves while I return to Brock. Fill her in on our visit and our suspicions. Get the warrants. Have her get officers to Dr. Wood's home, see if Brock is his patient and what they can get out of him. It's unorthodox, but necessary. What he has to say could be the difference between saving two more lives or calling in an ME. Best to find out what we can ASAP."

"Yet, you're going on ahead *without* that knowledge."

"If I thought we had time to spare, I'd wait. But Brock has his guard up from our visit. If Leanne and Gracie are inside or on this property somewhere—which I strongly feel they are—we just moved up their execution."

"I'm not disagreeing, but this guy is dangerous. Unhinged, Amanda."

His words of caution drilled home what was at stake. Not just her life but Zoe's. Could she really afford to put herself in a dangerous situation that could leave that little girl motherless again? But what about Gracie Reilly? She might not make it to her next birthday if she and Trent didn't step in and do something. "I can't just sit here."

He scanned her eyes. "This is when I could remind you Sergeant Graves told us we were just to talk to Brock."

"You could, but you're not," she flipped back, calling him out.

"Of course I am. Think of Zoe."

"No." She shook her head. "Don't bring her into this. I'll play things as cool as I can with Brock. Ask if I can use his bathroom. All low-key and casual. But if I find just cause then we're golden. I will make a move if it means saving lives."

"I don't know if you should—"

"Not up for discussion. Call Graves."

"I don't like this."

"Which you've made abundantly clear. But you don't need to like it. We promised to serve and protect, and I'm not letting Brock kill the Reillys. And given the shifty way he was acting, they are here and they are still alive."

Trent held her gaze and eventually said, "Keep *your* eyes open."

"I will." And she was. She thought she'd caught a flicker of movement in the upstairs window a while ago. But she wasn't confident enough to mention it to Trent. "And make sure Graves knows I'm inside. It might speed things up." She didn't wait for Trent to acknowledge and got out of the vehicle. She hurried to the door and knocked.

The dog barked, but it sounded like it was far away. Maybe it was still closed in that back room.

Brock opened the door. "Oh, Detective, what is it? Did you forget something?" His question was casual, but his tone and shadowed eyes communicated his guard was certainly up.

She became conscious of the weight of her gun holstered on

her hip, giving her a sense of bravado. "Sorry to intrude like this, and it's not exactly appropriate, but I am desperate. Could I use your bathroom?"

He glanced over her shoulder to the car where Trent was still behind the wheel, the vehicle idling. "I'm not sure that's a good idea."

"Oh, please. I'll be quick." She winced to sell her story.

"Okay. Be quick, though, please."

A killer with manners... And a dog.

He showed her to a bathroom on the other side of the staircase. As she followed behind him, she took in the house again. Sparsely furnished, and there weren't any framed photographs on the wall. Odd there wasn't a single one of Cheryl or Holly. But if he had killed them looking at their faces might cause him too much pain and guilt.

"Thank you. I'll be quick," she told him.

She shut the door behind her and locked it.

Now what?

The wallpaper was peeling, and the mirror over the sink was lightly tarnished. The sink was light green with staining around the drain. The room was in need of a gut and remodel. Inconsequential observations that didn't help get her closer to the Reillys, possibly her mind's way of serving up a mild distraction—the calm before the storm. After all, she was certain mother and daughter were here. She'd hoped to have discovered just one little inconsistency or clue that would give her that just cause to move freely through the house. *No such luck.*

She flushed the toilet with her foot and turned on the faucet while she searched the cabinets under the sink. Nothing to advance her purpose.

There was a tapping in the pipes. Amanda figured it was an older house, so such noises could be expected. But when she turned the water off, the noise continued. If she wasn't losing her mind, she detected a pattern to it.

Tap, tap, tap, taaaapppp, taaaapppp, taaaapppp, tap, tap, tap.

Was that SOS in morse code? It had been a long time since her father taught her the basics. The pattern of tapping repeated.

Yes, it was SOS!

Leanne Reilly was sending her a message. That moving shadow in the window hadn't been her imagination. Now, if she could only remember how to respond...

Think, Amanda!

She paced in a circle, and she had it. Bending down, she tapped her gun against the pipe beneath the sink.

Tap, taaaapppp, tap—R for received message.

The tapping from above stopped.

Amanda twisted the handle and pulled on the door. It didn't budge.

He must have locked her in from the outside.

Overhead, footsteps padded and floorboards creaked.

Leanne and Gracie Reilly were up there, and she was sure Joshua Brock was too.

FORTY-SEVEN

"She's what? Why didn't you stop her?"

Trent had held his phone away from his ear, but Sergeant Graves's voice still rang in his ear. He hadn't told her he'd tried to talk her out of it. What would be the point? The result was the same: Amanda was inside with a suspected serial killer.

He'd brought the sergeant up to speed, including a request that Dr. Wood be contacted at home. All of this had been five minutes ago.

What was taking Amanda so long?

Trent peered in the car's rearview mirror at the house, tapping his hands on the wheel. He couldn't just sit here if she was in trouble.

He turned the car off and jumped out. He'd tell Brock he received a call and him and Amanda needed to hit the road.

After knocking twice, with no sound of a dog barking or the man coming, Trent pulled his gun.

Something was way off. He tried the handle, but the door was locked.

He backed up and rushed at the door, putting his shoulder to it. No movement. Again, and this time it gave way.

"Trent?" It was Amanda's voice calling out.

He was torn about whether to respond but he figured his breaking down the door would have already notified Brock of his arrival. "Where are you?"

"Bathroom, other side of the stairs. He's locked me inside."

Trent moved across the space, gun at the ready, ever cognizant of his surroundings. The door she'd indicated was shut and secured by a latch and closed padlock.

"I'll get you out." *An epiphany could strike any minute...* One did, but he wasn't too excited about trying it out.

"He has the Reillys. Hurry."

No pressure... "All right. Stand back from the door."

"Okay, I'm tucked behind the cabinet. What's going on?"

"There's a padlock. I'm going to shoot it." He got in position, extending his shooting arm, holding the gun pointed down at the padlock. Shut his eyes, drew some courage. Eased some on the trigger.

"Wait!"

"What?" His heart thumped, and he lowered his arm.

"Stand as far as you can to the *side* of the lock. If you're in front of it, the bullet could ricochet back and hit you."

He shimmied to the left of the handle, extended his gun arm again. "I've got it. All good."

Thank God she warned me!

He fired off a round. Direct hit. The padlock slapped open. The bullet pinged toward the staircase. He resumed breathing.

The sound of the shot and it hitting the lock had been loud, though. He certainly wasn't making a quiet entrance today!

Amanda emerged from the bathroom as his phone rang.

"Are you freaking kidding me?"

"Answer it," Amanda told him. "I'm heading up."

"Wait—" She was already up a few steps. Caller ID said Connor Wood. Trent answered, curious what the therapist might tell him. "Detective Stenson."

"This is Dr. Wood. You should know that Joshua Brock is a dangerous and volatile man."

Tell me something I haven't figured out!

"Joshua served with a SEAL team on a mission in Syria nine months ago. Three members of his team returned stateside in coffins. He blames himself."

Trent listened, unsure how this helped in the situation. But he trusted the therapist had been briefed on the urgency.

Dr. Wood continued. "The mission took him deep into a compound of insurgents. As the team's leader, Joshua was responsible for ensuring intel was reliable. But he trusted the wrong people. He got close to a woman and her young daughter, Janna and Fatimah. They ended up leading Joshua and his men into an ambush."

"I'm still not sure how this helps—" Trent wanted to move but felt locked in place for this conversation.

"Detective, Joshua is battling with severe PTSD. He has flashbacks, and he sees that woman and child everywhere. He might have... might have acted on urges of retaliation."

"Every time he kills, he's taking out the enemy?" Trent wasn't sure if he was making proper sense of the therapist's words.

"That's right. And now I hear that Joshua's wife and daughter may be dead. In my professional opinion, and in retrospect, Joshua may very well have killed them. His mind could have slipped back to Syria, to that insurgent mother and daughter."

What the doctor was telling him explained the signs of affection and remorse at the burial sites, the reason he targeted women who were abused and took care of them. It also shed light on why he'd be hugging them one second and breaking their necks the next. "I've got to go. But thank you!"

FORTY-EIGHT

Amanda had her gun at the ready and tore up the stairs, taking them two at a time. "Joshua Brock, Prince William County PD!" Her voice rattled off the walls of the old farmhouse.

"Stop it! Stop it!" The cries of a child.

Gracie Reilly. Amanda picked up speed and followed the noise to a room at the end of the hall on the right. Its door was open and sunlight spilled into the hall. She tucked against the wall and peeked through the doorway.

Joshua Brock had his hands around Leanne Reilly's neck. Gracie was kicking and punching his legs. She slowed when she caught sight of Amanda. She gestured for the girl to move away, and she retreated to a far corner of the room.

Amanda stepped into the doorway, gun raised. "Prince William County PD! Let go of her now!"

"You don't understand!" Joshua's scream bordered on hysteria. "I can't... I can't..."

"I have my gun leveled on the back of your head, Joshua."

Trent entered the room and made eye contact with her. She nodded, picking up on his silent communication that his call armed him with something to help. He was moving ever closer to Joshua. Each time the man turned back to Leanne, Trent ate up some distance between them.

But Trent had to hurry. Leanne's face was turning bright red.

"You don't want to do this, Joshua. It's not who you are," Amanda talked consolingly all the while Trent inched closer to the man.

"How do you know? I've killed many times before."

"When you were told to for your country. This is different." Amanda took a stab that he'd seen an active war zone.

There was silence except for Leanne slapping at Joshua's hands to break his grip.

"This is Leanne Reilly and her daughter, Gracie. Do you hear me, Joshua?" Trent asked.

Amanda noted Joshua released his grip, if minimally.

"Leanne and Gracie," Trent repeated. "They have done nothing to you and your men."

"You're wrong." Spittle hurled from Joshua's mouth, and tears fell down his cheeks.

"Please, listen to me." Trent moved forward, slowly.

Joshua glanced over his shoulder to look at Trent. "They lied to me. Deceived me." Snot bubbled in his nostrils, and his eyes were dark.

"Janna and Fatimah. They deceived you. Leanne and Gracie are innocent."

Joshua took one hand from Leanne's neck and swiped his wet cheek. "They killed my men."

"That's right. Janna and Fatimah. It's their fault. *Not* yours."

Amanda was listening and piecing together what Trent's caller might have told him. She'd guess a military mission went sideways, leading to unnecessary bloodshed.

"But it *is* mine," Joshua roared and lost his balance.

Trent moved in quickly, clocking Joshua on the head with the butt of his gun.

Joshua stood there, dazed. But the shock of the strike had him releasing his hold on Leanne.

She crumpled to the floor. Her face and neck were bright red, but she was alive. She rubbed at her throat and coughed.

Amanda heard approaching sirens and breathed easier. The entire cavalry would be coming. She ushered the girl from the room and told her to go outside. She ran off crying. Then Amanda attended to Leanne. "Help is almost here. Hang in there."

As she comforted Leanne, she kept glancing at the situation between Joshua and Trent.

Joshua was staring at Trent, fire in his eyes, and lunged toward him.

Trent skirted away, putting several feet between them, and held his gun on Joshua.

"Stop! Or I will shoot you." Trent held his ground, his stance strong.

Joshua rushed toward Trent, wrapped one hand around his gun, raised the muzzle to his heart, and pulled the trigger with the other.

It all happened so quickly, there wasn't time to prevent it or react.

The force of the shot pushed Joshua back.

Blood blossomed from his chest, and smoke rose from the gun.

Trent stared on in shock, his arms shaking and lowering.

Joshua sunk to the floor, holding a hand over the bullet hole. "Now I will be with them again." His eyes fluttered shut, and his body fell limp to the side.

Amanda rushed to check his pulse.

Joshua Brock was dead.

EPILOGUE

TWO WEEKS LATER...

Friday Afternoon

Amanda and Trent had closed another case by the time they
had all the answers they were after about Joshua Brock—the last
of which came through that morning. They were tidying up
paperwork on a Friday afternoon, and her mind was working
through everything.

They'd discovered that he had briefly met or interacted with
all his victims at one point—the Archers at the school, the rest of
his victims at Prince Park. She and Trent had spoken to regulars
who took their kids to the park, and they identified the Cohens,
Reillys, and Riggs from their pictures.

Further conversation with Dr. Wood revealed Joshua did
speak affectionately of his family and expressed a deep desire
for the flashbacks to stop. He told the therapist they were
destroying his life. While there was no way to know for sure,
Dr. Wood said Joshua may have left Leanne Reilly's car behind
in a subconscious endeavor to be caught. Whether Joshua had
known about the camera's coverage on the parking lot and
parked intentionally out of sight, went to his grave. But it

seemed to Amanda he hadn't given surveillance cameras any thought.

Purses belonging to each of the women were recovered from the house. Crime Scene also lifted their fingerprints from the room. DNA was collected but still being run through the system. Either way, they had solid proof the women and their daughters had been there.

A search of the Brock property revealed two graves containing two human bodies each. One marked the resting place of Cheryl and Holly Brock, and their autopsies confirmed severed spinal cords due to broken necks. Same for those in the second grave. It was believed it contained the remains of Abigail and Mia Cohen.

Cheryl's and Holly's time of deaths were estimated as eight months ago, only about thirty days after Joshua's return from duty.

The canine hairs on the toys were a match to Brock's dog. Jill Archer's Chevy Malibu was in the barn. Her wedding ring was in the console—why or who put it there would remain unanswered. They also found work boots that matched the partial left near the Archers' grave.

The outcome was equally sad as it was tragic. No one would be going to prison, and truly, Joshua was a victim himself. He'd gone overseas to defend his country and had returned broken. Unfortunately, a sad story on repeat for many who served in the military.

And Amanda suspected Trent was having a tougher time than he let on. After all, a man had used his service weapon to kill himself. The fact it had happened so fast did little to offset the aftermath of guilt and what ifs.

One good thing to result from this was that Leanne Reilly had left her husband, and she and her daughter were now living at the shelter.

Her phone rang, and it was Sergeant Graves. "Could I see you for a minute?"

Amanda had been sitting at her desk, thinking about everything. "Ah, sure." The clock was showing it was just a few minutes from five.

Once she reached her office, Graves closed the door and told Amanda to take a seat.

Why does it feel like I've been called to the principal's office?

"I know you've noticed me..." Graves stopped talking, letting her gaze dip over Amanda's face. "At Hannah's Diner."

"I have." Things between them had continued to grow more awkward over the last several days. She'd spotted the sergeant outside Hannah's Diner on more occasions, and as far as she knew, she still hadn't entered the place.

"Then you're probably curious why I've been there." Graves wrung her fingers, shifted in her chair. Whatever she had to say was making the sergeant as uncomfortable as it was making Amanda. "You saw that article back a couple weeks ago now that spoke of my past coming close to the Brock case?"

"You know I did."

"My stepfather was an abusive man. I saw him beat my mother." Graves stopped talking, though Amanda got the sense it wasn't for sympathy, but rather she was drawing inward strength to continue with her story. "My mother was murdered about a year before I came here."

For all the internet sleuthing Amanda had done on the sergeant, she'd never discovered that.

"Her husband did it. And he's in jail now. It was pretty open and shut. The evidence was indisputable."

"I'm sorry... That's horrible about your mother."

"I'm not telling you this for your sympathy, but just building to my point here. My mother died as Tori Kidd, but was born Hurst."

That was May Byrd's maiden name.

"My mother was May Byrd's sister," Graves clarified. "May is my aunt, but I've never met her. Well, she would have known me when I was quite young. But the sisters became estranged. May had tried to get my mother to leave her husband, but my mother was too blind to see him for who he was. When he ended up killing her, Mom had been in the process of leaving him. She never got far enough away."

Amanda was having a hard time finding the right words. Tragic and heartbreaking to be sure.

"The reason I'm telling you all this is because you're close with May. Am I right?"

"She's like an aunt to me. I've known her most of my life."

"Would you... I mean, don't feel you have to. It's not like what I'm about to ask is as your sergeant."

"What is it?"

"Would you introduce me to her? I mean she probably won't even want to meet me."

"She would." Amanda knew May well enough to feel confident saying that much. For her not to ever mention a sister, it must have hurt too much to talk about. "Family extends beyond blood, even death, in my opinion. And even though your mother and her sister may have had a falling out, I can tell you May probably never stopped loving her. She isn't someone who holds a grudge."

"You're sure?"

"I am."

Graves's shoulders relaxed.

"I can introduce you tomorrow if you'd like." Amanda was determined to get home on time for Zoe tonight.

"That would be... I couldn't thank you enough."

"No problem." Amanda smiled at the sergeant, liking how the last few weeks had given Amanda a glimpse of her boss's human side. Prior to that she was like a highly functioning robot doing the bidding of its programming, or in her case trying to impress the higher-ups.

Amanda returned to her desk and found a handwritten message left on her notepad.

Have a great weekend! Trent

"You too," she said to the air. He was feeling better having seen his aunt last week. He'd confided in Amanda that he ended up knocking on her door. He had put his heart out there one last time, giving his aunt another chance. While she had ended up sending him away, it was the final closure he'd needed to release her and his guilt and move on.

Amanda had a rather uncomfortable personal situation to deal with herself. She and her half-brother were meeting up for coffee this weekend. It might be tough putting her father's affair out of her mind to connect with Spencer, but she was willing to give it a try. And Sunday was the weekly dinner at her parents' place. For the first time, she'd invited Logan to come along, so that ought to be interesting. And in every spare minute, she'd be hugging Zoe—even if she protested.

Amanda flicked her monitor off and snatched Trent's note. She was smiling as she tucked it into a pants pocket. Despite all the death and the ugly, there were always some things worth living for.

A LETTER FROM CAROLYN

Dear reader,

I want to say a huge thank you for choosing to read *Her Final Breath*. If you loved the book, I would be incredibly grateful if you would write a brief, honest review. To stay informed about new releases in the Detective Amanda Steele series, just sign up at the following link. Your email address will never be shared, and you can unsubscribe at any time.

www.bookouture.com/carolyn-arnold

Every day, women and children retreat to the safety of shelters around the world. It's such a sad statement that their existence is even necessary. When it came time to write *Her Final Breath*, I wanted to shed some light on this global epidemic and stress how if we know a woman or child in need of help, that it's our responsibility to do what we can to offer it.

With this novel, I also wanted to express my gratitude for those who serve either in law enforcement or the military. They not only risk their lives in the line of duty, but also their mental and emotional health. They see humanity at its worst and are left to process that. Sometimes it's too much to ask. As a society we need to speak up for mental health, and as individuals, make sure we are there for those who need us.

I'd like to thank Lindsey Paul, my niece and a teacher, for

her insight into how reporting suspected abuse works in the school system.

Another shout-out of gratitude goes to Yvonne Van Gaasbeck, a former coroner in the state of Georgia, who answered my questions about broken necks and contusions.

While I do my best to get police procedure accurate, if you're familiar with the Prince William County, Virginia area, you'll realize differences between reality and my book. That's me taking creative liberties.

If you'd like to continue investigating murder, you'll be happy to know there will be more Detective Amanda Steele books. I also offer several other international bestselling series for you to savor—everything from crime fiction, to cozy mysteries, to thrillers and action adventures. One of these series features Detective Madison Knight, another kick-ass female detective, who will risk her life, her badge—whatever it takes— to find justice for murder victims.

Also if you enjoyed being in the Prince William County, Virginia, area, you might want to return in my Brandon Fisher FBI series. Brandon is Becky Tulson's boyfriend and was mentioned in this book. You can read about when they first met in *Silent Graves* (book two in my FBI series). These books are perfect for readers who love heart-pounding thrillers and are fascinated with the psychology of serial killers. Each installment is a new case with a fresh bloody trail to follow. Hunt with the FBI's Behavioral Analysis Unit and profile some of the most devious and darkest minds on the planet.

Last but certainly not least, I love hearing from my readers! You can get in touch on my Facebook page, through Twitter, Goodreads, or my website. This is also a good way to stay notified of my new releases. You can also reach out to me via email at Carolyn@CarolynArnold.net.

Wishing you a thrill a word!

Carolyn Arnold

www.carolynarnold.net

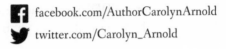 facebook.com/AuthorCarolynArnold
twitter.com/Carolyn_Arnold

CPSIA information can be obtained
at www.ICGtesting.com
Printed in the USA
BVHW032238020223
657747BV00003B/55